Powers of Darkness by Fred M White

Fred Merrick White was born in 1859 in West Bromwich in the Midlands of England to Joseph White and Helen Merrick who had married the previous year.

Joseph was a solicitor's managing clerk, who by the time the family moved to Hereford a few years later, had become a solicitor's article clerk.

Little is known of White's early years but what is known is that he followed in his father's footsteps and worked as a solicitor's clerk in Hereford. His father by now had also become a solicitor and times seemed quite prosperous for the family.

However in the late 1880's something went badly wrong for his father and he was imprisoned.

White had by now decided that writing was a more preferable career for him than the law. By 1891 Fred M. White, now 31 years old, was working full-time as a journalist and author, earning enough to support himself and his mother, Helen. By this time Fred's younger brother, Joseph A. White, had left home and working as a glass-blower.

In 1892, White married Clara Jane Smith. The wedding took place at King's Norton, Worcestershire, and the couple went on to have two children; Sydney Eric White (1893) and Ormond John White (1895).

As the century closed Fred's father had been released from prison and was living as a "retired solicitor", together with Helen, in Worthington in West Sussex.

By the time of the 1911 census, Fred M. White, now 52 years old, and his wife Clara were living at Uckfield, a town in the Wealden district of East Sussex. As the ominous shadows of the First World War gathered White had established himself as a popular and extremely prolific author. Indeed whether it was novels or short stories they flowed from his pen with a startling speed and many of them were initially serialized in the popular weekly and monthly magazines. His clever use of science to create imaginative and highly adventurous story lines was a particular talent of his.

During the First World War, both of his sons served as junior officers in The Royal Inniskilling Fusiliers.

The titanic struggle of the First World War and his sons' war-time experiences in it greatly influenced this phase of his writing. His novel The Seed of Empire (1916), describes early trench warfare in great and gritty detail. He went on to describe how the social changes after the war created many problems for returning soldiers as they attempted to fit back into a now peaceful society.

Fred and Clara spent their twilight years in Barnstaple in Devon, an area which also provided the backdrop for his novels The Mystery Of Crocksands, The Riddle Of The Rail, and The Shadow Of The Dead Hand.

Fred Merrick White died in Barnstaple in 1935.

Index of Contents

CHAPTER I

A MATTER OF NERVES

As the girl drew back from the window, the soft silk curtains fell from her hand. A thick, white fog rose from the valley, blotting out the landscape; here and there a great elm stood out of it, like a ship becalmed on a moonlit sea. The warmth of the atmosphere chilled suddenly, and the girl in her thin evening dress shuddered. Probably there was a fire in the drawing-room; at any rate, she hoped so. An hour earlier she had been sitting in the garden amidst the full glow of summer roses. But it was often like thus on Dartdale.

How gloomy and depressing it had become all at once, and yet how characteristic of the atmosphere of the place! Time had been when Rawmouth Park was a house of love and sunshine, but that was before the death of Mrs. Martin Faber and her husband, who had followed her into the Silent Land less than six months afterwards. And now the girl was here as the ward and guest of Raymond Draycott, who had succeeded to the property.

From the bottom of her heart Alice Kearns hated Raymond Draycott. It counted for nothing that he was more or less kind to her, that he insisted upon giving her a home until she came into her property some time hence. She was in his hands, for under Martin Faber's will Draycott became her legal guardian. It was absurd that a stranger should have such power over her future; but the fact remained.

Up to a year ago she had never heard of the man except through Mr. Faber's casual references. Draycott had been his great chum in the old days before the former set out for the Argentine to make a fortune, and after Faber had been found cut to pieces on the railway it appeared that he had left everything—Alice included—to Raymond. There was very little, so it seemed, beyond the lovely old house and the grounds round it, but it was discovered that Faber had been insured for a large amount, so that Draycott found himself master of nearly a hundred thousand pounds.

He offered a home at Rawmouth to Alice, expressing a desire to have her near him. He would not hear of any other arrangement. From the first she was afraid of him. He was dark, so dark as to suggest Spanish blood in his veins, his hair and moustache were black, though his eyes were blue. This latter fact was only apparent when he removed his glasses. He disliked any allusion to the subject.

There was something mysterious about him. He was furtive and watchful, and apparently found it always necessary to keep a guard upon his tongue. Yet, reserved as he was, he had an extraordinary knowledge of things and places in the locality. Episodes that had happened years ago were perfectly familiar to him. He was a rigid teetotaller, moreover, though he spoke learnedly in unguarded moments on the subject of wine. Deep down in her heart in a blind, unreasoning way, Alice detested him; loathed him more than anything else in the world—with the sole exception of Carl Moler.

On the whole, this clever, silent, watchful German doctor was the worse man of the two. Alice knew by instinct that Draycott hated him more than she did. That being so, what was he doing at Rawmouth? Draycott was boisterously friendly, outwardly pleased with Moler's society; but there were times when, unthinkingly he regarded him with a glance absolutely murderous. He was like a cat waiting to spring and yet pausing to pounce. Moler had come at first on a chance visit, protesting he had found Draycott quite by accident. Now he was settled at Rawmouth as if the place belonged to him.

There was something amiss here, some mystery that troubled Alice. Nor was she the only one that was under its influence. Jane Mason, the old housekeeper, could unfold a tale if she liked—Alice was sure of that. But when sounded, Jane merely turned white and anxious and changed the subject. "It was no business of hers," she said.

"We've all got our troubles, and I have got my share, miss," she would remark. "Let sleeping dogs lie. And if anything happens, you've got a friend in me. It would be different if we had Mr. Hugh back again, poor innocent dear!"

Ah, if Hugh Grenfell were only here once more! Alice's heart throbbed with pain as she thought of him. It was the full weight of her own hopeless misery. She was thinking of nothing else as she finished her toilet and went down to dinner. The cold, white fog that lay over Rawmouth enshrouded Hugh Grenfell's quarters, too. The truth as to that sad story would be told some day, if there were any justice left; it must—

Alice always dressed early, especially at this time of year, when the weather was warm and it was possible to go into the gardens before the others came down. There were happy occasions when Draycott and Moler were absent from the meal altogether, but Alice did not very often have such a lucky interlude, which mostly happened only when Draycott was ill. Still, his attacks did not grow less frequent. Indeed, Alice thought that they were more regular now than they had been before Moler arrived. What was Moler doing here? Why had he come? The girl asked herself these questions over and over again. Alice remembered his arrival quite well. He had not been expected. Draycott had been moody all through dinner; had changed his mind a dozen times whether he would drink or not. He passed for a teetotaller, and boasted that he drank little or nothing save under the doctor's orders. Sometimes when attacks of fever were imminent he indulged himself, but then he professed to take the liquor as a medicine and against his will.

He had been very moody and shaky that night. Anybody but Alice would have refused to believe Draycott's protestations; a man of the world would have said bluntly that he was suffering from the very thing that he affected to despise. The bloodshot, watery eyes, shaking lips, and trembling hand proclaimed it as if from the housetops. It was Draycott's fancy to call it ague, and Alice was constrained to humor him. He had passed many years in foreign parts, and it might have been malaria.

Still, it was very unfortunate, the girl concluded, to have to live under the same roof with him after her experience with Martin Faber, whose drinking having recurred at intervals of about six weeks, and lasted for a few days. At such times he was more or less dangerous and one of the men servants had to keep a close eye on him. Then the fit would pass away. Faber would come down sullen and shaky, and in a short time be himself again.

Was history repeating itself? It mattered little what Draycott called it, seeing that the effect was practically the same. How strange that Martin Faber should have gone out of his way to make this man rich! Poor as he was, he had insured his life for a prodigious sum, only that Draycott might have a good time of it. It must have cost him a serious struggle to pay the premium, and he must have known that it would be impossible to discharge a second premium, in which case the policy would have been forfeited, and Faber have literally wasted his money. Perhaps he had committed suicide in the most cold-blooded and deliberate manner? Had Draycott compelled him to do it? Alice had read of diabolical crimes of that kind.

But Faber's will was dated some years before. For a long time he had meant, it was clear, to leave everything to Draycott. Alice wondered what the relationship between them was. They were alike, and yet there was a wonderful difference. Though Draycott was much stouter, and his features and expression were different, there was a queer, subtle likeness. Draycott vaguely gave Alice the impression that he was afraid of something, that he expected something to happen. The sight of a stranger made him restless and uneasy. He was just like that the day Moler came.

They were seated at lunch, and Draycott was unusually amiable. A servant brought in a visiting-card, which he laid by Draycott's plate. The latter glanced at it and started instantly. His face paled, his lips trembled, and Alice could see that his eyes had a wicked gleam in them. Whoever the newcomer was, Draycott had no liking for him. Alice never forgot the singular sense that overtook her of a spirit of tragedy in the air. A second later Draycott burst into a torrent of profanity. He pulled himself up suddenly.

"I beg your pardon, my dear," he stammered. "An old friend of mine. I—I never expected to meet him again. He reminded me of a most unpleasant time in my earlier career. But I am glad to see him, though I wish he had given me notice he was coming."

Alice felt that Draycott meant this by the expression in his eyes. He wished this man had arrived quietly, without anybody knowing; in which case—Alice fairly shuddered at the suspicions that crowded her mind.

"Don't you think you had better ask the gentleman in?" she suggested.

"Oh, yes, of course," Draycott said with feigned ease. "Ask Mr. Moler in. My dear fellow, I am delighted to see you again. It was a shock at the moment—"

"I guessed it would be," the other said drily. "There was not time to write. Pray present me."

He bowed low to Alice and held out his hand. He was not a big man, though he gave a suggestion of strength; he was not handsome, yet his face was attractive in a way. It was a fine, intellectual head, with high forehead and flowing hair, and clear eyes, set a little too closely together. Nevertheless, this man was a mental force, beyond question, a being born to have his own way. The glance of open admiration which he turned on Alice made her hot and uncomfortable.

"I am pleased to meet you," she said coldly. "Are you staying here?"

"I have come for a few days," Moler explained, "on business. Quite by accident, I discovered that my dear old friend Raymond Draycott was living in the neighborhood. I am a doctor, Miss Kearns. I have a series of most delicate experiments going on, and I want quiet for them. I am going to ask Mr. Draycott to put me up for a while."

Once more the singular gleam lit up Draycott's eyes.

"Miss Kearns is mistress here?" he suggested.

"I—I am sure there can be no possible objection," Alice stammered. "We have plenty of spare room."

Alice fancied that Draycott expected her to make a reply like this. It seemed to her that Moler took the answer as a matter of course. He laughed quietly.

"Then that is settled," he said. "A light luncheon, if you please; a little of that delicious fruit. I rarely touch meat. After luncheon I shall enjoy a talk with Draycott. My dear friend, you will give me an hour or so?" It was not a question, it was a command. With a sullen air, Draycott rose and followed Moler into the library. Alice sat at the table with a curious sinking at her heart.

How long had this state of things lasted? She asked herself the question as she came down to dinner. Had Moler been dominating the house for months or years, making covert love to her? He was going to marry her one of these days—he had told her that plainly and calmly. He had fallen in love with her; and hoped to use her money in completing his wonderful experiments. He had Draycott under his thumb absolutely.

What would it all mean, and where would it end? How much longer would this menacing air of mystery hang like a cloud over Rawmouth? Did onlookers notice, or were they blind to what was going on?

There was no suggestion of mystery or crime.

The great hall was flooded with electric light under pink shades. There were ferns and flowers, pictures, and carpets, everywhere a fine combination of good taste and refinement. In the dining-room, dinner had been laid for three. A flood of light fell on the table, leaving the rest of the room in shadow. A feathery spray of pink orchids adorned the centre, and piles of the famous Rawmouth peaches were ranged on either side. Draycott and Moler were already seated. The latter smiled and rose as Alice entered. His glittering eyes gloated over her figure; the fair hair was brushed back from her forehead, and her white arms gleamed between the meshs of her black dress. The man always made her uncomfortable.

"You are rather late, my dear," Draycott said.

Alice almost started. There were times when Draycott's voice reminded her of Martin Faber. It was only now and then, but to-night the resemblance was marked. It gave her a strange, odd feeling that she had been through all this before. It is a sensation that comes to everyone at times. Draycott had a little gesture with his hands, too, that Faber had also used. Strange she had never noticed it before! It was a night of small surprises and coincidences, for Draycott actually had a glass of champagne before him. Faber had been partial to champagne—too partial; for there were frequent intervals when he suffered from 'nervous headaches' in the seclusion of his room! Draycott suffered from 'muscular neuralgia,' accompanied by intense pain. He also had to lie up from time to time, at tended by Moler. For the first occasion it flashed across Alice's mind that these periods of suffering coincided as to their intervals with the bouts that Faber had indulged in. She wondered this had not struck her before. Was it possible, that Draycott was a relative of Faber's—a relationship kept in the background for prudent reasons? A brother perhaps—

"I am trying a new remedy," Draycott said, as if reading the girl's thoughts. "I am afraid another of my attacks is coming on. Moler permits me a glass of champagne."

The German said nothing, though Alice imagined there was something sinister in his smile. How dark and mysterious he looked, in keeping with the fog and the gloom and the air of mystery that always seemed to brood over the old house now! The dinner dragged on with frequent pauses, and little or nothing in the way of conversation for Alice. She dreaded this long ceremonious hour, and looked forward eagerly to the moment when she could escape. She sat with downcast eyes, taking little besides fish and fruit. She slowly peeled and ate a peach. Draycott was talking faster than usual, and said something presently that attracted Alice's attention.

She looked up quietly. The servants had gone. Draycott was pouring out the last glass of champagne. Obviously he had finished the bottle. It must have been so, for Moler never touched anything. Draycott tossed off the glass and reached for the liqueur brandy. There was a peculiar, uneasy gleam behind his spectacles.

"How long is it since old Toolman met with that fatal accident?" he asked. "I mean—"

"That was before your time," Alice said. "It must have been four years ago."

Moler rose to his feet. The smile was no longer on his face; obviously something had happened to disturb him. He crept quietly behind Draycott's chair and gripped him by the shoulders.

"You are overdoing my instructions," he said. "It is time to take your medicine. You will come with me to your room at once, if you please."

It was not a polite request, so much as an imperative order. Just for the moment the wild murderous expression that Alice had seen before crossed Draycott's face. She could see his hand gripping the dessert knife till the knuckles stood out white and hard.

"Perhaps you are right," he stammered. "I have had one or two of those infernal twinges during dinner. I'll ask you to excuse me, my dear. Excellent fellow, Moler. A little too arbitrary for my taste, but very anxious for his patient. When you are married to him, you will learn to appreciate his good qualities."

Alice flushed scarlet. This was by no means the first time this hateful topic had been mentioned. As she stood in her turn she noticed that Draycott lurched as he moved towards the door. He burst into song as he staggered into the hall—the same song that Faber had indulged in on many a similar occasion. It was as if Martin Faber had come back from the dead—the ghastliness of the idea made Alice shudder. A sudden fear set her trembling from head to foot. She seemed to see the whole mystery laid bare as one sees things in a dream, only to lose sight of them again. Yet Martin Faber was in his grave. It was impossible in the circumstances—

Jane Mason was standing there, white and horrified as was Alice herself.

"Did you hear that?" the girl demanded. "It is like a voice from the dead. But you heard it, Jane, or you would not tremble like that. I believe you could tell me what it all means."

Jane shook her head sorrowfully.

"Don't ask me, miss," she whispered. "Don't ask me. Let sleeping dogs lie."

CHAPTER II

THE UNEXPECTED

"You always put me off like that," Alice replied. "At any rate, I don't see what you have to fear. I am sure you could tell me a great deal if you chose. Who is this man that has all the habits and mannerisms of Mr. Faber, who speaks like him, and who has to hide himself from everybody for a few days every six weeks or so? You may say that it is Mr. Raymond Draycott, who came into the property under Mr. Faber's will, but—"

"Is there any resemblance between them, Miss Alice?" Jane interrupted.

"Oh, I admit the difficulty. One is dark and the other fair. Mr. Faber had a blunt nose, and Mr. Draycott has a regular one. Their mouths and teeth are different, and Mr. Draycott is shorter than my late guardian was. Yet they speak alike, and have the same gestures and the same weaknesses."

"My present master has a painful form of neuralgia," Jane suggested.

"So he says," Alice replied scornfully. "I refuse to believe it. He had too much wine to-night. It was just like Mr. Faber before his attacks began, and these come to the same regular intervals. Mr. Draycott sang the same song. Though he is a stranger here, he knows of things that happened in the house years ago. Moler watches him as a cat watches a mouse. I cannot make out this bewildering mystery. Did Mr. Faber have a brother who disgraced the family? I am sure Mr. Draycott is a relative. If we did not know that Mr. Faber was in his grave, I should be inclined to imagine—but that is absurd."

"I can tell you nothing whatever about it, miss," Jane Mason said.

Alice turned away, baffled and disappointed. Mason's words carried no conviction to her. She did not for a moment believe what the woman was saying, and longed for some friend in whom she could confide. She had but one in the world, and she could think of him only with tears in her eyes. She passed the drawing-room door on the way to her own room. She had no heart for the music that was her one comfort and consolation.

She heard the clicking of the switches presently as the lights downstairs were extinguished, and threw open her window and looked out. The white mist had lifted and a silver moon was hanging in the blue sky. There were lights dotted over the wide stretch of country, and a row of pin-points of flame was visible to the left. By their means Alice made out the outline of Dartdale convict prison.

She crept on to the balcony that ran along the whole of that side of the house, moved by an impulse of curiosity that it was impossible to resist. A light burned dully, as if from behind drawn curtains at the end of the balcony, picking out a bush of crimson roses on the lawn below. The gleam came from Draycott's window, as Alice knew quite well. It would be no hazardous matter to go along the balcony and ascertain what was taking place inside. It seemed to the girl that she was justified. The dark mystery involved her future happiness, and possibly even more than that. A glimpse of the pin-points of flame from the windows of the prison decided her. She would find out what was passing in the room at the end of the balcony. Snatching up a long black cloak and extinguishing the light in her room, a moment later she was listening to the sound of voices in Draycott's room. The window was closed and the blind drawn. All Alice could hear was a confused murmur. The two men were disputing over something, and a violent quarrel seemed to be in progress. There was a noise presently, as if a chair had been overturned, then a shadow pantomime on the blind indicated a struggle. Somebody suddenly burst out into a peal of laughter.

"Grenfell!" a voice cried. "Go and ask Hugh Grenfell! He's the man to tell you all about it. He stood in this very room and told me to my face that I was a scoundrel. I told him he should pay for that, and by heavens, he has. Ask Hugh Grenfell!"

It was Draycott who spoke. He shouted the name again and again at the top of his voice, till the room rang with it—the mere mention of it filled him with drunken amusement.

"You fool," Moler hissed. "You thrice-besotted fool, be silent. Do you want the whole world to hear that story? If any of the servants are listening—"

"Let 'em listen," Draycott chuckled. "You're too cautious, Moler—that's what's the matter with you my boy. You're very cunning and very clever, but not half so clever as I am. What you lack is imagination. Ask Hugh Grenfell!"

He yelled out the name once more, followed by a crackle of laughter. Alice distinctly heard the curse that broke from Moler's lips. A chair fell over with a crash, Draycott burst out into a spasm of rage, then there ensued a prolonged silence. The blind was flung up, the window was opened, and Moler stepped out. He wiped his heated face, as Alice could see from her hiding-place behind a tub of flowers. He had something in his hand that glittered in the moonlight. Alice's heart almost ceased to beat, but she had no real cause for fear—the shining thing was nothing but a hypodermic syringe.

"That dose will keep his fool's tongue quiet till to-morrow," Moler muttered. "But for my presence here the whole thing would have been exposed before now. Yet he hates me like poison. Well, let him go on hating me—I am indifferent to his anger. I should have gone long ago but for the little girl. What an idiot I am to stay here! I should have taken my share of the plunder and left him to his fate. And here I stay for the sake of a pair of grey eyes and a mass of golden hair like spun sunshine. And she hates me worse—"

Moler withdrew sullenly to the bedroom and pulled down the blind. Red and hot and trembling in every limb, Alice crept back to her room again. After all she had seen and heard she supposed she would never be able to sleep again. She lay down on her bed from force of habit and closed her eyes to think—

When she awoke the sun was high in the heavens and breakfast was a thing of the past. Draycott had sent a message to the effect that he had had a restless night and would keep to his room for a day or two. Moler was busy, and excused himself. He would prefer to take his meals with his patient, he said.

Alice was not disappointed to hear it. The more freedom she had from these men the better. She wondered why she stayed at all. She had means of her own, money that nobody could touch, and her affairs were ordered and regulated by the Court of Chancery. The Court had been satisfied in the first instance to let Draycott take up the position of guardian rendered void by the death of Martin Faber. So far as anybody knew, Draycott was a man of substance, having inherited what appeared to be a fine estate, together with a large sum of money. At that time Alice was too young to trouble about such matters. One guardian was much the same as another.

She was old enough now to make application to the Court and have all this changed. She had a number of friends, whom she could visit, but she did not care to do that without returning their hospitality. She was free to ask whom she liked to Rawmouth Park, because, despite his faults, Draycott was not a mean man. But it was impossible to take advantage of this generosity. Alice had tried it once with disastrous results, and was not likely to repeat the experiment.

There was another reason why she had decided to remain for the present. Hugh Grenfell was not far off. She would get to the bottom of his story some day. The affair had happened when she was on the Continent. She did not believe anything she was told so far as Hugh was concerned. Draycott had, she thought, gone out of his way to conceal the truth from her.

"At any rate I'll stay here till the autumn," she told herself. "I don't think I could remain in the house another winter. Summer is a different matter, and there are things to discover. I am certain that Mr. Draycott could tell me all about Hugh, if he liked. That dreadful creature Moler is unspeakable, but for Hugh's sake—"

She walked into the garden amongst the flowers. It was usually her custom at this time of year to eat an apple or peach before breakfast. At the bottom of the kitchen garden she found Jane Mason. The latter started as if she had been caught doing something wrong.

"What is the matter?" Alice asked. "Jane, what are you doing?"

The housekeeper smiled faintly, and the color crept back into her cheeks again.

"I've the most dreadful headache that ever was, miss," she explained. "I've had a good many of 'em lately. I couldn't eat my breakfast, and I fancied some fruit. Nothing like an apple to cure a headache, I say."

She rambled on quickly and nervously, as if talking for the sake of talking. Alice saw how her hands were shaking, and laid her fingers on the woman's arm.

"Your nerves are in a dreadful state," she said. "Well, I am not surprised, Jane. If you leave this house you will be ever so much better. I'm thinking of going myself."

Astonishment, mingled with fear, struggled for the mastery in Jane Mason's face.

"You don't mean it, miss," she gasped. "And yet why not? You're young and have the world before you. Whereas I'm getting on towards the finish. It doesn't matter as far as I'm concerned. But for a pretty young lady to be wasting her life in this horrible house—"

She paused, conscious that she was saying too much. Alice faced round on her.

"You know a good deal, if you will only speak," she said.

"He has had one of his attacks and didn't come down to breakfast, and one of the maids heard Dr. Moler say that he will not be able to appear for some days to come. I swear that's all I know, miss."

Alice concealed the satisfaction that thrilled her. To breakfast alone was a pleasure. She escaped from the house presently for a long ramble over the moor. The day was fair and bright the air invigorating. She walked on and on till the grey walls of Dartdale were in sight. Down below in the quarries gangs of convicts were at work. She could see them moving, about and hear the click of picks and the orders of the armed warders. A feeling of pity for these outcasts filled her heart. There was a gang somewhat apart from the rest, excavating amongst the gorse and heather. A warder sat on a rock watching them. Alice observed that he had dropped his rifle and that his face had fallen forward on his hands. There was something in the attitude of the man that disturbed her. The convicts seemed to notice it, too, for they ceased work and began to talk in excited whispers. Other warders, however, being in sight, there was no great commotion or confusion. Somebody pointed to Alice, who was standing a slight figure on the skyline. There was a brief scuffle, a blow, and one of the convicts stumbled into a mass of bracken. A warder in the distance shouted and began to run towards his colleague, who sat, with his head still buried in his hands. Intensely interested, Alice stood watching. A pair of hands reached out of the bracken and pulled her down. The hands blindfolded her eyes, and hot lips were pressed to hers convulsively. She tried to shout, but words failed her. When she opened her eyes at length the world ceased to revolve dazedly around her.

"Hugh!" she gasped. "Hugh! Is it possible! What has happened?"

She repeated the question dreamily, as if not comprehending what she was saying, as if she did not contemplate a reply. For the miracle had happened, and here was Hugh Grenfell in the flesh. There was not too much flesh, as Alice could see, he was lean and brown and hard, and there was an expression in his eyes that brought the tears to hers. Her hands were in his, and she remarked the workings of the muscles in his throat, as if he were trying to speak and could not.

"Hugh!" she whispered. "It's a dream, isn't it? It can't be really you!"

Grenfell nodded. The words were a long time coming. He would recover himself presently. Alice had forgotten where she was and was taking no heed of the perils of the situation. At any moment they might be disturbed, but so far as she was concerned they might have been in the centre of a desert. To be interrupted was a contingency she had not considered. For here was Hugh, dear old Hugh, holding her hands in his and looking into her eyes with speechless rapture.

"It seems marvellous," Alice went on in the same intense whisper. "Are you not going to speak, darling?"

Hugh nodded again. If a word at that moment had been the price of his freedom he could not have uttered it. All he could do was to clasp the girl's hands and gaze into her eyes as if trying to recollect who she was and with what exquisite moment of his past she was connected with.

"It is Alice, isn't it?" the hoarse words came at last.

"Oh, yes, yes. Alice has come to see you. What a marvellous accident! I feel as if I shall wake presently and find that it's a dream. Won't you kiss me, dear?"

Still the man made no sign. Very slowly indeed everything was coming back to him. He had been so long out of the world, that it was in sooth little more than a vague memory.

"It is really and truly you?" he asked.

"Really and truly me, and nobody else," Alice said, with the tears in her eyes.

"And you haven't the remotest idea how you got here?"

"Indeed, I haven't. I blundered upon you and the—the—others by accident. I was taking a walk this way and had not the slightest idea that a gang was working here. The warder seemed to be asleep. He did not call out and order me back as I had expected. When I saw you, I would have come on, had there been a regiment of soldiers in the way—My poor, dear boy. How changed you look, and how rough and hard your hands are! I used to think they were the kindest hands in the world. Hugh, I must get you out of this; we must find some way of escape. We must expose the wicked conspiracy that brought you to this awful spot. I am beginning to find things out. I am watching and waiting. If I could only discover some real friend who would help me, I might be successful. I want a man, cool, clever, and resolute, and I am certain, that we could reach the truth in time. Raymond Draycott—"

Hugh started into something like life for the first time.

"I had forgotten him," he said. "He is your guardian. He is kind to you, Alice?"

"He is utterly indifferent, Hugh. I am free to come and go as I like, so long as I don't worry him. He is a bad man, Hugh, a worse man than Martin Faber."

Hugh passed a hand nervously over his forehead.

"I am trying to piece the puzzle together," he said. "I know a great deal, if I could only get the chance to say it. I suspect the full significance of the conspiracy. If only I could—but that is out of the question. They took good care of that. They took—"

Alice laid a hand on his arm again. She looked at him imploringly.

"Hugh, you have only kissed me once," she whispered. "Don't you know that I love you still, love you more than ever and know that you are as innocent as a child?"

The man in the convict garb kissed her again, holding her to his heart.

"Forgive me, darling," he whispered. "I couldn't help it. When I looked up and saw you standing there it seemed as if an angel from heaven had come down to help me. Our warder was taken suddenly ill, and not the first time lately, though they don't know down yonder. He used to be one of the boys in the old garden at one time. Heart trouble, I fancy. But don't let me waste the precious time, Alice. How I have longed to see you! I—I did not know whether you still cared for me till I saw your eyes just now—"

"For ever, Hugh!" Alice whispered. "As if I could cease to love you, Hugh! I knew from the first you were innocent. It was a great shock to me when I returned from Germany and found that you had been sentenced to penal servitude. I wondered why I got no reply to my letters, dear. But come along with me, Hugh. You cannot go back to that place now."

Hugh Grenfell hesitated. Here was the chance of a lifetime. But he shook his head.

"It can't be done like that, Alice," he said. "I should be detected at once within an hour, and you have been seen here. I have thought of a plan for escape. If I could get away from here for a week and and no suspicion were aroused, I could prove my innocence. I have my case all written out and stowed away in the lining of my coat. I was planning some means of sending it to you when this glorious opportunity came along. Here it is. You will have to find some man who will—"

"I know, I know," Alice said eagerly. "There will be no trouble about money. Mr. Draycott is my guardian, but I can borrow a thousand pounds if necessary without his knowing anything about it, Hugh. What am I to do next?"

"Write to Russell Clench—you will find his address on the paper I have given you. Ask him to come and see you secretly. Then you can discuss the plan with him. Now I must go before they miss me. Good-bye, and God bless you, darling."

Alice caught her lover by the arm. Her eyes were blazing.

"This warder of yours," she gasped. "He will have to leave the prison; they can't have invalids here. Tell me his name. I have a scheme, Hugh, a splendid idea. Give me the name, at once, dear."

CHAPTER III

AT THE WARDER'S COTTAGE

"What good could that do?" Hugh asked. "My dear girl, you must realise that you are proposing something very serious."

A sigh broke from Alice's lips. With all her quickness, Alice had not grasped the situation yet. All the same, Hugh Grenfell was very real. He was terribly drawn and thin, and his face wore a hard, hunted look, while that horrible drab uniform brought the tears to Alice's eyes. The mere look of it seemed to take the warmth out of the sunshine and to depress Alice, till she wept bitterly.

"My dear girl," Grenfell murmured, "I have said nothing to hurt you!"

"It isn't that," Alice sobbed. "It's—it's everything. You are dreadfully worn and ill—and that hideous dress! And you an innocent man!"

"I can look the whole world in the face and say that," Grenfell whispered. "I could prove it if I were free. If I could stand for a few minutes face to face with Martin Faber—"

"Who is dead, Hugh. My dear boy, you have forgotten that."

Grenfell passed his hand across his forehead like a man who brushes the sleep from his eyes.

"True, I had forgotten that. I shall forget my own identity if I stay in this ghastly place much longer. I have to thank Faber for everything, and regarded him as my friend! Still, I could prove any innocence."

"Do you mean without assistance from anybody," Alice asked.

Hugh smiled at the artlessness of the question. He was master of himself now, his mind working clearly and smoothly. His first shock of surprise was over and the listlessness had vanished. There was an eager glance in his eyes that Alice was glad to see.

"I don't quite mean that," he said. "Until a few minutes ago I'm sure that I should not have been able to explain what I mean. You have no conception of what this life is like. At the moment of your sentence your mind is a blank—you can't grasp it. If you are an innocent, as I am, you are too utterly stunned to understand anything. Then gradually it comes to you, and the despair of it is overwhelming. Seven years! It sounds like seven centuries. You feel that the time can never come to an end. Looking back, seven years are nothing. Looking forward, they are an eternity. After recovering from the first awful blow, I began to prepare my plan of campaign. But I could make nothing of it. In the first place, you can send nothing from here that is not read. If you say certain things, the letters do not go at all. You see how one's hands are tied."

"You could do nothing with the warders?"

"I never tried. I have no money or any inducement to temp them. I understand that such a thing has happened more than once. One learns many strange things in yonder prison, though we are supposed not to talk or communicate with each other in any way."

"Do you chance to know a warder called Copping, Hugh?"

"Copping, Copping! It sounds familiar. No relation to the Coppings that lived near the old place, I suppose? Oh, you mean the warder who is ill—the one I mentioned. He married an old servant of yours."

"The same," Alice answered eagerly. "I know him well, and his wife better. I see them both frequently. Mary Copping is a pretty, delicate little thing, who wants to get away from here. The doctor says that unless she can leave these terrible fogs she will not live very long. I have plenty of money, Hugh."

Grenfell smiled vaguely. It might be possible to do something in that quarter, but he could not see his way yet. Besides, he had other matters to discuss.

"All kinds of things would be needed," he went on. "I should want pen and ink, and paper in my cell. Such things might be smuggled in, but to hide them afterwards would be almost impossible. I'm told such things are done, but only by the old, cunning hands, who know all the ropes. I have quite another idea, Alice. Up to an hour or so ago, I had abandoned it. One loses heart in this dreary place, where one day is so like another. I was full of fight once, but all the steel goes out of one in time. Let's make the best of these precious moments. The warder will be here before long. He won't stay like that all the afternoon. Tell me something of your life, of the friends who are still true to you. Tell me that you are happy, dear."

She put her arms about him and kissed him tenderly.

"How can I be happy whilst you are here?" she asked. "It looks as if happiness and I have parted company for ever, Hugh. But I must not be selfish; I must think of you, darling. If you have a scheme for getting out of this place I should be glad to hear of it. Tell me."

But Grenfell seemed incapable of anything but passionate outbursts of affection. He held the girl close to him, devouring her with kisses.

"Nothing matters so long as you are here," he protested. "Why waste precious time in mere talk, darling? If you could only understand what it means to me—"

Alice was hardly listening. By craning her head she saw that the warder was on his feet again. His colleagues had resumed their duties. At some distance off a whistle was sounded. Grenfell started mechanically at the sound of it.

"I shall have to go," he said. "They are beginning to collect the gangs. Good-bye, sweetheart. It is like a glimpse of heaven to have seen you again. Go to Russell Clench or write to him. He is a man you can trust implicitly."

"But you did not say anything in regard to the warder, Joe Copping," Alice insisted.

"Oh, I had forgotten that," Grenfell said, with the faint suggestion of a smile. "Try Joe Copping, if you like, your Joe Copping, who lives outside the prison with his wife—being a married warder. How lucky you know them both so well! When you mentioned Copping I'm afraid I was not listening. I'm sure he'll help us, dear. I rendered him a service a while ago, and he does his best to make things easy for me. The man has something the matter with his heart, though he keeps it to himself. He has a sick wife, as you know. But you must not go near her, Alice; it would not be fair."

"You don't think it would be honorable?" Alice asked timidly.

"I'm sure of it," Grenfell said emphatically. "God knows, I would do much to get away from here, but not that way, child. Besides, my plan is the best, and Clench will say so. If—"

A whistle sounded harshly in Alice's ears; it seemed to be close by. Grenfell caught her in his arms and kissed her passionately. Then he put her aside almost roughly, and was gone. Like one in a dream, Alice watched the gang march off in files in the direction of the prison. She wept again and a pain was at her heart. It was so horrible, so cruel, so unjust. He was innocent, nobody could look him in the face and doubt that. He had lost none of his rigid code of honor either.

But Alice could not see how, situated as he was, his life ruined by foul play, he should feel the grip of honor. Short of anything dishonest, the end, she held, would justify the means. Everything was against him; he had been the victim of a vile conspiracy on the part of a dead man, and the law had punished him as guilty. The State had prosecuted him and condemned him for a crime he had never committed. It was not an occasion for scrupulous methods. Possibly he had thought out a wise plan, and Russell Clench might be as brave and clever as a friend need be. But there could be no harm in having an alternative scheme. Alice pondered the matter on her way home. She was only too anxious to help in the good work. Money would be necessary, of course, and, surely, she could command it. She had also valuable jewellery; which she could pledge at Exeter.

She wrote her letter to Clench, directing him not to reply by post, but to meet her in a quiet spot near the house, when she could give him details. She had been under the impression lately that her correspondence was tampered with, and intended therefore to take no risks. She dropped her letter into the box and turned her footsteps homewards. She had seen nothing of Raymond Draycott, and had heard nothing beyond a message that he was very little better, and probably would be confined to his room for the next two or three days. Carl Moler had gone into Exeter on business, and was not expected till late in the evening.

Alice had time to consider her plans, at any rate. She would go as far as the Coppings' cottage. She had never called there before, but felt certain Mary Copping would do anything for her. Still, she must be careful. Moler was out of the way for one thing, and Draycott was safe in his room. In these circumstances, Alice was greatly disturbed to meet Draycott in the woods at the back of the house, as she was making her way towards the cottage. What was more singular was that Draycott seemed to be more alarmed than she was.

"What on earth are you doing here?" he asked nervously. "It's very odd I can't go outside the house for a few minutes' peace and solitude without meeting—"

His voice trailed off in a gurgle, and he looked horribly white and shaky, and there were big, dark rings round his eyes. He had a furtive, guilty look as if he had been discovered in wrongdoing. Alice noticed that his shoes were muddy, and that there was mud on his knees. There had been no rain for days, and she wondered where the mud could be. It flashed across her mind that he had been following somebody on his hands and knees.

But it behoved her to keep these ugly suspicions to herself. She was doing nothing wrong in being there, and Draycott read plainly what was at the back of her mind.

"How long has this road been private?" she asked coldly "I have heard you say over and over again that the wood is too dark and oppressive for you. But I love its beauty, and it is my favorite spot when I have a book to read. Still, if you like—"

Draycott changed his tone at once. He began to realise how illogical his mood was. Moreover, he was filling the girl's mind with suspicions, and so he hastened to remove them.

"You must not pay too much heed to what I say, my dear," he muttered. "I have had a very bad attack this time—perhaps the worst I have ever suffered. Moler told me that I was to stay in, but I couldn't. I took advantage of his absence to have a stroll in the fresh air. I hoped if I came here I should not meet anybody. When I saw you I was foolishly annoyed. If you tell Moler—"

"I am not in the least likely to tell Dr. Moler anything," Alice said indifferently. "So far as I am concerned, I shall be heartily glad when I see the last of him. I have not taken any special pains to conceal my opinion of your friend—"

Draycott drew his breath in sharply.

"He's no friend of mine," he whispered hoarsely. "He's nobody's friend. He came for a few days, and has stayed—good heavens! how long he has stayed? Years. But don't make an enemy of him, nor let him know what I am talking about. What did I say?"

He drew his hand across his forehead with a touch of annoyance.

"You were warning me to be very careful with regard to Dr. Moler," Alice rejoined.

"No, I wasn't," Draycott snapped. "If I said so, I was only chaffing. Moler is a good fellow, and he will make an excellent husband when the time comes. There's not a girl in the country who would not be proud to become his wife. What are you staring at? I have had a fall and muddied my knees, but that's nothing very uncommon, is it?"

His voice fell to a murmur, and once more he rubbed his eyes.

"I'm not well," he went on, "as you can see, and when I'm in this poor, weak state I talk all kinds of rubbish. That infernal South American climate is responsible for everything, Alice. Don't take a bit of notice of me, and you'll be all right. I must go in and get my medicine. It is the most marvellous medicine in the world. It gives me the sleep I need so badly—it gives me—Walk in the wood, or sit in it, and come as often as you like, my dear. Good-bye."

Alice went on her way, feeling comparatively easy in her mind. At any rate, there was no chance of Moler watching her movements. There was a small colony of houses in close proximity to the gaol, and Alice had no difficulty in finding the cottage where the warder, Joe Copping, and his wife resided. She had gathered from Hugh that Copping was off duty after five, and had delayed her call purposely to catch him. It occurred to her that a few words with the wife first would not be waste of time, and therefore it was about half-past four when she knocked at the door of the honeysuckle-covered porch.

She knocked again and again without response. In the calm, clear air she thought she could hear voices in the garden. Apparently a woman and man were talking, the tones of the latter being harsh and threatening. Probably the woman was Mrs. Copping. Alice turned through an arch of hazel trees in search of the hidden pair. She distinguished the outline of a young and pretty woman, and by her side stood a man, the sight of whom brought Alice nearly to her knees behind the waving greenery of friendly bushes.

The man was Carl Moler, of that Alice had not the smallest doubt. She gasped for breath, for by the merest luck she had escaped detection. She crouched down, feeling fairly secure in her hiding-place. She could catch words here and there, but it was impossible to gather anything like a connected conversation. The two moved nearer her presently, however, so that she could catch snatches of their talk.

"I can't do it yet," the woman was saying. "Can't you have patience? You'll gain nothing by scowling at me like that, mister. Besides, I've my husband to think of. Yes, I know it's trifling, but if Joe caught you here he'd break every bone in your body. He may be back to tea at any moment. Why don't you go?"

"Oh, I'm going," Moler replied. "I will only come once more. You will have to make up your mind in a week one way or the other, Mary. Goodbye. I'll slip out by the back gate, so as not to meet Copping. Now, mind, this is your last chance."

The woman laughed as she made her way towards the cottage. Alice left her shelter by and by and followed. She had recovered from her alarm and surprise, and her courage was restored. At any rate, she had not wasted her time, for she had made what she was bound to regard as an important discovery. She was calm and collected as she knocked at the cottage door and asked for Copping. The woman was indescribably pretty, with a refined accent, but wore an aspect or fragility that told its own story. She started uneasily when she recognised her visitor.

"I want to see your husband, Mary," Alice said. "I understand that at one time he was a gardener at Felsted House with Mrs. Grenfell. It's rather strange that you never told me that, Mary."

The woman blushed, and the look of uneasiness left her blue eyes.

"I thought you were aware of that, miss," she said. "Though we were both children when first we met, Joe often speaks of the old days, and says it's a pity we ever left the village. The air here is bad for him, and it's bad for me. It's those cruel fogs that do the mischief. They get on my chest and keep me coughing for nights together."

Alice nodded, with ready sympathy. She knew that this woman was rehearsing a tragedy in these few words. The brilliancy of her complexion and the clearness of her eyes spoke plainly of the ravage of consumption. If Mary Copping stayed here she must die. Doubtless her husband was passionately fond of her. These pretty, fragile women have the knack of appealing to strong men. Alice was beginning to see her way.

"What does your doctor say about it?"

"Tells me to go away," Mary Copping laughed mirthlessly. "It's dangerous to spend even a summer here, and another winter will finish me. Joe's heart is all wrong, too. The doctor said I was to have a sea voyage, and when I came back to live on high ground. He might just as well have ordered me to go and stay at Windsor Castle. Still, that's what you've to put up with if you're poor. Nobody wants to prevent your dying; it's a free country, and you can die if you like, and all for the want of a hundred pounds. When I think of it, miss, I feel as if I could commit burglary."

The woman laughed with a hopelessness that touched Alice. She looked so pretty and pathetic withal, but it was evident that the iron had entered her soul. She had brooded over this trouble till she had justified any method for her own salvation. The matter was still under discussion when Joe Copping entered.

He knew Alice, of course, and was very glad to see her under his roof. At her request he walked with her presently in the direction of Rawmouth Park.

"You are in great trouble, Copping, over your wife?"

"We all have our anxieties, miss," Copping said. "Asking your pardon, miss."

"I understand what you mean," Alice answered. "It was a dreadful business, Copping, and the worst of it is that Mr. Grenfell is innocent. If he could get out for a few days he could prove his innocence. He says you have been kind to him."

"I beg your pardon, miss," Copping gasped. "Seeing that he's a prisoner—"

"Never mind that for the present, Copping. I have been talking to your wife. I suppose you know that if she stays here she will die. Do you want to save her?"

Copping's breast heaved with a deep sigh, and his brown eyes were full of pain.

"God knows I would lay down my life to save her," he said simply. "I'd do anything for Mary."

CHAPTER IV

A TACIT UNDERSTANDING

Joe Copping spoke from the bottom of his heart. It was exactly as Alice had anticipated.

"There is no occasion to go quite so far as that," she said, with a smile. "What you want is a hundred pounds. Mary must have a sea voyage without delay, and she must not return here. You will also get employment elsewhere, which will not be so difficult as it seems. We will play a game that we all used to be fond of as children—we will play 'Supposing.' Now suppose I ask you to do something for me. It isn't much that I am going to suggest. All I ask you to do is to be blind for a day or two, a week at the outside. We will take it that you have not a good memory for faces—men who are clean-shaven and dressed in that hideous convict garb are very like each other."

Copping's mouth grew hard and he shook his head resolutely.

"You ought not to talk to me like that, miss," remonstrated he. "It isn't fair."

"I thought everything was fair in love and war," Alice went on. She spoke lightly enough, but her cheeks were red and hot. "Besides, you forget that we are only playing a game. Of course you know Mr. Grenfell well enough, but he has changed a great deal. In the prison he has a number, I believe. By the way, what is his number?"

"484," Copping responded. "But, all the same, miss, I fail to see—"

"Oh, I will come to the point presently, Copping. When a chance like this comes, one is very loth to lose it. I know I'm doing wrong, Copping."

"We both are, miss," Copping urged doggedly. "You ought not to say this, and I ought not to listen to you. There's a big difference between you and me, miss, and I hope I know my place. But, all the same, if I did my duty I should order you to go home and warn you that you must not be seen here any more. Ah! and you know it, miss."

Alice flushed uncomfortably. There was no arguing the matter. Copping spoke no more than the truth, and, indeed, had not put the matter as bluntly as he was entitled to do. Quite illogically Alice felt annoyed with him. She was half inclined to change the subject altogether. But the reasons for persistence were strong, for Hugh's social salvation was at stake. If she drew back now she would be acting as a traitor. In her heart of hearts, too, she felt that Copping was yielding. If she could only win his consent, then all must work out rightly in the long run. She thought of the mystery of Rawmouth Park, of Draycott brooding and plotting mischief there. At all hazards, she must get to the bottom of that business. Had Draycott taken advantage of Martin Faber. Perhaps Faber had had an imperious reason for taking out that colossal insurance, and Draycott had heard of it. Possibly he may not have been in the Argentine for years; perhaps he had been waiting and watching his opportunity for months. Suppose he had lured Faber by night to the railway and then flung him on the line as the express passed; it was certain to cut him to pieces. There was some dark and criminal business on hand, Alice could not doubt. Hugh knew something about it, but so long as he was laid by the heels in yonder prison, his evidence was useless. He must be smuggled out of Dartdale at any cost. Copping must be induced to lend assistance.

All these thoughts flashed through Alice's mind as Copping was speaking. If he hardened now, all would be lost. Alice knew that she was touching the right place.

"You are very fond of your wife, are you not?"

A queer, unsteady smile quivered on Copping lips.

"I should not be here talking to you like this if I wasn't, miss," he said. "What you offer does not touch me in the least. Ten times the amount would not turn me from my duty. I'm thinking of Mary, and of her only. I couldn't do without her, miss. But if we bide here another winter I shall lose her. A strange thing love is. People laugh at it, but it's responsible for most of the good things and nearly all that's bad over all this world of ours. You know that, miss."

Alice flushed and smiled.

"You are sure of that, Copping?"

"Quite sure, miss. You wouldn't take all this trouble and run all these risks for Mr. Grenfell unless you cared for him. You think he's innocent, and so do I, and maybe there's somebody at Rawmouth Park who could tell the truth if he liked."

Alice started. So she was not the only one that noticed things.

"Do they gossip much hereabouts?"

"Did you ever know where they don't, miss?" Copping asked. "Mr. Draycott isn't what you call popular. There's folks who say there was trickery over that will. Not that it is any business of mine. And as to that other matter, really, miss, I don't see that I can help you. It sounds very dangerous."

"You mean as to Mr. Grenfell?"

"Yes, miss. I will do all I can, but so far as I can see—"

"Better let me go on," Alice said rapidly. "It is quite plain that when a man becomes a number he loses all identity. So long as you lock 484 in his cell at night you come home with the assurance that he is safely secured. You don't look at him each time you turn the key and see that his eyes and hair are the same color. The other convicts ask no questions, for the simple reason they dare not do so. If 484 is working one day a little apart from the rest of the gang, and you notice later that he looks different, you regard it as a mere idle fancy on your part. We are supposing all this, remember. We will also suppose that you come home the same evening and go into the garden. That is a fine asparagus bed of yours, Copping."

Copping wiped the moisture from his forehead.

"You are right there, miss," he said. "I've had a grand crop this year."

"Worth a lot of money, I daresay, and it may be worth a great deal more if you manage it properly. You might make up your mind to weed the bed on the evening in question, and in the far corner by the edge you might find a hundred sovereigns under the first plant in the row. Mind, I'm only 'supposing.' What a grand thing it would be! You could save your wife's life, you could give up your work here and move on to high ground. Directly you did that your heart would get stronger, and you would have no more such attacks as you had when you were on duty yesterday. If you have another of them, the prison doctor will examine you, and your occupation will be gone, Copping."

Copping listened with a white, set face. He was turning over the matter in his mind. He ought to have been furiously indignant, but showed no signs of anger. He was thinking of his wife and her future; and here was the chance he had prayed for. Mary would be saved; she would be restored to his arms, and they might yet spend a long and happy life together.

"What do you want me to do, miss?" he asked hoarsely.

"Nothing," Alice replied. "Only to be a little blind—blind as to one particular man for, say, a week. It might happen to anybody; it is only a case of carelessness. You may lose your post over it, but that will not matter, supposing you keep your eye on the asparagus bed. And the hundred pounds—may, will multiply by nine later."

Copping looked ahead with troubled eyes. But he made no protest; he did not reject the suggestion. The money was going to be his in any case. He had only to be a little careless, and the thing was done. All his resolution was melting like wax in the sun.

"I was always fond of the family, miss," he said, "and I honestly believe that Mr. Hugh is the victim of some deep-laid conspiracy. He has helped me on one or two occasions lately—if he had not stood by me, the people yonder would have found out, and I should have had to go. Mary is dear to me—more than I can say. And—and I'm going to save her life!"

Copping touched his hat, and turned on his heel. The action was abrupt, but Alice respected it. She had tempted this man, and he had fallen; she had touched on the one vulnerable spot. As she walked along, shame and elation strove for the mastery. She was sorry for Copping; but she was saving him from a lifelong sorrow, and at the same time had most certainly struck a blow for Hugh and her own happiness. Still, there was a haunting fear that everything was not as it should be. She was sorely troubled to account for the presence of Moler at Copping's cottage. What was the man doing there, and what was the gist of the conversation between Mary Copping and him? All this would have to be found out before Alice could feel the ground firm under her feet. Hugh had a plan of his own, which she had safely concealed in her pocket, but she was convinced that the scheme was not so good as her own. Besides, Clench could decide that when she saw him.

Carl Moler had returned to Rawmouth Park, by the time Alice arrived. He was quieter and more subdued than usual; the bold look was not so offensive as it frequently was. Mr. Draycott was better, but would not come down for a day or so.

"You mean that it is better he should stay in his room?" Alice asked.

"More or less," Moler replied. "He has enough exercise. I will take him out in the wood at the back of the house, and make a point of doing it every afternoon."

Alice listened uneasily, Moler had mentioned the very spot where she had appointed to meet Russell Clench. She would have to contrive to be there a little before the agreed upon hour to warn Hugh's friend. She did not care to suggest any change in Moler's scheme; to do so might arouse his suspicions.

"The attacks of pain are getting less?" Alice asked.

"They are not so severe," Moler explained. "It is a curious form of trouble and interests me greatly. I live in hopes of curing it altogether. It is perhaps fortunate for Mr. Draycott that I am here."

"You have known him many years?"

"Oh, dear, no, Miss Kearns; a little more than a year at the outside. I met him in Paris—"

"Really! I understood my guardian to say you met in the Argentine. But perhaps that is my mistake."

Moler bit his lips angrily, and his dark eyes gleamed.

"Paris first," he explained testily. "The Argentine afterwards."

Alice turned away listlessly. After all, what did it matter? The man was lying to her, and they both knew it. There were far more important things to think of such as the interview with Russell Clench on the following afternoon.

Alice slipped away directly after luncheon. It still wanted an hour of the appointed time, and there was nobody to be seen excepting an artist, who had set up his easel in one of the pretty wooded glades, where he was painting apparently in a deeply-engrossed frame of mind. In spite of her anxiety, Alice could not suppress a smile. Draycott had a perfect horror of strangers lurking about the place—even when they were above suspicion he had a dread of them. More than one party of innocent wanderers had been forcibly driven off. If he saw this man—

Alice saw him approach while she was still making up her mind what to do. It was easy to hide in the thick undergrowth and at the same time to watch the conduct of Raymond Draycott. She remarked how pale he was and noted the suggestion of fear and terror in his eyes as he came slowly along the drive, leaning on Moler's arm. The moody look left his face and a fierce spasm of anger filled him, as his glance encountered the stranger.

"Look at that, Moler," he rasped out. "Look at yonder scoundrel sitting there as if the place belonged to him. He's one of those confounded spies."

"Leave him alone," Moler said. "It's only an artist. What harm is he doing?"

But Draycott was not to be appeased. He strode angrily forward and grasped the unconscious painter by the shoulder. The latter looked up in mild surprise.

"Get out of this," Draycott roared. "Be off, you trespasser. I don't allow any tramps in my woods. Go, or I'll set the dogs on you. Here, give me that."

He made a grab at the wet canvas, but the artist anticipated him. Draycott's rage had over-taxed his strength, for he stood helpless and trembling. He urged Moler to take the canvas and pitch it over the hedge. In a few curt words the stranger defied Moler to do anything of the kind. The challenge was not to be evaded. With a gleam in his eyes, Moler took up the canvas and threw it on the ground. A moment later he lay on his back by the side of it, gasping for breath. The painter laughed.

"You have gone too far, my friend," he said pleasantly. "I am doing no harm here. If you want any satisfaction there is my card."

Moler took the card sullenly, but as he glanced at it his face changed and he forced a smile.

"Draycott, this is a hideous blunder," he said. "This gentleman is Mr. Russell Bassett, whom I have been expecting for two days. Mr. Bassett, my most humble apologies. Mr. Draycott is far from well, or this would not have happened. I'll take my patient back to the house and rejoin you in a few minutes. Where are you staying? At the village hotel? My dear sir, we must have your traps brought up to the house at once."

Moler hurriedly shuffled off with Draycott. Mr. Bassett sat down to the easel again, as if nothing had happened to disturb his serenity. When he was alone he took from his pocket a strong magnifying glass and examined his picture. With a pair of scissors he cut out a small square of canvas and carefully placed it in a tin case. As Alice was strolling by he took off his cap and held out his hand.

"I imagine you are looking for me, Miss Kearns," he said.

"I hardly know," Alice stammered. "But I think there is a mistake here. I am looking for a Mr. Russell Clench. I heard you say that your name was Bassett—"

"My nom de guerre," the stranger said gaily. "I will explain it in due course. In the meantime, I really am Russell Clench, very much at your service."

The stranger spoke with an air of lightness and gaiety that nevertheless carried conviction with it. A man so cool and yet so fertile of resource was the kind of ally Alice had longed for. Alice had expected—she knew not why—to meet a staid and middle-aged man. Perhaps when the disguise was removed Russell Clench might appear older. But his voice sounded clear and resolute, and the mould of the chin spoke of power and determination.

"This is quite romantic," Alice remarked. "I never thought of meeting you under an alias."

"My dear young lady," Clench retorted. "I have two exceedingly clever and absolutely reckless criminals to deal with. Whether I shall have to fight the two of them is a point I cannot decide at the moment. I know already that Moler does not love Draycott. That Draycott hates the other man is certain. I understand that Moler came for a few days originally, and has remained ever since. There are black secrets here that we have to solve. It is fair to assume that Moler is aware of these secrets. He is blackmailing Draycott. That, I may say, is a point in our favor. We must try to separate the two."

Alice listened intently. It was a wonderful relief to her to have such an adviser.

"Have you formed any plan yet?" she asked.

"Not one," Clench confessed. "I purposely refrained from drawing up anything in the nature of a programme. In the first place, I desired to see how the land lay. Is Draycott still having his attacks? Does he hide himself for days at a time?"

"As usual," Alice explained. "Strange that he and Martin Faber should both—"

"Yes, yes; I know what you are going to say. Perhaps before I have finished it will not look so strange as it appears to be on the face of it. Have you any theory?"

"Oh, a dozen a day," Alice replied wearily. "Mr. Clench, ours is a dreadful house to live in. I am not timid or frightened, but the place is getting on my nerves. I feel as if something horrible were going to happen. There are days when Draycott is dangerous. I am sure he will kill somebody in one of his fits. He has done something wrong, and is afraid of being found out. He declares he came from South America, that he is a stranger in England, and yet he knows the gossip of years, is familiar with the principal law cases, scandals, and other things that come from a careful study of the daily papers. Every now and then he betrays a close and intimate knowledge of local affairs, incidents that happened years ago. When he makes a slip like that he is mad with himself. Sometimes I fancy he found out that Faber made a will in his favor, and came secretly here and murdered his benefactor. I dare say you will laugh at me—"

"My dear young lady, I shall do nothing of the kind," Clench answered grimly. "From inquiries I have made, I believe there is much to be said for your theory. Probably Faber was induced to take out that huge, non-forfeitable life policy on false pretences. After he had paid one premium, the chief conspirator had a year in which to act. I should not wonder if you were right. It is to ascertain that definitely that I am here."

"Well, I am more than glad to meet you," Alice said, sincerely. "Why did you put that scrap of canvas so carefully away?"

Clench shook his head gravely.

"Ah! we shall see in due course. That was a little trap of mine, and the mouse walked into it. I should not be surprised if that bit of painted rag hanged Raymond Draycott."

CHAPTER V

FLESH AND BLOOD

Though Alice expressed no surprise, she was trying to feel easy in her mind, for, to some extent, she had to take this man on trust. For all she knew to the contrary, he might be an impostor, a creature of Draycott's introduced to blind her. But after his last assertion she put any fugitive suspicions aside as unworthy and absurd. Clench met her gaze frankly; there was a friendly gleam in his brown eyes, a suggestion of strength and fearlessness in his square jaw and firm lips. He might make a good enemy, but assuredly he would make as good a friend.

"It is odd we should meet in this dramatic manner," she said gravely. "I was looking for you—I wanted to warn you that Mr. Draycott was coming here this afternoon. It is a most unusual thing for him to do, and I began to fear he had discovered something."

"I don't think so," Clench replied. "He is clever and, far-seeing, but not so acute as that. Depend upon it, this woodland scenery has no charm for him; but he must have exercise—his peculiar complaint requires it."

"But how do you know?" Alice exclaimed. "How could you guess that Mr. Draycott's malady—"

"My dear young lady, you forget that you have already discussed the matter with me. In my profession, not to know such things would inevitably lead to disaster. I am a solicitor, you understand. We do a confidential business, and the handling of delicate family matters is our strong point. With scarcely an exception, we are responsible for more legal diplomacy than any firm in London. It may surprise you to learn that I have spent several days making inquiries. I know perfectly well what is the matter with Draycott. He is a dipsomaniac of the worst type—the sort of man who keeps clear of drink for weeks, and then breaks out like a lunatic."

"He calls it muscular neuralgia."

"Muscular fiddlesticks! I beg your pardon. You will see that I am right later. You have said that it strikes you as queer that both Faber and Draycott, his successor, should suffer from a malady that drives them into complete retirement for some days every six weeks?"

"That is what puzzles me!" Alice said. "I may go further, and say that it frightens me. There are so many points of similarity. Occasionally there is the same tone of voice, and there are even the same gestures. I have mentioned how familiar Mr. Draycott is with details of local history. It is as if the spirit of Martin Faber had found its way into Raymond Draycott's body."

"Let us admit that there is some amazingly ingenious fraud here."

"Well, of that I am absolutely convinced," Alice observed. "But how is it possible? Mr. Faber is dead. Before he died he told me more than once who should have his money. He confided in me when he was in good health before his accident. I know he had a high opinion of his friend in the Argentine. The will leaving everything to Draycott was made long ago. Now, beyond question Mr. Faber is dead; I saw his body brought into the house, I am prepared to swear to the man, to his hair, his face—what was left of it—the hard, brown hand with the peculiar warts he could never cure. I forget what they call them, but they are described as a species of blood poisoning. My impression is that Mr. Draycott is a relative of Mr. Faber's in disgrace; perhaps he got into trouble and changed his name."

Clench had followed Alice's views with flattering attention.

"You are quite correct," he said. "My inquiries have satisfied me that there is a very close relationship between Faber and Draycott. There are reasons why this must not be mentioned—we don't want to spoil our game at the start. And now, as to the German, Carl Moler. What is his part in the drama?"

Alice shrugged her shoulders carelessly, but there was a tinge of color on her cheeks.

"I can't say exactly," she murmured. "He turned up unexpectedly one day and made himself at home. He professed great pleasure at meeting Mr. Draycott again. I was present at the time, and if there was any pleasure it was all on one side. Mr. Draycott's face was positively ghastly, even malignant, for the moment. It was terrible. Mr. Moler has been here ever since. He has some hold on Mr. Draycott."

"Blackmail," Clench said, thoughtfully. "I expected this. It tends to confirm the conclusions I have formed. He is an impudent scamp, too, and has a strong sense of his own importance. My dear young lady, I shall know how to get rid of Moler when the time comes. Meanwhile I have baited a nice trap for him. The man is undoubtedly a clever surgeon and scientist, and his fame has travelled. So has his reputation. Certain people in South America would like to meet him again. You heard him call me Russell Bassett, and I shall be obliged if you will keep up the deception. I may be supposed to come from South America, and am greatly interested in scientific pursuits. I am very well off, and Moler hopes to secure my money. He asked me to meet him here. I fancy I am going to be a guest at Rawmouth."

"That will be a great comfort to me," Alice exclaimed. "But your meeting was not very propitious."

"Don't be too sure of that. In a way I played up for it and luck gave me a magnificent chance. I told you that little bit of smeared canvas you saw me put aside so carefully will go a long way to help us when the time comes. You have heard of fingerprint evidence. Well, I have got that. I won't spoil the dramatic side of my plot by saying anything more at present. Now let us discuss Hugh Grenfell and his future. I want to hear what his plan is and whether it is practicable or not."

Alice unfolded the outline of Grenfell's suggestion. Clench shook his head.

"Not much good, I fear," he said. "Too many loose ends and too many 'ifs' in it. We can do something better than that, Miss Kearns. It would be far better if Hugh knew nothing of it till the critical moment arrives."

"That is my own opinion," Alice answered eagerly. "I have a scheme and feel sure it will be successful. By good chance one of the warders of Dartdale—but here comes Mr. Moler. I must postpone my explanation till a more favorable opportunity."

Moler came up, looking worried and anxious.

"I have had some trouble with my patient," he explained. "Quite ridiculous things upset him, even the trifling incident that happened here just now. But I have given him some soothing medicine, and he will be at dinner tonight. I have sent for your traps, Mr. Bassett, and I hope you will stay for a few days. I see you have made Miss Kearns' acquaintance."

"That has been my privilege," Clench said, politely. "It is really very good of you. If I won't be in the way, I shall be delighted to accept your invitation."

"I am sure it will be a pleasure to me," Alice smiled. "I hope Mr. Draycott will be well enough to have a chat with a gentleman who knows his part of the world."

Alice turned away, leaving Moler with a startled countenance. She saw nothing of Clench till dinner-time, when Draycott came into the room pale and shaky, but with a pleased expression and a somnolent look about his eyes that attracted Clench's attention.

"Morphia," he said, sotto voce. "Morphia, or I am greatly mistaken. Not that it very much matters at present. Still, it is significant."

Draycott sat at the head of the table smiling pleasantly. His appetite was good, but Clench noticed that he passed the decanter with a suggestion of dislike. He spoke in a sleepy voice and his wits appeared to be constantly wandering. Clench was watching discreetly, and veiling his keen eyes behind the plants on the table. It struck Alice, listening demurely, that Clench talked both agreeably and well. He spoke of places on the other side of the globe. Suddenly he appealed to his host for confirmation on some point.

"Haven't the least idea," Draycott said, abruptly, "I've never been there."

Moler exploded into loud laughter. He bent over and laid his hand on Draycott's shoulder. The grip was that of a vice, forefingers and thumb meeting in a cruel pinch.

"You're chaffing Mr. Bassett," he said. "He's speaking about your own country in the back of the Argentine, Carados, you know. Wake up, Draycott."

"I was half asleep," Draycott apologised. "I have had such bad nights lately. If Mr. Bassett has no objection I shall retire early. Carados, of course. I thought you were discussing some place in Australia. Sometimes I wish I was back there."

Clench did not labor the point. He had found out all he needed. He began to speak presently of a mine in which he was interested. He illustrated the plan by the help of wineglasses and a few nuts. The cigarettes had been passed round, and the servants had vanished. It was an interesting story, and even Draycott was listening closely. He stood by Clench's side with his hand on the table.

"This is where the gold lies," Clench went on. He took his cigarette from his mouth and waved his hand with an excited gesture. "This spur of rock runs up the valley as far as the place where the stream enters. If you draw a line from north to south and—really I beg pardon, Draycott—I hope I haven't burnt you."

Draycott dashed a little pile of ashes from the back of his hand on which the hot cigarette had come down in the excitement of the moment. He shook his head.

"Oh, dear, no," he said. "I assure you I felt nothing, the merest touch. Go on! As an old prospector, your story interests me."

The story came to an end at length, and the talk became desultory again. Draycott sat with his head buried in his breast, half asleep.

"Really, I'll ask you to excuse me," he said. "I can hardly keep my eyes open. I could do with a good night's rest. Come and see me to bed, Moler."

Moler and his host vanished. Alice saw Clench's eyes gleam.

"I hope you will find your gold," she said. "At any rate, I gather from the expression of your face that you have found something."

"The gold is fairy gold," Clench laughed. "But I have found something. I've come precious near to a solution of the whole mystery."

There was no more to be said for the time being. Alice was glad to know that Clench was established as a guest in the house, and was sure her anxieties were relieved. It was not yet the hour for retiring, and there was more than a chance that Moler would come down again. Clench confidently expected him.

"He does not often leave his patient," Alice explained. "He is a devoted attendant."

"He has no intention of killing the goose that lays the golden eggs," Clench chuckled. "Such a shrewd doctor has no difficulty in patching the goose up after the foolish bird has gone beyond bounds. If anything happened to Draycott, Moler's position would not be so pleasant. He'll stick to his patient so long as he has a sovereign left."

"You think there is nothing the matter with Mr. Draycott?"

"Well, not what you call physical infirmity," Clench replied. "Neither do I think there is anything wrong with his constitution. The trouble is drink."

"You are absolutely certain of that?"

"My dear young lady, I have no doubt of it. I am a man of the world, and in my time I have had all sorts and conditions of clients. Out of my experiences I could make the fortune of a dozen novelists. I have seen some very sad cases. It is astonishing how people with nothing to do and plenty to do it with drift into that vice. Draycott has every symptom of it, but by way of keeping him more or less under control, Moler plies him with morphia."

"But there is no necessity for that," Alice protested.

"You are wrong. There is one class of drunkard that never gets any worse. His drinking habits are as regular as the clock. He goes on in his own dogged, stupid way, and very often lives to a good old age. Then there is the savage drinker, who drinks fitfully and has that awful thing called delirium tremens. That's the kind of man Draycott is. Don't you see that some day in a fit or madness he might tell the truth about the mystery of Rawmouth Park? He might come down now and blurt out the whole story for our delectation. If that were done, the pretty bubble would collapse and Moler would be thrown on the hard world again. This is the one thing he dreads. He has one effectual means of keeping Draycott quiet, and that is to dose him with morphia when an attack is imminent. That glassy eye, those shivering fits, even on a hot night like this, the sudden changes of his mind, all point to morphia. Now, if you don't object, I'll take a stroll in the garden. There is a moth peculiar to this district I am interested in which I wish to add to my collection."

"I didn't know that you collected moths."

"My dear, Miss Kearns, I have been interested in moths all my life—moths and butterflies. The butterflies are comparatively harmless, but the moths are different. There are two in this house, which I should like to get under my net and pinned down to the board. But this is only an excuse for Moler in case he returns. If he comes down, please let me know. He will be pretty certain to come, I think, for he will be anxious to find out whether or not I have discovered anything. Even a poor, harmless old scientist like myself must not be overlooked. Now, do I talk in the least like a man to be suspected?"

Alice surveyed her benign-looking companion with a smile. He looked the last person in the world to distrust or dislike anybody.

"You look quite a dear old thing," she laughed, "like the elderly, benevolent comedian one sees on the stage. You are Benjamin Goldfinch in 'A Pair of Spectacles.' You would deceive a judge."

Clench chuckled as he passed out into the garden. He peered about among the trees, as if eager to come up with his prey. He was indeed the very ideal of the type of amateur who has less knowledge than he imagines himself to possess.

Out of the darkness of the garden, Clench could see the lights in the upper windows, and caught a glimpse of Moler and Draycott in one of the bedrooms. The window was up and the blinds were undrawn. Moler was leaning against the sash smoking a cigarette, while Draycott paced up and down the room restlessly. On the still night air it was possible to hear nearly every word that was said. Clench crept along till he was half hidden by a mass of flowering shrubs in one of the beds. He might or might not hear something to his advantage and he was not going to lose the opportunity for the sake of a few scruples.

He had a fair view of the figures. He heard a laugh come from Moler's lips, followed by a growl from Draycott. There was the hint of a scuffle, but only for a moment. The watcher thought that Moler held something shining in his hand.

"Well, if you think you can manage it better than I can, go on. Perhaps you prefer the tablets you used when I first came."

"Curse the tablets," Draycott muttered. "They give me indigestion till I can't breathe. What's the use of getting your nerves steady, if you'll have a pain under your heart like a knife. Let me have the needle; nothing like the blessed needle."

"And nothing so accursed," Moler retorted. "Why don't you pull up, man? How long do you suppose this kind of thing can go on? You've had two doses to-day already."

Draycott laughed horribly.

"Not strong enough. Why didn't you give me one more before dinner? You saw how near I was to making a fool of myself. My nerve cracked at the wrong moment. At times you are so stingy with the drug. Lucky that old fool saw nothing."

Clench smiled to himself; this was exceedingly interesting, especially to the old fool, who was listening eagerly. At any rate, his suspicions were being confirmed. Draycott was a dipsomaniac, and Moler was keeping his brain clear by morphia. He saw the needle flash, saw it plunged in the arm that Draycott extended. He heard the sigh of relief that followed later. Draycott shook himself like a dog fresh from sleep.

"That's better," he said, with a long drawn breath. "I feel a man again. Wonderful what a difference that little needle makes, Moler. I'm not afraid of anything now."

"Nor need you be, if only you took more care of yourself," Moler retorted. "You're pretty safe, you must be safe so long as Grenfell is out of the way. Do you suppose a single soul in the world has the slightest notion of the truth? I'm the one man, and, so long as I am paid for my silence, you have nothing to fear, absolutely nothing."

"Yes, I have," smiled Draycott. "I've got you to fear. Half my money has gone to you already."

"Your money," Moler cried. "What would the insurance company say if—"

He dropped his voice to a hissing whisper, and Clench heard no more. He stepped back into the house to find that Alice was still in the dining-room.

"Did you catch the moth?" she asked.

"Two of them, I hope. I have not wasted my time."

CHAPTER VI

Alice asked no further questions, for the simple reason that she knew it would be useless. Clench would tell her everything in good time. Meanwhile it was a source of satisfaction to know that her ally had so speedily and cleverly got to work.

"I must not be curious," she said. "But there were one or two things I could not help noticing at dinner. You introduced that place in the Argentine on purpose. Mr. Draycott had never heard of it."

"That certainly was the idea, wasn't it?" Clench smiled. "Draycott is supposed to have lived within a mile or two of it for years. You heard what he said, and saw how his answer affected Moler. He laughed it off, of course, but he was greatly upset. Did you notice how he pinched Draycott? It wasn't a bad excuse of Draycott's either. He was nearly half asleep, and besides had had a liberal dose of morphia."

"What object could Moler have in that?"

"I have already told you. Just a nerve tonic in the first instance, but to keep him from blabbing. But all this is nothing to the discovery I made just now. Meet me in the garden to-morrow morning, as I have much to tell you. I also want to hear more of your scheme for giving Grenfell his chance. It is sure to be an ingenious one. Whether we can acquaint Grenfell with it is another matter."

"Well, you can make your mind easy on that score," Alice answered. "I can promise that Hugh shall know everything within twenty four hours, and the authorities in the prison will be none the wiser. How thankful I am that you are here! I was beginning to lose nerve and courage with those two men always conspiring. Now I feel as if I could do anything. Had you better not keep up your role as an artist, Mr. Clench? You can ask me to point out the beauties of the place."

Clench deemed the idea excellent. Nor was there any difficulty in carrying it into effect the following morning. Draycott had passed a good night; but he was not so well after breakfast, and needed Moler's attention. Clench expressed his regret, and inwardly blessed the reaction from the dose of morphia.

"We will defer our discussion till after luncheon. Meanwhile, Miss Kearns has kindly volunteered to show me some of the best bits for painting. It is my favorite hobby after science. Don't worry about me."

Clench went out presently with a cigarette. He chose a fairly open spot, where he could sit painting and talk with Alice. He mistrusted Moler, and meant to give the wily German no opportunities for eavesdropping. He listened with grave attention till Alice had unfolded her scheme.

"On the whole, it is smart," he said. "It is evident Copping will do all you ask him. In similar circumstances I should yield also. But this part of the programme I must leave to you. It would never do for a solicitor to be found guilty of tampering with a prison official. My legal career would cease. It's a pity you're not a man; but that can't be helped. But, after all, only a woman could work the thing successfully. No man could touch the proper sentimental note. So far, your scheme is excellent, and I don't see why it should not come off. It will not be difficult to smuggle a letter into Dartdale to Grenfell. We could arrange the day and hour, so that he could be ready. There is one thing, however, that is difficult. Have you thought about a substitute?"

"Frankly, I haven't," Alice admitted. "We must have a substitute, but where to find him baffles me. He must be bold and resolute, ready to accept punishment if it comes his way; but he will be well paid. I can find a thousand pounds."

"For a thousand pounds I can find hundreds of men willing to do anything, not even excluding murder. What would nine out of every ten men not do for that sum? One could write a whole volume on a text like that! Now, in all seriousness, you must not let this go any further, or I shall lose my standing in the profession. I don't think you want a hireling at all. You need some fine fellow who will run the risk for sheer love of adventure and novelty of the thing. He will play the part better than one you pay, and will go into it con amore. An enterprising journalist might do it. The risk of detection is not so very great. The dull routine of the prison presents that."

"If you only happened to know such a man!"

"Well, as a matter of fact, I do. I'll wire to him at once. I'll get him to fix up an appointment which will give me an excuse for saying that I have important business in London tomorrow. I'll leave the telegram about, so that Moler is certain to read it. I'll return next day, and tell you what I have done. It's pretty certain Wilfred Collier will do all I ask."

The telegram came in the course of the evening, apparently to Clench's great annoyance. He would have to go to town on the morrow. It was a nuisance, but could not be helped. If he might, he would leave his things and return as soon as possible. Moler was sorry, too, but interposed no difficulties.

At two o'clock next afternoon Clench was sitting in the chambers of his old friend and college chum, Wilfred Collier. Collier was by way of being a barrister, but the main part of his income came from his pen, and a decided turn for the stage. He was an enthusiast in his profession, and prepared to take any risks in search of fresh 'copy.' He listened to Clench carefully.

"A story in itself," he said. "I'll write it when I have time. By Jove, what an adventure! Do you really mean it, Clench?"

"My dear boy," Clench said solemnly, "I was never more serious in my life. Directly the scheme began to take shape, you came into my mind at once. I said to myself, 'Here is a magnificent chance for Collier.' The story must come out sooner or later, and it will make a fine stir. The public will idolise the man who was ready to suffer in order to clear the innocent and punish the guilty. You may pay for your temerity, but public opinion will pull you through."

"I'll do it," Collier said. "I'll do it, and glad of the chance."

"That's what I expected you to say. You're nothing if not a sportsman. Will you be able to put up with the dreadful existence for a week?"

"Of course, I shall," Collier said scornfully. "Look at my record, old man! I was for a whole week in an earthquake district without food. I've been shipwrecked, and a prisoner with the Moors. There is no kind of hardship and danger I've not been through. Why, a week in a convict prison will be luxury compared with some of my experiences. Besides, the love story appeals to me. I met Grenfell once, and he struck me as being a good fellow. You can count me in, old chap. I'll get all the necessary properties together and slip down to Rawmouth at the proper time. If you can provide me with a photograph of Grenfell, so much the better. I'll make up as nearly like him as possible."

Clench went his way well satisfied with his work. He walked as far as his office and dropped in upon his partner, Dallas Smith. The shrewd little man, his eyes sparkling behind pince-nez, greeted him eagerly.

"Well, did you get hold of Moler?"

"Oh, Moler and I are quite good friends, Dallas; and as to the rest, we're progressing. A happy thought occurred to me on my way to Dartdale, and an accident gave me the desired opportunity. Here is a scrap of canvas. As a matter of fact, it is the fragment of a picture. Handle it carefully, please, and put it back again into the box. Then take it to Scotland Yard and ask them to photograph it."

Dallas Smith nodded meaningly. He had too intimate a knowledge of his partner's ways to ask unnecessary questions. He wanted to know what the next move was.

"I shall return to Dartdale to-morrow," Clench explained. "It is likely you may not see anything of me for a few days. Meanwhile, I am going to Somerset House to inspect the will of Martin Faber, whereby everything he had to dispose of went to his dear friend, Raymond Draycott, some time of the Argentine. I am casting a fly over a stream that I know nothing of, but it's always possible to hook a fish."

Half an hour later Clench was at Somerset House with the will in his hand. He read it carefully from beginning to end, and made notes in his pocket-book. Finally he held it up to the light and made a rough drawing of the water-mark. After that he drove to a firm of law-stationers in the city and asked for paper of a similar character.

"I suppose you have it in stock?"

"Certainly, sir," the polite assistant said. "How much do you need?"

"Well, say a ream," Clench said. "Send it to Dallas Smith and Clench. I daresay the firm have an account with your people. Very nice paper."

"And very popular, sir," the assistant said. "We sell a tremendous quantity of it. It a looks like handmade; in fact, only an expert could tell the difference. We have sold tons of it since we introduced it, two years ago."

Clench started. He had hoped for this, but still he started.

"Longer than that, surely?" he hazarded.

"Not at all, sir. Two years at the outside. That water-mark was only registered in 1906. I ought to know, as that kind of thing comes in my department."

Clench went away thoughtfully but joyfully.

"What's the game?" he asked himself. "Here's the will purporting to be signed some years ago, and written on paper that was not made till five years afterwards! Now, what did Faber mean by doing a thing like that? The plot is thickening!"

In the circumstances, Clench deemed it proper to talk over the matter with his partner before proceeding further. Dallas Smith had not left the office when Clench returned.

"I didn't expect to see you again today," the latter said. "I was just leaving."

"Well, you are not going to do anything of the kind," Clench smiled. "My dear fellow, I have made a most interesting discovery. More out of curiosity than anything else, I went to Somerset House to look at Martin Faber's will."

"Seems a waste of time, doesn't it?" Smith asked. "The will was all right, made and signed years ago."

"Probably correct, my dear fellow. The fact that the will was made some years ago seems, on the face of it, to strengthen Draycott's position. I examined the will, which, by the way, appeared to be perfectly regular and held up the paper to the light. I amused myself by taking a sketch of the water-mark. Not that I expected to find out anything; but when you are investigating a case that reeks of fraud, when you know that things are altogether wrong, you don't let slip any chance. After I'd left Somerset House I took a taxi as far as Rosland and Bullocks, in the city—our law-stationers, you know."

Dallas Smith nodded. His partner was about to tell him something important.

"I saw an assistant there," Clench went on. "I produced my rough sketch of the water-mark and asked him whether he could tell me where the paper came from and who made it. As it happens, they have the very same paper in stock. Seemed funny, didn't it?"

"After seven years, certainly," Dallas Smith muttered. "It's very seldom the same paper keeps in the fashion in lawyers' offices as long as that."

"That's what I thought, Dallas. We examined the sketch and the water mark on the paper, and beyond all doubt it was the same stuff. When I asked Gibson, the assistant, where he got it he startled me by saying that it had been designed and made for his own firm, and that nobody else had any. But the point of the story is, that the paper has only been made for two years."

Dallas Smith jumped from his chair.

"So that's the dodge," he said. "Faber makes a will dated seven years since and written on paper he could not have purchased until a couple of years ago. My dear fellow, let me compliment you on an exceedingly good day's work. Now, why on earth did Faber date his will back, and how did he manage to obtain his witnesses?"

"Probably they did not notice. They would be told they were witnessing a will, and put their signatures to it as a matter of course. This looks like a very complicated affair, Clench. Did you take the names of the witnesses?"

"Upon my word, I didn't," Clench continued. "I forgot all about it. I must return to Dartdale without further delay. Goodness knows what may be taking place. Perhaps you'll get the names of the witnesses and phone them to me. It's a long way to telephone, but I'll be at the other end of the wire at Cullingford to-morrow at one o'clock. As I'm staying at Rawmouth Park, it will never do to write me a letter. I don't think for a moment those fellows suspect me, but neither would hesitate to steal a letter if it were worth while. Let me have the information and I'll look the witnesses up."

This being arranged for, Clench made his way to Paddington. Once more he was disguised as Russell Bassett, and was ready to take up the trail again. He strolled up the platform with his books and papers, looking for a first-class compartment which he might have to himself. The first stop would be Exeter, and he wished to make himself comfortable. In front of Clench was a lady and her maid, the former a tall, handsome woman, with dark eyes and hair, and the haughty carriage of one who knows her position and makes others feel it, too.

"The Countess D'Arblay!" Clench exclaimed. "Now this is a slice of luck. This appears to be one of my happy days. I'll dally about till the train is ready to start, and get into her carriage."

The train was actually moving when Clench took his seat. The lady favored him with a haughty stare and settled down to a magazine. There was no chance of interruption till Exeter. Clench bent over and touched the lady on the arm.

"I am very fortunate," he said, "very fortunate indeed. Probably you may not recognise me, but there was a time when I was proud to reckon myself amongst your admirers. It will facilitate matters if you tell me what is the name you are assuming at present. One of your most charming attributes was the quiet way in which you vicariously adopted a different nom de guerre."

"Really, this is an outrage," the woman protested. "If I summon the guard—"

There was an ominous flash in Clench's eyes.

"Pray don't take that line. I see you can't place me, and for the moment I have no intention that you shall. But you won't summon the guard, for if you do I may have something to say. I could reveal a good deal about the picturesque career of the Countess D'Arblay."

The woman's indignity vanished, and with a smile she showed an exquisite set of teeth.

"I am beaten," she said. "There are times, dear sir, when discretion is better than valor. As to my name, that of D'Arblay will do as well as anything else. Only you have a great advantage over me—"

"That advantage for the moment I prefer to keep," Clench replied. "It will be something of a novel sensation for you. May I ask where you are going?"

"To Newquay," the Countess said, with a touch of hesitation. "I have not been well lately."

"I am sorry," Clench murmured. "You are prosperous as ever. I can see so much for myself. Do you remember the old days when you had Hugh Grenfell and Oliver Partridge and Marcus Gainsforth in your train? Those were brave times, Countess. And that pretty maid of yours—what was her name? Mary Something. You might have got her into very serious trouble."

Again the Countess showed those exquisite teeth in a dazzling smile.

"You puzzle me," she said, "and I hate to be puzzled. Please tell me who you are."

But Clench declined to be drawn. He talked glibly till Exeter was reached, interesting his companion with a score of reminiscences, but as to his identity she guessed nothing. As the train pulled up at Exeter he grew more serious.

"It is possible I can render you real service if I choose to do so. On the contrary, I may need your assistance sometimes. Will a letter or a telegram sent to the old address find you?"

"The letters will be forwarded," the Countess said smilingly. "Good-bye."

She held out her hand and vanished. Clench laughed as he closed the door.

"What luck! I'm getting on famously. She'll be very handy latter. Why did she say she was going to Newquay, when her bag was labelled to Delveston? She is evidently going to be very close."

CHAPTER VII

THE MARTYR'S CROWN

Clench's visit to Somerset House had been something in the nature of an afterthought. In his own words he had cast a fly over a stream with the waters of which he was not very familiar. There was a possibility that he might land a fish, but he had not expected to hook a fine salmon. There was a chance of discovering something useful between the lines of Martin Faber's will, and his expectations had been exceeded.

At the same time he was puzzled. There was not the slightest reason, as far as he knew, why Faber should not dispose of his property as he chose. He had known for years that his invalid wife was not likely to survive him, and he was not on good terms with his relatives. He was just the kind of man to leave everything in some unsuspected quarter. A year or two ago there was not very much to leave, for Faber had been recklessly extravagant, and the property was subject to a heavy mortgage. For some reason best known to himself, however, Faber had insured his life for an enormous amount, and within eighteen months had met with a dreadful accident that resulted in his death. Thus Raymond Draycott had become the fortunate possessor of over a hundred thousand pounds.

But why had the will been antedated? What was the object of an apparently unnecessary fraud like this? Was Draycott at the bottom of it? Had he obtained private knowledge of Faber's will and come home secretly to put his benefactor out of the way? Suppose he had returned to England sub rosa, and visited Rawmouth in disguise. Suppose he had murdered Faber and left the body on the line so that the express train should cut it to pieces. He might even have inveigled him to the line in the dark and thrown him in front of the engine. The authorities would never suspect anything of that kind; there would be no post-mortem examination, and nothing to reveal if there were.

Such a crime was possible to a man of imagination and courage enough to carry it into effect. Still, there was another theory, and Clench made up his mind to test the alternative first. It counted for much that he had obtained evidence of fraud on the part of somebody, and the alternative solution that was uppermost in Clench's mind was also daring and original.

It was all the more necessary to have speech with Hugh Grenfell. He would probably be able to throw some light on the heavy insurance Faber had effected on his life. The way was clear, and Clench lost no time in putting his latest plan into operation. Alice listened with breathless interest.

"You really have found the man?"

"The very man for the purpose. Wilfred Collier could not be bettered. He will carry it out the more effectually since he is a volunteer."

"How can I thank him for his kindness?' Alice murmured.

"Oh, there's no kindness about it," said Clench. "It is a matter of business with Collier. He would tell you, if you asked him, that the kindness was on your side. He has never had the chance of an adventure like this. He will come here to carry out the plan directly we are ready for him. You had better see Copping and arrange a convenient date. I should say after Saturday—the first fog we get. I'm told that you don't wait long for a fog even in the height of summer."

"Rarely more than a week," Alice answered. "A few days of this hot weather and a thick white fog is inevitable. When it comes it generally lasts two or three days. You can rely upon me for my part of the contract. I was in Exeter yesterday, and obtained the money. I'll go to Copping's cottage at tea-time and pay him the hundred pounds—at least I will place the gold where he is certain to find it. Only one thing troubles me, and I can't understand why I did not tell you before."

"You are not afraid of anybody here?"

"Indeed, I am, Mr. Clench. I am afraid of Moler. Perhaps you can keep him out of the way. He thinks you are a simple-minded Colonial with a taste for science, and he hopes to make money out of you. At any rate, I am reckoning upon this. But you will be surprised to hear that Moler knows Mrs. Copping."

"The deuce he does!" Clench exclaimed. "That's awkward. I certainly did not count on this. Do you mean that he is on familiar terms with her?"

"I think so. But let me tell the story."

Clench's face was grave enough when Alice had finished. Here was a complication that went far towards upsetting his carefully laid schemes. Moler was playing some deep game, and had not taken Draycott into his confidence. There could be no doubt that the German had only renewed Mary Copping's acquaintance since he had been at Rawmouth, and was cultivating it for the purpose of learning something about Dartdale prison or communicating with one of the inmates. Was that inmate Hugh Grenfell? Clench wondered. He would have given much to know.

"It was extremely fortunate you told me this," he said. "I'm bound to confess that, for the present, it has knocked me out of time. Have you any idea what kind of influence Moler has gained over this woman?"

"I fancy she is afraid of him. I gathered as much from the way in which he spoke and the tone of her replies. He did not use threats exactly, but spoke as if he intended to be obeyed."

Clench turned the matter over in his mind.

"I must keep an eye on Moler," he said presently. "He's evidently a dangerous chap. You must bind Copping to secrecy—he must promise that his wife shall not know where the money is to come from. You will appreciate the reason for this."

Alice readily understood what Clench meant. It was more than probable that Copping would keep the secret for his own sake; indeed, he was not likely to let his wife know he had been guilty of a dereliction of duty.

"Still, it's serious," Clench went on. "Perhaps I can get Moler out of the way for a day or two directly Draycott is better. I might send him on a wild-goose chase, under the impression that he is going to make a good thing out of it. Once Hugh Grenfell is free, Moler will cease to count."

"Anyhow, you will take care that I am not followed this afternoon," Alice said. "After I have seen Copping, my part of the conspiracy will be finished. I will go just before tea-time."

Clench gave the desired assurance. He would keep an eye on Moler all the afternoon, so that Alice might accomplish her journey with the comfortable assurance that the way was clear. She was fortunate enough to meet Copping in the lane leading to the cottage. She thought he regarded her somewhat guiltily, yet with an air of expectation on his face.

"I was on my way to the cottage," she said. "I wanted to have another look at the asparagus bed. I have brought the seed for it as promised."

She spoke lightly as she handed a small heavy bag to Copping. He flushed to the eyes as he put it in his pocket, yet his sigh of relief was unmistakable.

"I think you said a foggy day," Alice went on in a low voice. "The first foggy day rather late in the afternoon. We understand each other, Copping?"

Joe clenched his pocket tightly. The touch of it spurred his flagging courage.

"I fancy so, miss," he said hoarsely. "I am sure I am much obliged to you. It's—it's taken a load off my mind. Mary will be able to go away at once, and as for me I should not be able to stay here much longer in any case. Still—"

He turned his head away sorrowfully, but he knew not that he had all Alice's sympathy. She felt horribly mean and ashamed of herself.

"Perhaps you will give me a cup of tea," she said; "and mind you, your wife must know nothing of this. She is bound to know you have the money, but must not learn how. I have your word for that?"

"Oh, I will say nothing, for more reasons than one," Copping said bitterly. "Very pleased to give you some tea, miss, if you will honor us with your company."

Mary Copping welcomed her visitor cordially. It was a proud afternoon for her, she declared; but there was a forced gaiety about her that Alice noticed at once. She looked ill and drawn, despite the brilliancy of her complexion. It was all the humid air, she said, and the fogs. If she could only get away she would soon be herself again.

"And so you shall, my dear," Copping exclaimed. "I've had a bit of luck, lass. I kept it from you till I was certain—one of those newspaper competitions—a matter of a hundred pounds. What is more, I've got the money. We'll leave here as soon as we can and buy a bit of a business where the land is higher. It's a miracle, Mary."

The woman gave a gasping cry, and the cup fell from her hand. She swayed and would have fallen, had not Copping caught her in his arms.

"I should have broken it gently," he said. "But joy never kills."

"No, no," Mary Copping said slowly. She spoke like a woman in a dream. "Joy never kills. It's—it's a bit startling, Joe, but I'll get used to it in time. Go and get Miss Alice some of those new yellow roses, Joe. When you come back I'll feel myself again."

Alice discreetly led the way to the door. She was alarmed and uneasy. This was an emotion deeper and more painful than mere surprise would have caused. Mary Copping was frightened. When Copping had vanished she crossed to the window and opened it. She was panting for breath, her face was wet and hot, and her head ached.

"So it's come," she whispered. "The thing I have prayed for on my knees—life and health and happiness. And now, I can't go—I dare not!"

Alice glanced at the speaker in astonishment. Had Mary Copping deceived her in any way? Was she playing a part at Moler's instigation? The question trembled on Alice's lips. But it might be indiscreet to mention Moler, and if Mary were playing some deep game, to betray any knowledge of it would be foolish. She did not look as if she were doing anything of the kind. Unless she were a born actress she would never have stimulated longing and despair like this. Her eyes were full of misery, her lips quivered. Alice decided to appeal to the better side of her nature.

"I don't understand you, Mary."

"Come to that, I'm not sure that I understand myself, miss," Mary said, forlornly. "I know you mean well. I know you would like to help me. I believe you would do as much for me in any case, had you known my trouble."

"Certainly I would; but, unless you tell me what the trouble is—"

"Miss Alice, I can't do anything of the kind," Mary went on. "You wouldn't believe me if I did. I've got a big trouble, and I must fight it in my own way."

"But things, troubles, are always so much easier if you have people to share them," Alice urged. "When we hug troubles to ourselves, they always look so much more terrible. I daresay if you told me yours I could show you a way out of it altogether."

But Mary shook her head resolutely. Like most gentle, fragile creatures, she had a strong vein of obstinacy. The quivering lips grew firm, and the look of anguish faded from the blue eyes.

"It's very good of you, miss," she said, "and I don't know how to thank you. I'll do what I can as far as I can. But I've got to stay here. If it kills me, I must remain in the neighborhood. That is why your suggestion does not tempt me so much as it might have done. My trouble is my own, and I've got to bear it by myself. I am paying for my folly. Heaven knows it was no more than folly. You'll say nothing to Joe about it?"

"My dear Mary, why should I mention it to your husband? You have told me so much on the spur of the moment. Well, think it over. Don't make up your mind definitely. Be sure there must be some way out of the difficulty."

It was very disturbing and unsatisfactory, Alice thought. The woman was only too anxious to quit Dartdale, where she had not enjoyed much in the way of delight or pleasure. She knew her life depended upon going right away, getting from the chilly mists and cold fogs. Some strange terror must root her to this dangerous spot.

It would be necessary to mention this development to Clench. There was no immediate hurry for the present, and Alice walked on across the moor, bent on a healthy exercise. It was always good to steer clear of Rawmouth Park, where she could forget its dark secrets and threatening troubles. Alice knew every bit of the country for mile's round, and was familiar with all the short cuts; there was not a sheep track she could not have followed. The road here was narrow, with boundary fences on each side, and a stranger might easily lose his way.

Somebody had gone astray apparently, for a large car had pulled up by the roadside, and a sullen-looking chauffeur was being violently scolded by his solitary passenger. Alice glanced at her as she passed. She saw a tall, strikingly handsome woman, with dark hair and eyes, her face marred at that moment by an expression of anger and passion that gave it a sinister look. She was beautifully dressed, and evidently patronised Paris for her clothes. The car, too, was of the most luxurious type, the flowers that decorated the interior being costly orchids.

The hard glitter of the eyes softened, and a smile came to the parted lips, as the occupant of the car caught sight of Alice. She made a gesture to the driver and he sulkily opened the door. Alice paused for a reason that she would have found it hard to explain, she would have preferred not to speak. Something about the woman repelled her. But the stranger had lost her way, and had descended from the car on purpose to make inquiries.

"I am sure you will excuse me," she said, with a fascinating smile, "but my man has gone wrong. He is an excellent driver, but he has a genius for taking the wrong turning. As a rule, if he says one direction, I insist upon another, and invariably reach my destination. On this occasion I was so weak as to be over-persuaded. As there appear to be no guide-posts in this delectable country, I am helpless. Will you be so good as to show me the way to Delveston?"

Alice gave the desired information. She would have passed on, but the woman detained her.

"Really, I am very grateful to you," she said. "How nice to know the country as you do! I suppose you live in this neighborhood. That is a lovely house among the trees."

"Rawmouth Park," Alice said. "That is my home."

For a fraction of a minute a queer smile played about the stranger's mouth. Alice wondered where she had seen that smile before. Why did she connect it with Dresden?

"A lonely place," the woman went on. "As I am staying not far off, I hope to come and see it. Thanks so much for your help. Good-bye."

She smiled and bowed, and the big car slipped over the shoulder of the hill. The queer smile was still on the woman's face as she sped along.

"So that is the fair Alice," she muttered. "Well, you did not gain much by your change of affections, Mr. Hugh Grenfell. I wonder what she would say if she knew."

Alice watched the car out of sight. She was asking herself a question or two.

"Now, where did I?—I know. It was in the Imperial, at Dresden. The diamond bracelet! That's the woman who tried to steal it!"

CHAPTER VIII

"DR. GORDON BLAYDES."

But there were other matters to think of besides mysterious women and diamond bracelets. The success of her mission more or less assured, Alice made her way back to Rawmouth. She had done what Clench required of her and, so far as she could see, there was no flaw in the arrangements; but, in a vague way, she was uneasy. Mary Copping's attitude had alarmed her. Mary should have expressed the wildest and most extravagant joy to know that she could leave Dartdale; but, instead, she looked like a woman who had received her death sentence. The news that her husband had found the means to take her away had fallen like a bolt from the blue. In an indefinite way Alice felt that Moler was at the bottom of it all. Anyhow, the circumstance in itself was disconcerting, and it would be interesting to watch how Russell Clench would tackle it.

Clench had no explanation to offer.

"I don't like it. The woman is not likely to prove a stumbling block in our way, but she is certainly in Moler's power. Now, why should that be? Moler has only been here for a short time, and Mary's has been a humdrum existence ever since she was born. There is no suggestion of the woman with a past about her. Yet this man has some tight hold on her. I will make it my business to find out what it means when I have a little time to spare. Meanwhile let me congratulate you on the way in which you have done your work, Miss Kearns."

"You are going to move almost at once?'"

"On the first favorable opportunity. But you can safely leave that to me. You won't see much of me for the next day or two, but I shall not be very far off. The fact that I was staying in the house makes it a little difficult for me; but, on the other hand, the situation has its advantages."

Alice was content to leave matters to Clench. He appeared to have a deal of correspondence to attend to, and she noticed that, on one pretext or another, he usually contrived to post it himself. Evidently he was taking no risks. He generally vanished for an hour or two after dinner, hinting at mysterious meteorological observations, whereat Moler smiled in a covert manner. Moler would make use of Clench presently. The man whom he took to be Russell Bassett would be worth money to him.

But Moler might have modified his opinion had he chosen to follow Clench a few nights later. The latter made his way across the woods to a solitary farmhouse on the far side of the moor. Close by was a trout stream, which sufficiently accounted for the presence of a visitor who had been attracted by reports of the good fishing. It was not the first time the people at the lonely farm had had a lodger on a like errand, so they had no occasion to view their visitor with suspicion, the less so, indeed, that he proved to be wonderfully expert at his pastime.

The lodger sat in the small parlor reading a sporting volume by the light of a lamp. The casement window was wide open, and Russell Clench had no difficulty in entering the room. Wilfred Collier turned as Clench came in.

"Glad to see you," he said. "Sit down and smoke. Don't he afraid to talk—my honest landlady and her husband are in bed and asleep long ago."

"Rather dull, isn't it?"

"Not a bit of it, my dear fellow. I'm an outdoor man to the backbone, and the fishing is all that it was represented. I'm quite happy, but ready for work all the same. When will the curtain rise on the first act of the drama?"

"We are only waiting for the weather," Clench explained. "Miss Kearns tells me that a real moorland mist is considerably overdue. It generally comes up about four in the afternoon. At the first sign of it you are to meet me at the appointed spot. Only, no time must be wasted in preliminaries."

"No time will be wasted by me," Collier said. "The fishing is so good that I am never far away, and, I repeat, I am in readiness. The people here know that I am only waiting for letters, and may have to leave at any time. I settle up with them day by day. When I enter on my sphere of usefulness elsewhere, all you have to do is to get a telegram forwarded from Exeter, purporting to come from me, informing my landlady that I have been called away on urgent business, and asking her to send my few traps to a place where I can pick them up when I need them again. I am merely reminding you of all this. Thus my exit will seem natural and not arouse gossip or suspicion. Is there anything else you need?"

Clench expressed himself as perfectly satisfied. Moler was perfectly satisfied also. Two days later the fog rolled up unexpectedly about lunch time, blotting out the blue sky and filling the air with a raw dampness. Clench shiveringly complained of the cold. Damp and mist always had a depressing effect on his spirits, he said. He would keep to his room and write up his letters. Half an hour later, he was making his way to the rendezvous.

The fog left nothing to be desired. It lay everywhere like a blanket; shutting out the world altogether. Behind the thick curtain the sun was shining brightly, and a few miles away the country lay open and smiling in the gold and verdure of a typical summer day. Whence the fog came and where it went was a mystery. It was strangely local, too, and almost as well defined as a physical feature on a map. Scientists had in vain tried to explain it. Only one thing was certain—it would go as mysteriously as it came. It might last for a day or an hour, it mattered little, whether there was wind or not. It came and went like a dream.

Meanwhile it was raw and chilly, and everything dripped with moisture. The white roads were dry and hard and dirty, but from the trees overhead great drops of water descended with the noise of a failing stone. The butterflies lay with folded wings on the lower side of the leaves, and the birds had suddenly ceased to sing.

Here, then, was the ideal opportunity the conspirators had been waiting for so long. Clench shivered, as he turned out. After the brilliant sunshine of the last few days it struck cold to the marrow of the bones. He could imagine the effect of a startling change like this on a constitution, such as Mary Copping's. There was another thing he was conscious of—that he had not the remotest idea which way to go. He had flattered himself that he had learnt the neighborhood thoroughly, that his bump of locality was perfect. But after he had walked a short distance along the road he felt absolutely lost.

"Confound it!" he muttered irritably, "where am I? It was lucky I put out those stones to mark the moor. When I reach the moor I shall know where I am, but I have to get as far as Collier's diggings. I'd better wait till somebody comes along. I only hope it won't be Moler."

As he spoke, a slim figure emerged from the mist. Clench was thankful to recognise Alice.

"I thought I would follow you in case of accident," she said. "This fog is unusually thick, even for Dartdale. Has it puzzled you, Mr. Clench?"

"It has baffled me altogether," Clench confessed. "I took the most elaborate precautions against being lost on the moors. But it never occurred to me that I could lose my way in the wood. One has evidently to be educated up to this kind of thing."

"It is strange how fog and snow confuse one," Alice said. "I've known old inhabitants go astray in fog and snow. That's why I followed you. I knew you would object if I had volunteered my assistance in the first place. So I came out with you as far as the gate leading to Mr. Copping's farmhouse. Mr. Clench, you have no idea how nervous and anxious I am."

Clench nodded sympathetically. Despite his native coolness, he was feeling anxious himself. From a strictly practical point of view, he was doing a very foolish thing. If the experiment failed, he was likely to get himself into trouble.

"I quite understand your feelings," he said. "It was good of you to follow me for, if you had not, I should have had to return to the house. Surely, this is the gate."

"That is the gate."

"Then I am immensely obliged to you," Clench replied. "Please don't come farther. Go home and keep up your courage. We are not going to fail."

Collier awaited him. He wore a big cap, heavy shoes of indiarubber, and large, baggy stockings. A brown sweater completed his outfit. Clench looked disappointed. The make-up was calculated to attract attention.

"Not a bit of it," Collier said cheerfully. "Have you arranged about that telegram?"

"I did all that as I came through the village," Clench explained. "But where is your change? I like the way you have made yourself up to look like Grenfell, but still—"

"My dear fellow, it's all right," Collier broke in. "I've thought out everything carefully. Now, listen to my scheme, and go one better if you can."

Collier went into all the details, and then said, "What do you think of that? You'll find everything where I left it, and the instructions are plain. As an old hand at amateur theatricals yourself, you will know exactly what to do. I flatter myself the idea is a good one."

Clench was more than satisfied, and they pushed their way quietly and steadily through the fog till they reached their destination. They could only avoid mistakes by the careful observation of certain landmarks. They could hear the click of picks and the rattle of stones. Now and again a whistle sounded, and a warder uttered an order in a hoarse tone. With some difficulty, Clench made out the outline of Copping's burly figure. He had, of course, taken care to make himself acquainted with the warder's physique.

"That's the man," he whispered, as they crouched in the dripping bracken, "and that is the gang Grenfell is working with. It's impossible to say which is Grenfell; but, as he has had the tip to look out for us on the first foggy day, I don't suppose he's far off."

"We must contrive to get closer to them," said Collier. "How wet this bracken is! Still, it's good cover. Let's work past Copping."

They were actually in the midst of the gang presently, but the fog was so dense they could not distinguish any object five yards away. Clench hummed a bar of a popular song, and instantly one of the picks ceased working. A hand shot out of the gloom and Clench grasped it. A second later the three men were seated under a big boulder, overhung by a mass of bracken.

"I suppose it's you all right, Grenfell," Clench whispered. "Good! We have not a single moment to lose. Don't trouble to pull off your clothes. This fog is too risky for delay."

Collier had already divested himself of his sweater, his cap, boots and stockings, and displayed underneath these habiliments a perfectly correct convict's garb. Almost as quickly Grenfell was dressed in the cast-off garments. A dark moustache fixed to his lips and a dark curly wig adjusted on his head completed a wonderful transformation. It was almost as if a miracle had been wrought. With a rod in his hand, he looked the beau ideal of a fisherman. Collier, for his part, grasped Grenfell's pick with a cheerful smile.

"It's going to be all right," he said. "I will pass muster as long as Copping keeps his eyes shut and nothing unexpected happens, and my hands are every whit as hard as yours. I'd better slip back amongst those fellows, lest they grow suspicious."

"I don't think there is any need for hurry," Grenfell answered. "So far as I can judge, there is no sign of the fog lifting—and I have had some bitter experiences."

"There's no occasion to run any unnecessary risk, though," Clench suggested.

"That's what I am trying to avoid," Grenfell explained. "We have a few minutes to spare, and I am very anxious to give Mr. Collier a few valuable hints. The warders watch us pretty carefully, and they get to know a good deal about the characteristics of their prisoners. I am one of the silent lot. I never speak to anybody, but always go about my work with my head down. I have gained several marks for the way I keep my cell and the state of my tin and platter. Keeping the tin case bright is a pastime of mine. When you've had a day or two yonder, Collier you'll welcome anything you can do with your fingers, as a blessed relief to the monotony of it. Copping will say nothing, but there is another warder called Jacques, of whom you'll have to be careful. When he chaffs you, always smile, but, never look him in the face. I think that's about all."

The fog still lay thick as a blanket. Out of the denseness of it came now the sounds of pick and shovel, now a hoarse command or two, and now the cough of a prisoner. Collier asked a few more questions. He seemed as keen on getting into prison as most men are on keeping out of it. He had thrown himself heart and soul into the adventure.

"It is more than kind of you," Grenfell whispered.

That was not Collier's view of the situation at all.

"I should be jolly sick if I failed you at the last moment," he said. "I have put my back into the thing, and have worked it out on scientific lines. I flatter myself on my make-up, and consider the likeness between us is striking. By the by, you haven't any curious marks on you—no moles or anything of that kind? No family mansion tattooed on the small of your back?"

"Not even a pimple or a wort. I'm regularly free from anything of that kind."

"Well, that's all right," Collier responded. "Birth-marks are confoundedly awkward things. I'm looking forward to the issue of this business. Such adventures are the salt of life to me, and when our friend Clench offered me the chance, I could have embraced him on the spot. I shall make splendid 'copy' out of this. All the editors in London will be running after me. It's a pity I can't write under my own name and mention details. But there's always a something."

"You can't relish it, really?"

"I shall like it amazingly. My dear fellow, I love hardships. I am as fond of a good dinner and a good cigar as anybody, but I can do without them if necessary. Once I had nothing but bread and water for three weeks. I was never so fit in my life. Of course, there's a big difference between being a prisoner because one chooses that role."

Grenfell smiled bitterly. Nobody knew that better than himself.

"I see your point," he said. "The hardest part is the knowledge that you will be suffering the pain and degradation without the slightest reason for it. But I fancy there is going to be a change in the fog."

The thick blanket lightened for a moment, and glimpse of figures could be seen.

"By Jove, you're right," Collier whispered. "I'd better step into your place. I should hate to see everything spoiled at the last moment."

"I am trying to find words to thank you," Grenfell said hoarsely.

"My dear fellow, the thanks are all on my side," Collier responded. "Clench will tell you that I am under a deep debt of gratitude to you. I would not have missed the adventure for any money. Indeed, I would have paid handsomely for the chance of going into it. Hardship! Why, it will be a picnic, compared with some of the experience's I have had. So long."

Collier vanished without another word. There was no occasion for further misgiving; the thing was done, and not even Copping himself could have identified his late prisoner. They hastened back to the moor without encountering the suspicious glances of a single warder.

It was nearly 7 o'clock before Clench regained his room at Rawmouth. He had taken every precaution to see that his chamber had not been disturbed during his absence—the black silk thread from the door to the window was unbroken. He could declare, without the slightest chance of being contradicted, that he had not been out of doors. The fog had lifted, and it was a brilliant and warm evening as Clench came down to dinner. He did not dare to meet Alice's questioning eyes, and she did not glance at him a second time. Her opportunity would come presently; she would not spoil it by premature haste.

Clench strolled out into the garden by-and-bye, being followed by Moler. Draycott had not put in an appearance, though it was stated that he was better. A tall figure, in the garb of an old-fashioned clergyman, came up the drive and across the lawn. He was an elderly man, with faded cheeks and a cheery manner, his hair was silvery, and he wore a pair of glasses suspended from a broad, black silk ribbon. He might have been an archdeacon or a rural dean. He greeted Clench with a manner that was almost affectionate.

"My dear old friend," he cried. "Quite a delightful surprise, I assure you. I came for a short holiday, and heard by chance that you were here. I ventured on this liberty. May I beg the honor of an introduction to your companion?"

"My dear doctor," Clench exclaimed, "the pleasure is mutual. Miss Kearns, let me introduce you to Dr. Gordon Blaydes, the eminent authority on ecclesiastical antiquities. This is Dr. Moler, one of the foremost of the young school of German scientists."

Dr. Blaydes was delighted. He had not expected such congenial society. He had come for change of air, and rest. He prattled on amiably, and Alice was charmed. Clench had gone on ahead with Moler, and they were beyond earshot.

"Well, darling," the doctor whispered. "So you didn't know me! So much the better! A disguise that would deceive you would take in anybody. Let's go where I can kiss you, dear."

"Hugh," Alice gasped. "My dearest boy, is it really you? How wonderful!"

CHAPTER IX

THE CIGARETTE CASE

Hugh Grenfell smiled beneath his disguise. Even Alice had signally failed to recognise him. Not in the smallest degree did he suggest the man she loved, but he was the man, and that sufficed. She clung tightly to him, as if determined to detain him by her for evermore.

"But is this not exceedingly rash of you?" she asked.

"My dearest girl, have you not answered the question?" Hugh rejoined. "You had not the faintest notion who I was; my voice did not betray me. How much less likely is Draycott to suspect anything! He imagines that I am snug in gaol, where I am likely to stay for many a long day to come! It was a very clever idea, Alice. There is only one weak spot in it."

"And what is that?"

"Copping's health. So long as he keeps well, the deception is not likely to be discovered. The man who took my place will have to keep well, too. Still, there is no occasion to meet trouble half-way, and it need only be for a week. In a few days the conspiracy will be exposed and I shall be free."

"You must have had a very anxious time."

"The waiting was the worst of it. I got Clench's message and destroyed it. I thought the foggy day would never come. When it did come, the rest was easy. Collier changed a few of his garments with me, and the thing was done. He was in full convict garb, a regular quick-change affair. I carefully concealed my suit, so that I might know where to find it when required, and then Clench made me up as you see. And now I mean to have it out with the man who is responsible for all my sufferings."

"But you must proceed prudently," Alice urged.

"Oh, I am not likely to forget myself. I won't attack Draycott at his own table. Ostensibly, he is an entire stranger to me. What I want is the freedom of the house for a few days, and there should be no difficulty about that, seeing that I am a friend of Clench, or Russell Bassett, as Moler deems him to be. It is a very pretty conspiracy altogether!"

Alice refrained from further questions. She was easier in her mind. The wonderful disguise would deceive anybody if it deceived her, and she had been completely taken in. She must be content to leave the rest to Russell Clench. Grenfell put the girl away from him tenderly.

"We shall have to be circumspect," he said. "I must restrain my feelings. It would never do for anyone to see you in the arms of an elderly divine of benevolent appearance and the reputation of a great scholar and traveller. But we won't lead a humdrum existence by any means. If you watch carefully, without seeming to do so, you will see many interesting things. But the others are coming back."

"You will dine with us this evening, Dr. Blaydes?" Moler suggested. "It is a privilege to meet so distinguished a man. I hope our host will be able to come down to dinner."

"Really, it is very good of you," the pseudo-doctor said. "I had not anticipated anything of the kind, but I will come with pleasure. Unfortunately, I brought no dress clothes with me."

Moler reminded him that they were quiet people at Rawmouth, and stood on very little ceremony. Clench was delighted. It was a little before half-past seven when the 'divine' ambled up to the house and found himself alone in the drawing-room. The mere aspect of the place conjured up a flood of vivid recollections. There was the big armchair, where Mrs. Faber had been accustomed to sit over her knitting in the evening; on the other side of the fire place was Faber's seat, on the rare occasions when he visited the drawing-room. It was in the alcove behind the red silk curtains that Grenfell had first taken Alice in his arms and kissed her.

Things had looked rosy in those days. Hugh's prospects were brilliant, and he was to marry for love as well as money. He had no thought of the money, but, not being a fool, was sensible of its advantages.

From the first he had a vague notion that Mr. Faber objected to the arrangement. Sometimes Faber would slap him on the back with protestations of friendship and good wishes for the future, but at others he regarded him darkly with an expression on his eyes that Grenfell did not like. Moreover there were other suspicious circumstances. Faber was a struggling man; he had speculated most of his property away. He was careless and imprudent, like most men given to drinking bouts. It was singular that such a man, pressed on every hand, should find the money to insure his life for a hundred thousand pounds. Grenfell knew of this, because he occupied a responsible post in the company through which the policy had been taken out. He was at a loss to know how Faber had managed to pay even the first huge premium.

The premium was paid, however, but before the second became due, Faber, as we know, was cut to pieces on the railway not far from his house. This was six months after Mrs. Faber's death; Alice had been on the Continent till within a week of the fatal accident. During the short time she was away Hugh Grenfell had been arrested in connection with the death of one Oliver Partridge, who had disappeared not long before the accident that resulted in Faber's death. Partridge's watch had been found in the possession of Grenfell, who was unable to account for it. Because of these things, and certain circumstantial evidence, Hugh had been sentenced to seven years' imprisonment. Another person in the conspiracy, a certain Marcus Gainsforth, could not be found, and Hugh had no doubt but that he was being kept out of the way by somebody. He had a presentiment that Faber was at the bottom of the whole thing. Now Martin Faber was dead, and Raymond Draycott reigned in his stead.

During the last few hours Grenfell had been carefully posted in the current events by Clench, and knew pretty well how matters stood.

"I have always had my suspicions," he remarked to Clench. "If I told anybody what I think and believe, they would not credit me—they would say the thing was impossible."

"Truth is stranger than fiction," Clench answered.

"Well, that is the familiar way of putting it. But it's true in my case. If I am correct, one of the most audacious and most original conspiracies ever hatched has been consummated at Rawmouth with brilliant success. It will be difficult, if not dangerous, to get to the bottom of it, but this must be done, and we shall accomplish it between us. The only one who appears to know anything besides Draycott is Moler. I thought of laying a trap for him, but after what you have said, we had better abandon the suggestion. Moler is far too clever to let us throw dust in his eye's, and the only thing to be done is to probe the mystery and confront those fellows with our evidence. Have you any plans?"

"I've been waiting for you," he said. "So far, my energies have been devoted to getting you out of prison. In that matter we have been successful, thanks to Collier. It was very plucky of him, and I hope he'll get the kudos and money he deserves. Now that we are both working side by side, free from espionage, we may do something. I'll think out the whole plan of campaign by morning. Meanwhile, let me ask you a question. How long is it since you saw the Countess?"

Grenfell started, and looked uneasy.

"A long time," he said. "I dropped her directly I discovered the manner of woman she was. We were great fools in those days, Clench!"

"There must have been a score of you altogether. However, I should not say that any of you were fools, apart from the fascination that woman exercised over you, of course. You were all in love with her, Hugh. I wonder there was no bloodshed."

"It nearly came to that once or twice," Hugh smiled, not too comfortably. "As a matter of fact, there were only three of us in the running—myself, Oliver Partridge, and Marcus Gainsforth. In a sense, Partridge was my undoing. I mean I was put into gaol for murdering him on a charge that I had put him out of the way, for, as you know, his watch was found in my possession. I always imagined that the Countess had something to do with that. She was very bitter against me when I told her we must meet no more. By that time I had found her out for what she was. She was my stumbling block; it was always her whim to have a score of us youngsters dangling after her. But why do you ask?"

"Because the Countess is not very far off," Clench explained. "I travelled from London in the same carriage with her. Oh! we were quite friendly. But she told me a lie about where she was going. It's odd she should be in this neighborhood just now."

"As blooming and prosperous as ever?"

"Rather more so," Clench laughed, "and very handsome still. I happen to know where she was going, and I'll look her up, if necessary."

"You think she could help us?"

"My dear boy, I am certain of it. I'm sure she could tell us all about Partridge. Now we must learn what Draycott has to say for himself."

Draycott was still shaky and nervous, but his manner was pleasant enough.

"Very glad to see you, doctor," he said. "Moler has been telling me about you. It is an honor to have so distinguished a man under my roof."

He advanced with hand extended, and Hugh took it formally. Then he gasped and stared at Draycott as if he had seen a ghost.

"There is nothing the matter, doctor?" Draycott asked.

"A mere nothing, my dear sir," Grenfell hastened to say. "One can't give oneself over to physical exertion without paying a penalty. Mine is a nervous trouble, the result of experiments with snake poisons. Sometimes the attack lasts for hours, sometimes it goes like a flash—I am better already."

Others came into the room, and conversation became more general. Alice watched her lover anxiously, but not for a single moment did he betray himself. He had had too hard a lesson for that, and was not likely to lapse when he had victory in his grasp. The other two were palpably taking him at his own valuation. He had more than his share of talk during dinner, relating interesting experiences as the table was cleared and the butler produced cigars and cigarettes.

In a mechanical way Grenfell pulled a case out of his pocket. Draycott was bending over the silver box, carefully selecting one of the little white tubes of tobacco.

"Would you mind trying mine?" Grenfell suggested. "They are treated in a peculiar, way. My own process I may say. I am anxious you should sample them."

Draycott held out his hand for the case—a silver one of peculiar construction, evidently of Oriental manufacture, with a dull, copper-colored beetle on the front. As he touched the case it fell from his fingers to the table and a choking cry escaped him.

"You infernal juggler!" he yelled. "What trick are you playing upon me?"

The word came with startling effect. Dr. Blaydes looked up with mild surprise and reproach on his face. Draycott was wet and ghastly.

"My dear sir," the doctor protested. "Really, my dear sir! Mr. Moler—"

Moler had furtively drawn a couple of tiny green pellets from his pocket.. He dropped them into Draycott's glass and forced him to drink. In the pause that followed, the color gradually returned to Draycott's face, and he regained control of himself.

"I humbly beg your pardon," he said. "An attack of nerves. I am subject, to them. That cigarette-case recalled painful recollections. Why, I couldn't tell you."

"It was given to me by a man who has disappeared," Grenfell said. "He was a remarkable man in his way, and his name was Marcus Gainsforth."

For a moment Draycott showed signs of renewed panic. His face paled under the dark mask of tan, till he looked like a white nigger, as Clench told himself.

"A friend of yours, I presume," Draycott stammered.

"A friend of mine, and, I understand, a friend of Martin Faber's," Grenfell went on. "But as to that, I may be mistaken. He disappeared in the most amazing manner. I had need of his services, but he left me, and has never been seen to this day. Remarkable case, very, but I wish you would try one of my cigarettes."

Draycott helped himself to a cigarette with fingers that shook strangely. At the same time, a servant entered and whispered something in Moler's ear.

"I can't possibly see her to-night," Moler said sharply. "Who is she?"

"She gave her name of Copping, sir."

With a snarl, Moler rose and excused himself. Alice looked up and caught Clench's eye. She nodded almost imperceptibly, and slipped quietly out of the room. From under his brows Clench had been taking careful note of what was going on.

"Our friend is a squire of dames," he said. "Who is the fair Copping?"

Draycott replied indifferently. Assuredly the name of Copping conveyed nothing to him, and his indifference was not assumed.

"Moler is a very clever man," he observed. "I suppose there is not a more brilliant surgeon in England. He likes to try his hand on certain people here. He has effected one or two remarkable cures where the ordinary practitioner has been wholly at fault. I daresay this is one of his patients. Moler never takes money from them."

"Oh, there is no doubting his qualities," Clench said warmly. "The thing that puzzles me is why such a man is content to remain in a village."

Draycott's eyes glittered dangerously.

"He is a spendthrift, a gambler," he said. "Moler has made a lot of money in his time, but he never has a penny. He wants a huge amount for a series of experiments, and declares that if he can get it he will startle the world. I believe that, but I'm not going to find the money. It would be gambled away directly. I tell him I will see his—"

Draycott paused, conscious that he was saying too much. His lips were firmly set, and the gleam in his eyes was dark and angry. He had told Clench something. He had confirmed the latter in his opinion that Moler was blackmailing his host.

"In Germany they help these experiments," Clench said. "The State finds the money. We ought to have a fund of that kind in this country."

Draycott laughed, his hands moving restlessly over the table.

"Moler would want the lot," he said, "and he'd have it. He hopes to cure criminals by some surgical operation. He had better practice on himself first."

The last words came in a hissing whisper. It was as if Draycott, talking to himself, had said the words aloud. He looked down moodily at his plate. Clench exchanged a significant glance with Grenfell.

"I am intensely interested," he said. "Has Dr. Moler had any subjects?"

"One or two, but only in a small way. He wants some famous criminal to work upon, somebody notorious. He says women make the best subjects. If you know of some brilliant adventuress, Moler would be grateful for an introduction."

Clench smiled, as he lighted a fresh cigarette.

"As it happens, I know the very woman," he said. "She possesses all the qualities Moler is looking for, and more. Whether or not she will be willing to be operated on is another matter. You have seen a great deal of the world, Mr. Draycott?"

"Well, yes—I mean, no," Draycott said, confusedly. "Most of my time was spent in the Argentine. I had to work hard there, and I saw little of society. It is only in recent years—"

"But you know something of Paris?" Clench ventured.

"Never been in the place in all my—what am I talking about? This confounded neuralgia makes me quite stupid now and then. I did spend a few months in Paris on my way home after I had come into the property. Why do you ask?"

"Because the woman I speak of was in Paris at that time. It is probable Moler knew her. She used to call herself the Countess D'Arblay. Ever met her?"

Draycott started restlessly, and his cigarette dropped into a glass. It expired with a hiss.

"What do you mean?" he demanded. "What you do—Oh, that pain again! Would you mind finding Moler? I'd like to go to bed if you will excuse me. No, I never heard of Madame—I mean the Countess D'Arblay, never, never, never. Why doesn't Moler come, damn him!"

CHAPTER X

"TO BE OR NOT TO BE!"

Once Copping had given his promise, he did not stop to ask questions. Beyond the shadow of a doubt he was doing wrong. He was guilty of a gross betrayal of his trust, and made no attempt to justify his failing. It was neither difficult nor dangerous to convey a letter to Hugh Grenfell, and the thing was done, effected, nobody appearing to be a penny the wiser or the worse. The prison authorities were in absolute ignorance of the deception which had been practised on them, and the convicts in Grenfell's gang asked no questions. Possibly they failed to notice the episode; not that it would have mattered had they done so, for Grenfell had always kept steadily aloof from the rest of his fellow prisoners, and had hardly ever exchanged a word with any of them. For all they would know to the contrary, he might have served his time and been released. In any case, one convict in prison garb is very like another.

Joe Copping had carried out his part of the contract and Grenfell was free. Copping was the richer by a hundred pounds, and there was nine times as much to follow. According to the bond, Grenfell would be in gaol again at the end of a week, the exchange of prisoners would be made the next foggy day, and society would not suffer loss or damage. Copping would apply for his discharge without a stain on his character, would go elsewhere, and start on his way to fortune. He had saved his wife's life and his own. In the circumstances, conscience could not expect much of a hearing, and on the whole Copping felt on good terms with himself.

This being so, he could not make out his wife at all. He had expected her to burst into a flood of grateful tears, to cling round his neck and thank God for His goodness. It came almost as a blow to see how she took her salvation. She might have been in the dock before a black-capped judge. She sat with her hands in her lap when Copping came back to the cottage after seeing Alice on her way; her head was bowed sorrowfully.

"Come, cheer up, lass," Copping said boisterously. "Not feeling bad, are you? I don't believe you understood what I said just now."

The woman raised her head wearily, and tried to smile. She quite realised what her duty was. This access of riches meant new life to her.

"Tell me all about it again, Joe."

"Well, there isn't very much to tell," Copping said, as he paced about the room. "I've had a bit of luck. Had it in an assumed name from one of those newspapers. Time drags on our hands yonder, and I thought it all out. I didn't tell anybody, and I'm not going to. It's nobody's business but our own. And I've got the £100. There's—there's another prize of £900 that may come to me in connection with the same competition."

"Show me the paper, Joe."

"The paper had to be returned with the coupons," Copping lied, glibly. "It's an American paper. I'll remember the name of it presently. Anyhow, I've got the money in my pocket, and at the end of this week I shall give notice. We can clear out in a fortnight. Go to London first, and then to France till you're well again. Give me a kiss, old girl."

Mary Copping complied in a dazed way. Her lips were cold and clammy.

"Why, what on earth's the matter with you?" Copping demanded, with pardonable irritation. "You look as if you had seen a ghost. And telling you all this good news. Don't you want to go?"

"Of course, I want to go," Mary Copping whispered. "I'd like to turn my back on the village now and never see it again. I have dreamt in the night that we have gone, and woke up with tears in my eyes, to find it was a dream. But—but I don't want to go yet. I—I promised to see Mrs. Duncan through her trouble first, and she's a delicate woman."

Copping respected the motive, but was not convinced.

"How long is that likely to be?"

"I don't know. Perhaps two months, perhaps less. If—if her sister comes over from America, it may not be necessary for me to help at all. So long as this weather lasts I can't take much harm. It isn't as if we were in the depth of winter."

Copping shook his head, but argued the matter no further. He never could understand the ways of woman, and began to think he knew even less than he had imagined. It was clear that Mary was frightened about something, but she would not have learnt what was going on. He walked back to the prison moody and disappointed.

He left his wife sitting with her head in her hands and the tears on her cheeks. Her thoughts were far blacker and bitterer and more rebellious than his.

This grand chance had come to her and it was useless now that it had come. She had prayed for this on her knees, and the fruition of her hopes was as Dead Sea fruit in her mouth. She should have wept for joy on her husband's neck, and instead of that she was glad to see his back lest he should ask any more awkward questions. Joe would not return till late, so that she had some time to ponder the situation. She yearned for an hour with Alice Kearns. She must have the sympathy of another woman, and it was out of the question to confide in any of her neighbors. She would go to Rawmouth Park in the first instance and see Moler. Perhaps he would be merciful; he could make all the difference if he chose. She would go after dark and appeal to him.

"I never did anything wrong," she told herself. "God knows I was not a guilty party, but if the police set on the track, nobody will believe me. They would say I was as bad as my mistress. As if any woman could have been as bad as she was! They would have all been happy to-day but for her. Mr. Grenfell would never have got into prison, and Mr. Gainsforth and Mr. Partridge might have been honorable men to-day. I've a good mind to go to the police and tell the whole story. But how did Moler know that I used to be in the service of Countess D'Arblay? He was never one of that set, and yet he knows everything. With him I feel like a mouse trying to escape from a cat."

She put out her husband's supper, so that he could find it if he returned sooner than she expected; she could easily make the excuse that she had gone to see a neighbor. She set off across the moor towards the Park. It would not be dark for some time, so there was no cause to hurry. She sat down presently on the dry heather, enjoying the calm of the evening. A solitary figure came slouching along the road towards her; a man dressed in clothes which at one time had been in fashion. They were well cut, but frayed and shiny. The man wore a white bowler hat jauntily on one side of his head, he had a muffler round his neck, despite the warmth of the evening, and the way his coat was buttoned up suggested the absence of a shirt altogether. He came along with an impudent swagger, pulling at the fag end of a cigarette. He gave Mary a glance as he passed, then favored her with a harder stare. A smile broke out on his face and the mouth with its black teeth trembled humorously.

"Well, this is an unexpected pleasure!" he said.

Mary regarded him uneasily. She was some distance from home, and the spot was lonely. The man was by no means the typical tramp, and looked capable of anything.

"I've nothing to give you," she said. "Please go away."

But the man made no attempt to move. He stood smiling, as if amused by something.

"Do you mean to say you don't recognise me, Mary?"

"No, I don't," Mary said freely. "And you don't know me."

"Perhaps you'll say your name is not Mary?"

"Perhaps, but I should be telling a lie if I did. My name's Mary all right, but anybody might have guessed that. If you get into the hands of the police they will lock you up. They are terribly sharp on loafers in Devonshire. If you take my advice you'll go on about your business. I've met your sort before, my man."

The swaggering, seedy tramp did not appear to be in the least offended.

"I'm certain sure you have," he said, "but not here, Mary. If was different when you lived in George-street, Longdon Square, with the Countess. You met plenty of my sort in those days. But we looked a sight more respectable than we do now, my dear. We had money to spend then—Gainsforth and myself, and the rest of them. The Countess had not sucked us dry then. We thought it a fine thing to be seen about with her, to be regarded as one of her set. As a matter of fact we were lucky to keep out of gaol. How did you manage it, Mary?"

The woman dropped on to the heather. It seemed to her that all the ghosts were rising. Moler had come first, then Grenfell, and James Waterhouse, and now this man, who was beginning to shape oddly familiar, though as yet Mary could not put a name to him.

"I—I see you know what you are talking about," she stammered. "Will you tell me your name?"

"Am I so altered that you don't recognise Oliver Partridge?"

A cry of astonishment came from Mary's lips.

"Good heavens!" she exclaimed. "Have you fallen so low as this, Mr. Partridge?"

There was no contempt in Mary's voice—she had no idea of being in the least offensive. She was purely astonished, and that was all. How different things had been when she last saw this man. Then he was well set-up, prosperous, and had the world before him. It was impossible to credit that this was the same man.

"It is a bit of a change," he said bitterly. "I was all right so long as my money lasted. When that was gone the Countess chucked me. She tried to get me into trouble as she did with Grenfell and Gainsforth. If she did not actually land them herself, she was a party to it. You were wise to leave her when you had the chance, Mary."

"I ran away. I was afraid to stay any longer. She said the police were after me."

"Lies!" Partridge cried, bitterly. "The police were after nobody. After all, you would have had no great difficulty in proving your innocence. But she got away right enough. They tell me she is better-looking and more prosperous than ever. The only man that ever got the better of her was Russell Clench, and I believe he was the only man she ever cared for. She ruined me body and soul, and the only way I can get a living now is to foot it from town to town, doing a bit of conjuring in public-houses. I was always clever at that kind of game, as you know Mary."

"You don't seem to have done very well at it, Mr. Partridge."

"I should if I could only keep sober. I get thinking, and that drives me to drink, and there you are. I had a little unpleasantness with the police at Newton Abbot. I'm tramping back to London. Once there, I'll stay there. But I'm nigh half dead for want of food, and I haven't a copper. It's a pretty humiliating thing to have to ask, Mary. But if you could let me have a bob or two—"

"Oh, I'll do that," Mary said. "Many's the pound I've had from you, Mr. Partridge. My husband is a warder at the prison here, and we have done pretty well. At any rate, I can find five shillings and not miss it. Follow me to the white cottage yonder."

Partridge dropped behind briskly. He got his five shillings presently and jingled the coins in the pocket of his ragged trousers.

"You always were a good sort, Mary," he said, gratefully. "Rum thing I should run against you like this, isn't it? I'll get along now. Good-night, my dear."

He strode off jauntily, leaving Mary to her thoughts. For the moment she abandoned the idea of going as far as the Park. She might go later, for it was still daylight. But this meeting with Partridge had disturbed and upset her. Joe rose, like an accusing vengeance, before her.

"What must he think of me?" she asked herself. "What would Joe say if he knew everything? And no woman ever had a better husband. How happy he looked as he came in just now! And how disappointed when he went out! He thinks I don't care, he thinks I have ceased to love him. Why don't I tell him, why didn't I tell him before we were married? He would have forgiven me. He would have felt for me, he would have seen that I was not so much to blame. I did not know that I was going to take service with an adventuress. I might, perhaps, get Moler to release me—I might manage what he needs before the week is out."

It was late before Copping returned to the cottage. Mary had got herself more in hand by this time, and greeted him with a smile. The warmth had crept into her caress again, and her kisses on his lips were fervent. If she could only tell him everything, if she could bring herself to speak! But her courage failed her.

"What is the matter?" she asked. "How pale you are, Joe! Has anything happened?"

"I've been a bit put out my dear," Copping explained. "Rather a nasty business with some of the hands. Bit of sheer carelessness on the part of one of the young warders. There was a scrimmage, and I was dragged into it."

"I see you were, Joe. That's a nasty bruise on your head. Let me bathe it."

"Oh, that's nothing," Copping said carelessly. "One of them hit me a bit of a rap. I was his match in the ordinary way, but it's my heart that gives out. After the scrimmage I had to lie down for half an hour. Couldn't get my breath properly. The governor noticed it, too, and I had hard work not to see the doctor. A week or so later it would not matter."

"Why a week or so later, Joe?"

"Oh! you know what I mean," he answered. "Now that I've got the money. Still, I daresay I am worrying you unnecessarily. One of those chaps got a mauling. He's in the hospital with two or three broken ribs. He didn't look like a strong man, but he fought for us like a score. But he never did lack pluck."

"Who is the man you are speaking about?"

"One of our old hands," Copping explained. "At least he's been with us over a year. He was the hero of a big case some time ago that everybody was talking about—James Waterhouse, the forger and blackmailer."

Mary Copping suppressed a cry. She rose with a mumbling excuse that she must give Joe his supper. She bent over the fireplace, anywhere so that Joe should not see her face. The ghosts were rising again, and stood mocking her in grisly array.

They stood by the side of her sleepless pillow; they were with her in the daylight all the next day. Her husband had gone on duty; she was glad it was one of his long spells, and that he would not be back till late at night. She wanted to be alone and to see the prison doctor. He took an interest in her case—he had warned her of the danger of the mists. She caught him in the evening as he was returning with a fishing-rod in his hand.

"Oh, I don't suppose a month or so of this weather will hurt you," the doctor said. "But you never know how long it is likely to last. We may get a few weeks of fog and then, well, then don't blame me, Mrs. Copping. I don't wonder that you feel nervous."

"I'm nervous for my husband, sir," Mary, said. "He tells me there was trouble in the prison last night. One poor fellow was hurt. Is he very bad?"

The doctor responded in a few curt, professional words, hinting casually at the worst, and passed on. He was not hard or flippant, but the atmosphere of death was familiar to him, and familiarity breeds contempt. Mary Copping stood watching the doctor till he was out of sight. He had told her something she had desired to know, and now she was trembling between hope and fear. It was possible that the release from all her trouble was at hand; it was also possible her anxiety might be multiplied a hundred-fold. She walked homeward, a prey to nameless fear.

The mists began to clear presently. She had the long evening to herself, she would slip over to Rawmouth and back again before Joe returned for his late supper. She must see Moler without delay; it was imperative she should do so. He might be angry with her and, on the contrary, he might be more angry if she delayed.

Presently she stood trembling in the hall at Rawmouth. Moler came out, with a smile on his face and a polite inquiry on his lips.

"I am sorry to have troubled you, Mrs. Copping," he said politely. "The little matter of those bees of yours would have kept for a day or two. But come this way."

He waved his hand towards the morning-room, and closed the door. Then the smile died from his lips, and his face grew hard and black.

"You fool!" he hissed. "Why do you come here? Do you want to make your name a bye-word in the parish? Have you any sort of sense? Out with it, don't stand gaping there. What is the matter?"

Mary struggled for breath, and then she regained some courage.

"Jim Waterhouse is in the hospital badly hurt," she said, "the doctor says he will die. If Jim opens his mouth, as he may do when he sees that life is finished for him, what will you do then?"

A curse broke from Moler's lips.

"Why didn't you tell me this before?" he demanded. "Speak, you white-faced fool!"

CHAPTER XI

THE PRISON DOOR

Moler got over his anger, for he was face to face with a problem likely to tax his ingenuity to the uttermost. He paced about the room, his lips compressed, muttering to himself in momentary forgetfulness that he was not alone. The unexpected had happened and his calculations were upset. He could not have counted on such a disaster.

"Do you know anything about it?" he asked. "Have you any details? Was Waterhouse trying to get out of prison, or what? Who told you?"

"My husband, in the first place," Mary explained. "I was not listening carefully—I had so many things on my mind at the time. When Joe spoke of Waterhouse I was interested, of course. I asked the prison doctor for details."

"Which I have no doubt are grossly exaggerated."

"You may think what you like," Mary Copping said warmly. "The doctor took a very serious view of it. I managed to gets a few details on my way here. Waterhouse was not trying to get out of gaol. There was a disturbance, and he went to the assistance of the warders. When I come to think of it, my husband told me as much. Anyhow, Waterhouse is pretty bad and not likely to recover. I thought you would like to know, and that is why I came here. I can't do more for you than that."

Moler turned on the speaker with an ugly sneer.

"And don't want to," he suggested. "You'd be glad to hear that Waterhouse was dead. There would be no more anxiety so far as you are concerned in that case. I should have no further need for your services. But I haven't done with you yet."

Mary Copping's face grew grey. She was terrified to find how correctly Moler had been reading her thoughts. She had almost hoped for the death of the convict, Waterhouse. Her contract with Moler would be at an end then, and she would be free to leave Dartdale.

"I was annoyed with you for coming here to-night," Moler went on. "It was a foolish thing to do, and it was still more foolish to give your name."

"I had to," Mary protested. "They would not take my message without. But the name would not convey anything to anybody besides Miss Kearns."

"Miss Kearns! What should she know about it? Is she a friend of yours?"

"She knew me when I was a child. My husband used to be a gardener's boy with poor Mr. Grenfell's people. Miss Kearns has only been to see us once."

The explanation sounded simple, but it disturbed Moler considerably. He started to ask a question, then checked himself. He seemed to be turning over some problem in his mind. The hard look returned to his eyes.

"I don't like it," he muttered. "This is too much of a family party arrangement to please you, Mrs. Copping. Still, that must stand over for the present. I'm glad you came now, because you can do something for me. As I have already told you it is absolutely necessary that I should communicate with Waterhouse. You must smuggle a letter into him, as the price of my silence about those years you spent in London. I made that clear before."

"And I have done my best to do the impossible."

"My good woman, nothing is impossible; difficult and delicate, no doubt, but not impossible. At any rate, the danger of discovery is less, and this accident may be really a blessing in disguise. It makes your work ridiculously easy. You have only to go to the hospital and ask to see Waterhouse—"

"You must be mad to suggest such a thing."

"On the contrary, my dear Mary, my suggestion is peculiarly sane. What course could be more natural? You know Waterhouse—at one time you were on very good terms with him. He will be glad to see you, and you can take a message to him from me. Say that I must see him, that I am here, and press him to ask the prison doctor to request me to call. Why are you looking so white and troubled? There is no longer any danger—it is as if I asked you to fetch me a reel of cotton. Do this, and you are free?"

"Free!" Mary cried, passionately. "Who talks about being free? I am your slave. I have to do as you tell me. But for the unhappy chance that brought us face to face I should have been far from Dartdale by this time. From that moment you began to persecute me. You threatened me with exposure if I refused to do your bidding. You set me what you knew was an impossible task."

The woman was wild and excited, and Moler's experience taught him that women in that stage are apt to be dangerous. He knew he must not push Mary too far.

"You never see or hear anything of the Countess now?" he asked suddenly.

"Never," Mary said. "I hope I shall be spared that. When I entered her service it was the worst day's work I ever did in my life. I thought it was a fine situation. I thought it would be a good thing to be maid to a great Lady like the Countess, but I didn't know till it was too late that I was under the roof of a notorious swindler. And you knew it, though you were not one of her friends."

"As a matter of fact, I was one of her intimate friends at one time," Moler sneered. "That was before she found the climate of Paris too sultry and decided to emigrate to London. We never met in London, though I kept a close eye on my lady. That is how I came to know all about her household, that is how I came to know you by sight. I never forget a face, a gift, my dear Mary, that I have found to be exceedingly useful. When I met you some time back and learnt that you were the wife of a warder, I recognised your value to me. When I discovered that your husband was a warder at the prison, my task was easier."

"It was a bad day for me when we met," Mary said bitterly.

"Not at all, my dear woman. I will pay you for your trouble. I understand that it is your ambition to leave this district as soon as possible."

"My ambition has nothing whatever to do with it, Dr. Moler. I am told that another winter here will be fatal to me. If I remain for the foggy season, I shall die."

"Then, in that case, my dear Mary, why don't you do what I suggest and get it over? The sooner you act, the sooner you will be free to do as you like. For goodness sake, don't get the idea into your head that I want to keep you. If you have consumption—"

"I did not say that I had consumption. I said it was my chest. If I can move to higher ground I shall not be troubled. It's you that stop me. It's murder."

"I should prefer to call it suicide," Moler said coolly. "Anybody would suppose that I was keeping you against your will in order to commit a crime. And really, what I ask is such a little matter. If you can only put me into communication with Waterhouse—"

Mary shook her head obstinately.

"I'll do nothing of the kind," she said. "Do your worst. Tell the police that I was the maid of the Countess D'Arblay, whom they have been looking for so long. If I give myself up, they'll possibly take my doing so of my own accord into consideration, and put me where I shall be a long way from these dreadful fogs. When I come out, Copping and myself can start again. I warn you that I am being driven to desperation."

Moler saw that he was going too far.

"Don't you want to earn a large sum of money?" he asked coaxingly.

"Not your money," Mary cried. "You're up to something wrong. You don't care anything for Waterhouse. He could rot and die in gaol, if you didn't want him for some purpose. I don't care for myself, but I won't get my husband into trouble."

"But you won't get him into trouble if you do as I tell you," Moler went on. "Be reasonable."

"Reasonable! How could a woman driven to desperation be reasonable?" Mary cried. "I'd like to kill you, I'd like to see you dead at my feet."

"Don't be theatrical," Moler sneered. "I only ask you to smuggle a letter into Waterhouse's cell. Of course you could not do it yourself, but you could induce your husband to do it for you."

"In which case I should have to tell him everything," Mary murmured.

"Well, why not? He is very fond of you. A wise woman can do anything with her husband. In any case he would get over his anger in time. But, if you don't choose to take your husband into your confidence, I'll write to him. He will not be quite so complacent after he gets my letter. Mind, this thing has to be done. If I don't hear by this time to-morrow that it is done, look to yourself."

Moler held open the door pointedly. There was a menacing gleam in his eyes that Mary knew only too well. Without another word she walked out into the darkness of the night. She knew how useless it was to appeal to his better nature. He was not likely to have the slightest mercy upon her. He would carry out his threat, unless she lent herself to his plan. Once that letter was written, it would be all over between Joe and herself. He was a good and just man, but his creed was strict and he had lived in a narrow groove all his life. He would never be able to appreciate the turmoil and temptation of the three years during which Mary had been in service in London—and elsewhere.

She could not tell him; he would never forgive her, he would not understand. If she could only carry this thing through and leave Dartdale, all would be well. She would take good care that Moler never saw her again. A sudden inspiration came to her. She would do this thing and rid herself of trouble for the future. There would be no occasion to tell a lie over it, for she knew Waterhouse well. She had seen a great deal of him in the three years she was so anxious to forget.

It was not too late even to-night. Copping would be on duty till after ten and it still wanted nearly an hour of that time. Dr. Flack was a good fellow, and would help her all he could. She might manage even to see Waterhouse that very night. As she had made up her mind to this, she began to feel easier. At any rate, she was doing something to get rid of the burden hanging round her neck, to be free from trouble and anxiety.

Her heart was beating painfully fast as she came to the block of grey stone buildings devoted to the uses of the prison staff. Dr. Flack rose, with a kindly smile, and put down the book he was reading.

"You want to see the man Waterhouse?" he asked, with elevated brows. "Rather a strange request. Do you know him? Does your husband know him?"

"I knew him in London," Mary said. She reddened under the doctor's glance.

"He was very kind to me at one time. In spite of his faults he was always a gentleman. And I—I don't want my husband to know this, sir. He might not understand."

Apparently Dr. Flack did, for he nodded with a meaning smile.

"It's very irregular," he said. "I ought not to do it, Mrs. Copping. Waterhouse was in much pain until I administered morphia. I hope he will sleep presently after he has had a little nourishment. I'll see what I can do."

Flack asked a question or two through his telephone, and a few minutes afterwards Mary found herself in one of the hospital wards. It was a bad case, the nurse said, and so far as she could see, there was small hope of recovery. The patient was cheerful and his pluck and good spirit had not been affected. He welcomed Mary with a pleasant smile, as she looked into the handsome, reckless face, with tears in her eyes.

"Small place, this world, Mary. Fancy meeting you again! You are the wife of Copping, the warder. Really, now! Do you remember our last meeting?"

"I should prefer to forget it, sir," Mary murmured. "My husband does not know; I was not aware till the other day that you were here. It must be some dreadful mistake."

"There was no mistake," Waterhouse interrupted. "The forgery was mine right enough. I was in a tight place and I had to do it. I felt certain I could replace the money and, well, I didn't. It's the old story. I got five years, which was not a day more than I deserved. Yet I am not a bad fellow, and never turned my back on anybody in trouble. I see you are in a trouble now. What can I do for you, Mary? What is the worry?"

The nurse had moved to a bed farther down the ward where another patient needed attention.

"It's Moler," she whispered. "He has turned up again. He is staying with a gentleman of the name of Draycott, who lives in a place called Rawmouth, near here."

"The devil he is!" Waterhouse cried. "All right—I'll try to keep cool. Poor little woman, no wonder you look anxious and worried. What is the rascal forcing you to do?"

"He wanted me to smuggle a letter in to you. He says he must see you. He promised to-night that if I could arrange this he would not worry me any more."

"So my accident has done somebody some good."

"Oh, I didn't mean that. Still, if you would not mind seeing him!"

Waterhouse made no reply for the moment. The reckless look had left his handsome face and he seemed to be pondering a problem. Mary waited anxiously for him to speak. Suddenly the smile flashed out again. It was hard to think of this man as a confirmed criminal.

"I'll see him," he said. "Oh, yes, I'll see him. Write and tell him so. It is likely to prove a most interesting meeting!"

"Do you mean that I am to write to him?"

"Why not? I'm sorry I am not able to do so myself. You can disguise your writing, if you like; you need not put any name to it. Only send a line to say I shall be pleased to see Dr. Moler here any reasonable time he likes to call. Would he care to meet the Countess as well?"

Mary looked puzzled. Did the whole world know the Countess? She began to wonder how many convicts in Dartdale she was acquainted with. Waterhouse seemed to read her thoughts, for he was smiling.

"As I said just now, it is a small world, Mary, and the longer you live in it, the more convinced of the fact you will be. I was at one time proud to call the Countess my friend. I may also say that to some extent she was my inspiration: the greatest I ever had. Nobody will do you any harm. You need not be afraid of the police. I will see to that, if necessary. I presume you have not heard or seen anything of the Countess since your marriage."

"I have tried not to think of her."

"Oh, well, it's not so bad as all that. Do you know where she is now?"

Mary shook her head. She did not want to labor the subject.

"That woman was insatiable where money was concerned," Waterhouse went on thoughtfully. "She could never have enough of it. As regarded men, she was a vampire. Kipling must have had that sort of woman in his mind when he wrote that wonderful poem of his. But, all the same, the Countess had her good points. I don't think she would have stood by and seen you get into trouble. If you wrote and told her how you are situated—"

"Oh, no, no," Mary cried. "I couldn't do it, sir, I couldn't indeed. I'd rather go on as I am and take all the risks. She was a dreadful woman. I should not feel comfortable if I knew that she was in the same county with me."

Waterhouse looked as if about to say something, and suddenly changed his mind. There was a queer smile on his lips as he asked for a pencil and paper.

"On second thoughts, I will write a note myself," he said. "I daresay I can manage it. And you will smuggle the letter out. No, it isn't to Moler. You will settle his affair as we have already arranged. The letter is to the Countess, and I will address it to a place whence it will be forwarded to her. I want you to be careful in this matter, because I am doing it entirely on your behalf. Anybody watching us? No? Well, here goes."

The note was brief and to the point.

"Dear Countess,—

"What are you doing in these parts? I suppose you thought that so long as I was shut up you could play the comedy in your own fashion. Let me warn you to do nothing of the kind. Don't forget that the arm of coincidence is long, my lady. Come and see me at the hospital here. They'll let you in if you ask for me, only give me a day's notice. But you've got to come, and you've got to do what I want you to do. Call this a threat! Well you can if you like." ..... "W."

"Post that to-night," Waterhouse said gaily. "It will be worth your while."

CHAPTER XII

A SHOCK FOR COPPING

Dr. Flack was pleased to meet Moler. He had heard of him as a daring and successful surgeon, as a man prepared to take risks and generally to justify them. It seemed strange that Moler should be wasting his time in a quiet village. As a matter of fact, it was strange. Moler might have had an established position in Harley-street before now, but respectability made no appeal to him. He could not settle down to a humdrum existence. Intrigue and duplicity interested him beyond measure. Besides, he was on the point of pulling off a big coup. He had not patience to pile up money slowly and steadily, he needed a fortune ready-made, and he began to see his way to it. When this was secured, he would startle the world. But he meant that Miss Kearns should share it with him.

He was on excellent terms with himself as he returned to Rawmouth. He had come to an understanding with Waterhouse, and had impressed Flack with the gravity of the prisoner's case. His friends should be sent for. Waterhouse's life might be saved, if he were removed to a house where Moler could give him personal attention; to which advice Waterhouse had listened with a peculiar smile. He had friends, and powerful friends, if only they cared to come to his assistance, and, seeing that he had suffered his injuries in support of law and order, the authorities would be inclined to consent.

Two days later Waterhouse was comfortably settled in a farm-house, with a nurse imported by Moler to look after him. The farm was about a mile from Rawmouth, so that Moler could readily pass to and fro. He appeared to be satisfied with the turn of events, as he stood by the bedside of his patient, smoking an after-dinner cigarette. The nurse was resting.

"You are feeling pretty comfortable?"

"Precisely," Waterhouse replied drily. "I am very sorry, however, to be under obligation to you. I am getting better. If I do, I shall take my place in the world again and let everybody see that I am—"

"Free till you are caught again," Moler sneered. "I have heard of those cases before."

"And will probably hear of them again, Dr. Moler. But my case will be different. I've had a lot of luck, and I'm grateful for it. I shall go to Canada to regain my character. But this does not concern you. You did not humbug Flack and put me on the road to health again from motives of philanthropy. What do you want?"

Moler smiled as if the speaker had paid him a compliment.

"You are quite right," he said. "I did not. I have been trying to get speech with you for a long time, and that's why I put pressure on Mary Copping. I was in a position to command her services, as you know. For the present she is free to go or stay as she pleases. She has served my purpose. Did you see Grenfell in gaol?"

"Not to recognise him. I heard about him; we manage to hear most things yonder. But get on, come to the point. How am I to repay you?"

Waterhouse put the question crisply. Moler had reached the critical point, and knew that any slip would be fatal so far as the information he was desirous of obtaining was concerned. He was far too clever to under-estimate the abilities of his opponent. He knew he was dealing with a mind as keen and brilliant as his own.

"Why do you speak of repayment?"

"My dear fellow, it is necessary to do so," Waterhouse answered. "It is an old axiom that one good turn deserves another. In these prosaic days a good turn is merchandise. It is an exchange of coin in another form. I asked you a simple question. Why have you done this for me? Why have you persuaded Flack practically to set me at liberty?"

"My dear fellow, surely you exaggerate by using such a term?"

"Not at all. I am allowed to do as I like. Nobody watches me and nobody is in the least suspicious of my movements. Moreover, I am better and stronger than people give me credit for. I could rise now and walk as far as the sea. My correspondence is not examined, and I am in communication with my friends. Some of them are pretty powerful. Big interests and big money are at my disposal. I could have a yacht waiting here to-morrow to take me to the other end of the world if I liked. I am reminding you of these things, though they are not new to you. Therefore I ask, again, why have you done this? Why have you put me under this obligation to you?"

"A fellow feeling makes one wondrous kind," Moler laughed.

"Honor amongst thieves, you mean?" retorted Waterhouse. "It doesn't sound so nice, but it is more true. Oh, we are a pretty pair, if it comes to that. And what good has our talent done us? We are both clever enough to have done anything in the world; we could have attained any position we wanted. We might have been presiding over the fortunes of a continent. And I am a broken gaol-bird, and you are sponging on, and blackmailing a murderer."

Moler started, and his face changed to a crimson hue. Waterhouse's cold, nerveless words cut him to the quick.

"It is not up to you to be so candid," he said hoarsely.

"It is up to me to tell the truth," Waterhouse retorted. "Man alive! why should there be any delicacy between two such rotters as ourselves? You know there is no such thing as what you call honor amongst thieves. You have some deep reason for helping me. I mean you have some good cause for putting me in such a position that we can talk without warders being by my side. Otherwise you would have seen me die in a ditch before holding out a hand to me. And when I ask for the reason, you palter with me."

"One has to be cautious," Moler muttered.

He was sore and angry, conscious that he was getting the worst of it, and he went on in this blundering way, knowing all the time that he was making a mess of it. Waterhouse watched him with grim amusement.

"You are too clever," he said. "You are almost as clever as the British Ambassador who acquired a tremendous reputation for his annoying diplomacy. His secret was simple—he always told the truth when the other fellows thought he was lying. As he told the truth, you see, he could never make a mistake. It sounds easy; why don't you try it?"

Moler forced a laugh to his lips. His expression became frank and engaging, and he went straight to the point without further prevarication or circumlocution.

"Well, tell me the real story of the disappearance of Partridge and Gainsforth," he said boldly.

"Really? Is that all? Don't you think you had better ask Martin Faber?"

"Faber is dead—he was killed in an accident on the line. He left everything to my friend, Raymond Draycott, from the Argentine. There are reasons why Draycott should not be approached by me. On the other hand, both Partridge and Gainsforth were friends of yours. Can you tell me anything about them?"

"I could tell you a great deal, if I felt disposed to," Waterhouse responded. "I could also throw a good deal of light on the latter doings of Martin Faber. But I don't feel inclined to do anything of the sort. That you are up to some dirty work, I feel certain. That somebody is to suffer is more than certain. Come again in the morning, and we'll talk it over, I'm too tired to-night. But I will not promise anything."

Moler did not press the matter. He would get all the information he needed in good time. There was a better way than an open threat. He nodded meaningly as he left the room. The nurse was not due on duty till ten o'clock, and Waterhouse would need nothing before that. Moler had barely gone, when the door of the bedroom opened, and Mary Copping entered.

She looked pale and anxious, but the suggestion of terror had gone from her eyes. She stole across to the bed as if afraid of being overheard.

"The front door was open," she whispered. "So I crept in. I got your message from the landlady's little boy. My husband had to go back to the prison for something, so I came along as soon as I could. What can I do for you, sir?"

"Upon my word, this is very good of you," Waterhouse said gratefully. "You are taking certain risks, and I hope you will come to no harm. Now, I need not discuss Moler with you—you know that scoundrel as well as I do. He thinks that he is using me and my accident to the best advantage. As a matter of fact, the luck is all on my side. My friends have taken me up again, and it is long odds that I don't go back yonder again. It was through Moler that I managed to get away from that hospital. He has humbugged Flack and pretends that by a new treatment he has saved my life. Moler thinks he will make a tool of me, but he won't. He is coming here to-morrow to learn everything. By that time I shall have concocted a pretty fairy tale for him. It makes me laugh to think of it."

"But what can I do for you, sir?"

"I want you to take this key and this envelope and post it for me. You will find pen and ink and paper on that little table. The key I have had with me all the time I was in gaol. Address the envelope to 'Russell Clench, Esquire, 17, Gray's Inn Court, London,' and mark it 'Private.' There is a scrap of paper round the key which will explain everything to Mr. Clench. If you will post that for me, I shall be greatly obliged. I need not detain you, Mary."

Mary made up the parcel and vanished. She had no need to stay any longer, and was more than anxious to return home. If she were back before her husband all would be well. She began to see her way to freedom; at any rate, Moler was done with her for the present. It would be no fault of hers if she was not out of the way and far from Dartdale before he saw her again.

Copping had not yet returned. That was so much gained, at any rate. It began to look as if the longed-for freedom were already come. A little longer and her troubles would be over. The door of the cottage opened, and Copping entered. There was no smile on his face, his eyes were hard, his lips set close together. Something seemed to catch Mary by the heart.

"Where have you been?" he demanded. "What have you been up to?"

"Up to!" Mary echoed. "Why, getting your supper, for one thing, Joe. And for another—"

"It's a lie," Copping said, hoarsely. "I ran back for something an hour ago, and you were nowhere to be seen. Where have you been? What's the matter with you? What do you know about that man Waterhouse they let out of the infirmary? Why did you go and see him? I'm not suspicious, and have always trusted you; but I'm not going to put up with this. It's been all on a par with your conduct lately, my girl. You were anxious to leave here, yet when the time came you seemed to be scared to death at the idea. Pretended you'd got to go and nurse some neighbor! Instead of which you were in love with a convict."

Mary trembled from head to foot. Should she tell Joe everything, should she unfold the story of those three eventful years she had spent in the Countess's service? Would he believe her if she did? She had done nothing wrong; she had merely been the innocent instrument of others. She had escaped from that bondage in time to save herself from serious disaster; she had gone back to her home and married the only man she ever cared for. Would he understand if she did tell him? She doubted it. Not now, at any rate; his present mood was unpropitious.

"You wrong yourself," she said, quietly. "I never cared for anybody but you, and I never shall, Joe. But we can't all do as we like, we are all in the toils of circumstance. I read that in a book somewhere; afterwards I found out how true it was. But I can go away now, Joe, and shall be glad if you will take me as far away from here as possible."

"Then you won't tell me?"

"Not to-night, dear. But what's the matter? Your clothes are torn, and you are all wet?"

Mary longed to pour out the questions that rose fast to her lips. Was this some fresh complication, and had she anything to do with it? She blamed herself bitterly for the way in which she had deceived her husband; but there was consolation in the fact that, on the other hand, he had been concealing something from her. Well, whatever he had done, she was ready to forgive him. If he was keeping anything from her, she was certain he was suffering the pangs of conscience as keenly as she was herself.

"Is it anything very bad, Joe?" she asked, huskily.

But Joe did not hear. He was staring vaguely into space, as if expecting some horror to materialise in front of him. He came to himself with a start.

"Did you ask me a question, lass?" he stammered. "I—I was thinking about something else. It's possible I've made a mistake, after all. Don't you worry, my dear. You've got quite enough to think of, as it is. I'm going back to the prison for a while."

"But not now," Mary protested.

"I must, lass; I've forgotten something. I'll be back in half an hour at the outside. Don't fret."

The advice was good, but unfortunately Mary could not take it. She was restless and anxious, wondering what new form of trouble was looming over them. She busied herself about the house, getting the belated supper ready, and half longing for, half dreading Joe's return. The atmosphere of the cottage seemed hot and oppressive, the air stifling. She was glad at length when everything was ready to go out into the soft, violet, velvety darkness of the night to breathe the cool and sweet air. She stood in her print dress and cotton bonnet at the gate, looking out across the moor. Away in the distance she could hear the purring of a car as it tore down the winding road.

It came nearer and nearer; the big acetylene lamps flashing on each side, the speed slackened and the car pulled up on the crest of the hill opposite the cottage. A tall woman with a fine, slim figure, and most beautifully dressed, stood up in the car and looked about her.

"Here is a cottage, idiot," she said shrilly. "You are the greatest fool I ever had in my service. You are always so positive, and yet you never know the way. Ask at the cottage."

Mary stood listening, with her heart at her lips. She wondered where she had heard that commanding voice before; then it came to her in a flash. She turned to fly headlong into the cottage, anywhere to avoid that vision. The woman hailed her, and she stopped.

"Come back! Where are you running to? Have you never seen a motor-car before? Have you never seen anybody from the right side of civilisation? What are you afraid of?"

Mary, shaking in every limb, was vaguely conscious that her face was hidden in the shadow of her cotton bonnet, that it was too dark to see her features.

"Tell me the way to Dartdale Prison. If you can show me how to get there I shall be all right for the next few miles. My chauffeur is the king of idiots, and, as far as I can judge, he is in congenial company in these parts. Which is the way?"

"Over the hill and then first turn to the right," Mary answered, in a voice that was not her own. "You can't possibly make a mistake, madam."

Madam said nothing by way of reply. The car started again with a jerk. Mary went into the kitchen and dropped breathlessly into a chair.

"The Countess!" she gasped. "Countess D'Arblay! What is she doing here?"

CHAPTER XIII

CONFESSIONS

Mary Copping forgot her immediate troubles in the contemplation of this greater evil. Shortly before she had been almost glad to find that her husband had a secret too, and now it looked as if they both had confessions to make. Had Joe been doing anything wrong? Should she tell him everything about her early days and ask his pardon? Was he as bad as she? He was the picture of dejection and despair, when he came in presently and sank moodily into a chair.

"What's wrong?" she asked. "What has happened, Joe? What's this new trouble that has come upon us, dear? Have I said anything to anger you?"

"Well, in a manner of speaking, you have," Copping said slowly. "Not that it much matters now. As sure as ever you do wrong it's safe to be found out. You can take what steps you like to hide it, but it's got to come to light. There's things nobody can foresee, be as cunning as you please."

Copping rambled on, obviously trying to collect himself. His anger was gone, and he had forgotten that Mary had deceived him. His weary and worried look filled Mary with alarm.

"What have you done?" she asked. "You had better tell me, Joe."

"It was for the best," Copping said, bringing his fist down on the table with a crash. "I'll swear that I did it for the best. I wasn't thinking of myself, either."

Mary crossed over and put her arm about his neck. She could see that he was trembling with emotion— this big, stolid man, at the touch of her, and the ghost of a smile hovered on his lips.

"We've got each other," Mary whispered. "Whatever has happened will make no difference. I shall go on loving you just the same, Joe."

"Ah, I know that," Copping said hoarsely. "I spoke like a jealous fool just now, and I ask your pardon my dear. Women have little secrets sometimes."

Mary slid down on the speaker's knee and laid her head on Joe's shoulder.

"I'm going to tell you something," she said. "I ought to have told it to you long ago. It was something that happened during the three years I was in service. Everybody said that I was lucky to get that place, and I thought so myself. The wages were good, my mistress was liberal, and she had a grand foreign style with her. There seemed to be no end to the Countess D'Arblay's money. I didn't know till long afterwards that she was no better than an adventuress. A few people may have suspected it, but only a few. I had all kinds of things to do, and I did them innocently. I carried stolen goods about, and got forged cheques cashed. I did a score of things that would have landed me in gaol, had I only known what they meant. Some of her friends were as bad as herself, but some were only foolish. The fools and the knaves were all mixed up together. About the greatest knave of the lot is Dr. Moler."

"What, the chap who is staying at Rawmouth?"

"The same—the man who is looking after Mr. Waterhouse now. He knew all about the robberies. When the crash came he was somewhere in the background. It was in that house that I first came in contact with Mr. Waterhouse."

"Go on," Copping said. "Go on lass. I begin to see daylight."

"Mr. Waterhouse was very kind to me. He was reckless and foolish, and I daresay deserved all he got in the end, but he was a gentleman and he took a fancy to me. Mind you, there was nothing, Joe—he never so much as touched my hand. He wanted me to leave and go elsewhere, and I wanted to stay, being innocent and ignorant of what was going on. There were two other gentlemen—intimate friends of his—Mr. Partridge and Mr. Gainsforth. It was Partridge that Mr. Grenfell was accused of murdering."

"They might just as well have accused me of it," Joe said contemptuously.

"Well, the evidence was pretty strong, Joe. And there was the missing man's watch. But I am wandering off the road. Only I wanted to tell you how kind these gentlemen were to me. When the game was up, and the Countess had to bolt, Mr. Gainsforth and Mr. Partridge made it easy for me. I think they called it covering my tracks. The police were looking out for the Countess's maid who had done so many clever things for her. They weren't clever, Joe—it was pure ignorance on my part. Had I been caught, I should have got into the most dreadful trouble. But I never was caught; I came back home and married you. Of course I ought to have told you all this before, but I was ashamed of the whole business and wanted it forgotten. I was beginning to forget it myself, when Moler turned up. You can imagine what a shock that was. He threatened to tell my story unless I did something for him. He wanted me to smuggle a letter into the prison to Waterhouse."

"You needn't go any further, my dear," said Copping, with a sigh. "I'm pretty slow at taking things in, but I understood that all right. Sort of blackmail, I suppose."

"I think so, Joe," Mary whispered. "I'm glad I've told you. It seems easy now, but I dreaded to speak. Oh! if I had only done so before."

Mary's eyes were full of tears, but there was a lightness at her heart to which she had long been a stranger. How incredibly simple it was! Joe had believed her story without question, and everything was straight between them. She might have known that it would be like this all along. They would be able to go right away now, out of the mist and fog and shame, and start life anew. She murmured something of this as she sat with her head on her husband's shoulder.

She felt his grasp relax, and a long sigh seemed to shake him.

"I had forgotten all about myself," he said, with a groan. "Your story was so very interesting. You're asking me to forgive you when the forgiveness is all on the other side. But what I did, I did entirely for your sake."

"Joe, don't you think you had better tell me what you have done?"

"I was coming to it, my dear. I was bound to come to it in time. It was just like this. If you stayed here you had to die, and as far as I could see there was no chance of our getting away. Then I began to be worried about my heart. If the people yonder found out that anything was wrong with me, it would mean the sack. We shouldn't have a penny between us, and—well, you know what such a prospect would be. Then Miss Alice comes to me and offers me a hundred pounds, with the promise of heaps more to shut my eyes whilst they smuggled Mr. Grenfell out of gaol—"

"But that was impossible, Joe."

"Impossible! It's done," Copping said gravely. "He's gone, and a friend of his is now in quod passing as Mr. Grenfell. Mind you, it is only for a week or until the next fog, and things are to be put on the old footing again. That's where I got the hundred pounds. What I told you about a newspaper competition was all lies."

Mary let that pass; she felt that much might be forgiven the man who had risked everything for her sake.

"Where is Mr. Grenfell now?"

"I can't say for certain, but I've got a pretty good idea," Copping said slowly. "My mind isn't quick to take up points, but we have what's called inspiration at times, and I've got it to-night. I can't tell you why, but I'm right. The old man you've seen about named Dr. Blaydes is Mr. Grenfell in disguise. I'm as sure of it as if he had told me so."

"We're a pair of fools," Joe said dolefully. "We should have confided in each other. Husband and wife have no business to have secrets. Look at the mess it's landed us in. I don't rightly know as we've made a full confession, either."

"Leave it till to-morrow, Joe."

Joe glanced at his wife with affectionate anxiety.

"Do you feel worse, my dear?" he asked.

"Only dead tired. There's a weight off my mind, and I know I shall sleep better than I've done for long. I brought it on myself, Joe, for I might have known you would take my part. I might have known you'd stick to me through thick and thin. But I thought I had put the old life behind me for good, so I made up my mind not to talk to anybody about it. But I was innocent, Joe."

Copping, stooped and kissed the trembling, white lips tenderly.

"Of course you were, dear," he said. "Anybody had only to look at you and see that. As to that Moler, if he comes here again I'll break his neck. Don't worry, Mary. I deceived you a sight worse than you deceived me, telling lies about a competition in a paper, when I took the money for doing a thing as would land me in gaol if it got to the ears of the governor."

"But, you did it for my sake, Joe," Mary whispered. "You were ready to do anything to help me get away from here."

Mary smiled gratefully. Only one thing troubled her now, and that was the knowledge of the Countess D'Arblay's presence in the vicinity. Was she residing in the district, or simply passing through? She would make a few discreet inquiries. A neighbor had a son in a motor-works at Newton Abbot. He might be able to tell her.

"I reckon I know who you mean," this man said. "Tall, handsome lady, in a red car. Bill was passing to-day, and looked in to tell me the news. She's a Countess. I don't remember her name, but it begins with a D."

Mary listened with a smile on her face. But there was no joy in her heart.

"I used to see a Countess like her once," she said. "I was in service near by. A very fine woman, that nobody knew much about. D'Arblay was her name."

"Then it's the very same. That's the name Bill mentioned. She's staying at the Tor Hotel, and is thinking of taking a place here for a few months. I fancy Bill said she was after Squire Taynton's place at Sawbridge."

Mary suppressed a tendency to scream. Were all her old associates drifting into the heart of Devonshire? Of them all, Mary was most anxious to avoid the Countess, and she was actually thinking of settling down in their neighborhood. True, it was probably only for a few months, but incalculable mischief might easily be done in that time. Sawbridge was only a few miles away, and Squire Taynton generally let the place for the autumn.

Mary thanked her friend, and returned to the cottage. She had not much to do that afternoon, and felt she must satisfy herself on the subject of the Countess's visit. Squire Taynton was absent, and she had some acquaintance with the housekeeper at Sawbridge. She would have an early cup of tea and go over. It was like thrusting her head into the lion's den, but she would risk that.

She came presently to the gates of Sawbridge and passed up the drive. There was a short cut through the shrubberies to the domestic quarters, as Mary knew. The place was quiet and secluded, and she could, if need be, hide in the thick bushes of evergreens. Mary fell back from the path, as she heard the flutter of a skirt in the distance.

It was the Countess herself. She stood in an open glade immediately opposite Mary's hiding-place, biting her lips impatiently. A summer-house made a frame for her, and a handsome picture she looked. Secure as Mary felt, she trembled as she studied the beautiful, angry face. She had once been this woman's willing slave.

Well, perhaps she might be again. The Countess meanwhile seemed as if she were waiting impatiently for another slave. He came a minute or two later, in the shape of Oliver Partridge. Mary expressed no surprise; she was no longer frightened, only intensely curious. She would remain on her knees and hear what passed.

"What are you doing in this quarter?" asked the Countess.

"Getting by easy stages to London," Partridge responded coolly. "I happened to spot you, my dear, and it struck one I should prefer going by train. You have the money and I have not. At one time I had the money, and you—well, we need not go into that. If I possessed to-day the stuff that I've lavished on you I should be a rich man."

"No, you wouldn't. It would have gone in some other way. Are you threatening me? Do you look upon my help as a right? What if I refuse it?"

"You won't, my dear, you won't," Partridge chuckled. "I'm too dangerous; I know too much. If I told half I know to some people here, you'd have to leave England to-morrow. I'm here by accident, but already I've discovered certain people who would be glad to know my story."

"Do you mean Draycott?"

"No, I don't; catch Draycott wasting his time in this country!"

Mary thought she noticed the Countess's face brighten.

"I'll give you five minutes, and then you must go. I am taking this place for a time, furnished. I do not want you—"

"Don't imagine I should be recognised as an acquaintance of yours," Partridge sneered, "though once you were glad enough to be seen about with me. But, to business. If I have any nonsense I'll drop a hint to the police at Exeter, and you'll reside in another place, rather scantily furnished, for a longer time than you care for. I want money—some of my own back, if you like—and I mean to have it."

He grabbed the woman by the arm and forced her backward into the summer-house.

"None of your damned airs with me," he went on fiercely. "Don't you drive me too far. Suppose I post those papers Ned Livingstone gave to me to—"

The rest of the sentence declined to a whisper; the door of the summerhouse closed, and Mary heard no more.

CHAPTER XIV

THE POCKET-BOOK

On the whole, Moler was satisfied with the progress of events. He was gradually getting all the strings into his hands. His next interview with Waterhouse was successful in a fashion, and he might be able to dispense with the aid of that brilliant criminal in future.

"I hope you are satisfied," Waterhouse asked with a smile.

"I am certainly obliged to you," Moler responded. "Did you ever contemplate writing a book?"

"A good many times," Waterhouse said grimly. "I could compile a most interesting volume out of our experiences. Why, I could fill a book with reminiscences of the various scoundrels I have met. You would monopolise a chapter."

Moler was not in the least abashed.

"You would not confine it to one alone?" he asked.

"By no means. I should like to include several women such as our fascinating friend, the Countess. Do you ever see her now, Doctor?"

"She has been beyond my orbit for sometime," Moler explained, "though I found her very useful on occasion. I fancy you and I are the only two who ever managed her properly. As a matter of fact, she is in this neighborhood now. She has had a prosperous spell lately, and her exchequer is comfortably full. She has reached the time of life when it is necessary to rest occasionally—nerves; you understand."

"They do find one out," Waterhouse admitted. "She is trying the simple life?"

"Oh, yes, plus a good cook and a French maid. She thinks that a couple of months here will set her up again. She is renting a place called Sawbridge. Young Sir Edward Treherne lives close by, and who knows? The Countess would not be the only lovely adventuress who has settled down to humdrum respectability."

"She has told you all this, Doctor?"

"No, I found it out for myself, more by accident than anything else. She does not know I am here, but will discover that pleasant fact before I go to bed. I telephoned for a cab from the Tor Hotel to pick me up at 10 o'clock. I shall walk back to Rawmouth. I am looking forward to our interview."

Waterhouse appreciated the keenness of Moler's anticipations.

"I'd give something to be there," he said. "But these pleasures are denied me for the future. I have made a solemn vow to turn respectable, and, with all my faults, nobody can deny I am a man of my word. Good-night, Moler."

Moler departed, feeling on the best of terms with himself. He had a pleasant conviction that his diplomacy had not been wasted, and was satisfied that he had gained some valuable information.

"Waterhouse is not the man he was," he thought. "Prison has sapped his intellect. It was like playing with a child at the finish."

At that moment Waterhouse lay on his back, smiling, and thinking much the same thing of Moler.

"That rascal fancied he was getting the better of me," he told himself. "I flatter myself I have started him on a good wild-goose chase. If he follows up my hints he will probably land himself in the hands of the Berlin police. I'm a bit of a wrong 'un, but I am an ignorant bungler by the side of Moler."

Moler reached his destination half an hour later. The season had not begun yet, and the hotel had only a few visitors of the less fashionable kind. Most of them had retired, but the Countess D'Arblay was still in the dining-room.

"The Countess is alone?" Moler asked.

"Quite alone, sir," the waiter said.

"Might I remind you, sir, that we close in half an hour?"

Moler intimated that half an hour would be sufficient. Neither did he see why his name should be announced. The Countess was expecting him.

She turned, with a start, as he closed the door behind him. The insolent courage faded from her eyes, and the haughty lips trembled, as Moler came forward. He saw her face quivering and that the hands by her side were clenched.

"You!" she said hoarsely. "What evil spirit has sent you here?"

Moler smiled gaily. He placed his hands on her shoulders and kissed her. Her lips were as cold as ice to the touch.

"My lovely Christine," he said. "By the way, is it Christine, or have we changed that sweet name? Are you not going to kiss me as you used to do? Ah, those were purple moments, ma belle, those passionate times when we were not acting a part. What are you doing here?"

The Countess dropped slowly into a chair. The man seemed to fascinate her.

"If I told you, you would not believe me."

"Perhaps not. Whatever you said would probably be a lie. You never would tell the truth, my dearest, even when it would have paid you to do so. Always tell the truth when you get the chance, Christine. So you are going to stay here for a time and enjoy a rest? You are wise, Christine, for ocular evidence compels me to say you don't grow younger. The edge of the charm is working off, darling, but I daresay a month or two here will make a great difference. You may come to like the life, and that young baronet you were driving with to-night might help you to enjoy it."

"If you should dare—"

"Pooh, pooh! What's the good of talking to me like that, duckie? I have only to say the word, and you will have to do exactly as I tell you. If you are reasonable I'll not interfere. You can marry a dozen young baronets if you like. It would be an interesting experiment to watch, as I was saying to our mutual friend, James Waterhouse, just now."

"Waterhouse!" the Countess gasped. "Why do you lie to me? James Waterhouse is in—"

"Dartdale Prison. But there are means and ways of managing these affairs, and when I tell you I have just spent an hour with dear Jim, it's your look-out whether you believe me or not. At any rate, he told me all I wanted to know about those Collesmore diamonds—"

The Countess appeared to be swallowing something with difficulty.

"You are a wonder," she said, with grudging admiration. "I—I never expected a complication like this. If you mean to do the fair thing by me—"

A steely glitter came into Moler's eyes.

"You are nothing to me," he said harshly. "You never will be—you never were. Waterhouse and I were the only two who read you from the start. Nevertheless, I wish you no harm. If you will only do what I wish, you will be safe as far as I am concerned. I am tired of the life here, and want to go back to the world and get on with my work. Only, I need money, dearest. My recent experiments have pretty well dried up, my intimate friend—"

"What you mean is, that you have dried him up yourself?"

"Well, put it in that way. I don't mind. I can see another fine source of profit, but I need your assistance. However, you will get nothing out of it for your services, my lovely one. I don't need you for a few weeks, so you can play the game with your baronet for the present, Countess."

The speaker proceeded to explain for the best part of the half-hour before he rose.

"I understand," the Countess said, when he had finished. "I will do as you say. Good-night."

A little later Moler returned to Rawmouth. He was on the track of certain information which he intended to turn to profit before long. Draycott was almost wholly in his power, but there were certain gaps he deemed it prudent to fill up. Draycott still had a large part of the hundred thousand pounds. Before long half of that must find its way into Moler's pocket. With such a sum he could devote himself to his scientific discoveries, which were destined to startle the world and place the name of Moler on the highest pinnacle of fame. This prospect, with Alice Kearns to share it, formed a picture that Moler did not find displeasing.

It seemed to him presently that somebody was following him in the darkness. He turned once or twice uneasily, for physical courage was not one of his virtues. He had an iron nerve and audacity, but the fear of assault did not leave him unmoved. Something stirred in a bush close by, and he gazed in that direction. Then a figure sprang upon him from behind; he was conscious of a hot, stinging sensation, and he knew no more.

An hour later a little procession, bearing a hurdle came into the hall at Rawmouth. An affrighted servant summoned Clench. Alice was in the drawing-room playing some dreamy music on the piano, and Draycott had retired for the night. He had gone off directly, after dinner, pleading a racking headache. Clench took command at once. The unconscious Moler was carried to his room, and a doctor sent for.

"Now, tell me how this happened," Clench said.

As far as possible, Mason, a prison warder, who was one of the bearers, told his story, but he had seen little in the dark, and had been drinking, and had not the remotest idea what the assailant was like. To Clench he gave a different description, from the one subsequently offered to Copping. Evidently there was little to be learnt at present, and the helpers were dismissed after certain hospitable rites had been performed. As some time must elapse before the doctor could arrive, it was necessary to communicate with Draycott.

Clench knocked quietly at Draycott's bedroom door. Three times he knocked, but no response came. He turned the handle and entered. The bed had not been slept in, and the occupier of the room had vanished. On his bed lay his dress clothes, and on the floor were a tweed suit, just discarded, and a pair of muddy shooting boots. The dressing-room also was empty.

Clench whistled softly to himself as he crept down the stairs. With a white face, Alice met him in the hall; she had heard what had happened.

"Is it true?" she asked.

"You mean about Moler?" Clench said. "Yes, he has either met with an accident, or somebody has tried to murder him. At any rater he is in a bad way, and I am waiting anxiously for the doctor. Till then, we can do nothing."

"But you don't think it was an accident, Mr. Clench?"

"Not for a moment," Clench said. "The man has enemies. In any case, it is no affair of ours. We have done all we can till the doctor comes. If Moler dies it will be a good thing for humanity; but he won't die, those fellows never do. You had better go to bed. The doctor will be sure to bring a nurse with him. I'll sit up till he comes."

Alice hesitated, but she did not relish the idea of looking after Carl Moler. Moreover, she saw that Clench wanted to be alone. Directly she had gone he ordered the servants to bed and sat listening intently, with the door of the smoking-room wide open. He was conscious presently of the sound of somebody moving on the stairs, and a moment later Draycott, in dressing-gown and slippers, came into the room. He seemed surprised and uneasy to find Clench there.

"I—I thought everybody had gone to bed," he stammered. "I came down for—"

His glance wandered to the decanter on the table, and Clench guessed what he had come for. Draycott put out a trembling hand and helped himself to a generous quantity of brandy. He tossed it down and took another almost as potent. A little color crept into his cheeks.

"What on earth are you sitting up for?"

"Moler has met with an accident," Clench explained. "I have sent for the doctor. You may leave everything to me, Mr. Draycott."

Draycott burst into a strange laugh. There was a peculiar gleam in his eyes.

"An accident!" he cried. "Is he dead? That is too much to hope for— What am I saying? Moler is a friend, one of the best friends I ever had. If you say anything to the contrary, you lie! Everybody knows we are the best of friends."

He slipped into a chair and began to weep in maudlin fashion. By and by he staggered to his feet, announcing that he was going to bed. Clench helped him up the stairs and remained by his side till he dropped into a drugged and heavy sleep. It would be hours before Draycott recovered consciousness, and Clench dwelt on this fact with satisfaction.

"And now," he remarked, "to do a little amateur burglary. It would be flying in the face of Providence to miss such a chance."

He fumbled about for Draycott's keys. If he could only find them, the opening of the safe in the library would be an easy matter. The keys were in his possession at length, and he went down into the morning-room again. He had hardly time to light a cigarette, when there came a tapping on the window. Clench drew up the blind and looked out. Grenfell, in his disguise, stood before him.

"I simply had to come, my dear fellow. As you know, I followed Moler to-night. It was no waste of time, because I discovered he has been attending Waterhouse."

"But Waterhouse is in prison."

"He's out, and, what's more, he will remain out. I'll give you the details, presently. But it's good to know that we can put our hand on Waterhouse when we need his services, as we shall before long. He will do anything for me. But this is not what I came to see you about. I followed Moler, but not so closely as to save him from an attack by somebody who had been shadowing him. The chap got away too quickly for me. While I was bending over Moler I was collared by a warder and was hard put to it to get away. I was foolish enough on the spur of the moment to call myself Blaydes. When I realised what I had done and the peril I stood, there was nothing for it but to bolt; but you see how this unfortunate business may ruin everything."

"Well, as a matter of fact, it hasn't," Clench smiled. "Moler is lying here now, and we are waiting for the doctor. The warder was not sober, and he has no more idea what you are like than Adam. For the present you are absolutely safe, Grenfell. I suppose you did not happen to see what the would-be murderer was like?"

"I was too late for that," Grenfell said regretfully.

"You could not give a guess?"

"I cannot. You may be sure Moler has plenty of enemies."

"No doubt, but this is a problem I fancy I can solve," said Clench. "Draycott went to bed early to-night on the plea that he had a splitting headache. When they brought Moler in I went to Draycott's room to tell him what had happened. He was not there! His dress clothes were on the bed, but of Draycott himself there was no sign. I waited till the house was quiet, and by and by Draycott came downstairs after brandy. He looked like a ghost, and was under the influence of morphia. He drugged himself with brandy, and I helped to put him to bed. On the floor I saw a pair of shooting boots with fresh mud on them, and a tweed suit just discarded."

Grenfell whistled, under his breath.

"Do you put the two events together?"

"Most assuredly," Clench said grimly. "Draycott leaves the house secretly and comes back secretly. He changes his clothes, and, when he presents himself, looks horribly scared, and he has the appearance of a man who has just committed some ghastly crime. We know he hates Moler from the bottom of his heart, though outwardly they are friends. We are aware that Moler is here for blackmail. Draycott has made up his mind to get rid of him at any cost, and the chances are he has done so. He was disappointed to find that Moler was still alive, and as good as said so. He blustered and tried to wipe out the impression afterwards, but it did not deceive me for a moment. I am convinced this thing was done by Draycott. And, what's more, I mean to prove it."

Grenfell could detect no flaw in Clench's argument. The evidence was strong, and there were many and urgent reasons why Draycott should want to put Moler away.

"I believe you are right," he said, "but I don't want Moler to die just yet. I am desirous of wiping off some old scores first. Is Draycott in his room now?"

"He is fast in a drugged sleep, and nothing can disturb him for hours. I took the liberty of borrowing his keys with a view to inspecting his safe. This is a case where it won't do to be too scrupulous. Let us see what we can find before the doctor comes; we may not get a chance afterwards."

Grenfell was nothing loth. The door of the safe was flung back, and the inside stood disclosed. Here was a suit of clothes, together with a package of linen and other articles, such as a pipe and a cigar-case. Letters and papers were laid in neat rows on the shelves, and these Clench proceeded to overhaul. He was careful to put everything back exactly as he found it. Draycott in his sober moments was a cunning man to deal with, and it behoved them to take no risks.

"It looks as if we shall have our trouble for nothing," Clench muttered. "I hope the doctor will not come yet. Halloa! here is something that looks familiar. It is only an empty envelope, but the writing is known to me."

Grenfell took up the envelope and turned it over in his hand. His eyes gleamed strangely.

"The writing is that of Oliver Partridge," he said. "The man I was supposed to have killed years ago. Look at the post-mark."

Clench snatched the envelope from Grenfell and regarded it eagerly.

"Not a month old," he cried. "By Jove! this is a tit-bit."

CHAPTER XV

THE PENNY STAMP

Grenfell examined the envelope carefully. He was not greatly excited at the discovery, for he had always known that he was the victim of a conspiracy, though the mystery of it was hard to unravel. Partridge had either been got rid of, or was a party to the fraud. It was, of course, possible he might have been robbed and murdered, but Grenfell never really thought so. Here was a striking proof of the correctness of his deductions.

But the envelope proved much more than the fact that Oliver Partridge was alive. It was conclusive evidence that he had himself been one of the conspirators. If not, why was he in communication with Draycott? Again, why had Draycott a part in the conspiracy? Perhaps Partridge, too, was blackmailing Draycott. Altogether, it was a tangle, and the more Grenfell dwelt upon it, the more puzzled he was.

"Anyhow, we have something to go upon," he said. "For the present it does not matter what sort of scamp Draycott is. We shall be able to classify him presently and put him in his right place in this rogues' gallery. The fact remains that Partridge is alive, and is a correspondent of Draycott's. If we can run

Partridge down, my character will be vindicated; for it will not be difficult to explain how that watch came to be amongst my effects."

"I had no idea Partridge was such a loathsome scamp," Clench said. "Seeing he is alive, he must know what has happened to you. He could have cleared you without sacrificing anything."

"Possibly," Grenfell said thoughtfully. "But, on the other hand, it may have paid him handsomely to keep quiet. Draycott may have bribed him for some reason of his own. I know Partridge has gone through a large fortune, and it has been hinted there was worse behind. He was a weak creature and easily influenced. But I hope you will meet him face to face."

Clench expressed an ardent desire to the same effect. He laid the empty envelope on a table and subjected it to a searching investigation.

"Not very promising, on the face of it," he said. "An envelope with the date and the post-mark, 'Brockley, S.E.,' is not much to go on. Still, here may lie the key to the riddle. There is a magnifying-glass on those etchings yonder—hand it to me, please. It's as well to do these things thoroughly."

The magnifying-glass was applied to the face of the envelope, and Clench grunted. The expression sounded like one of satisfaction. He smiled slightly as he took out a pocket-knife and drew the point of a blade over the stamp. The post-mark had rendered the stamp black and indistinct, but evidently Clench had found something.

"This is very interesting," he said. "We are not baffled yet. Let us go to the bathroom—I want to soak this stamp off. We shall find plenty of hot water, for I saw to that before the servants went to bed. It occurred to me that the doctor might require a supply."

They were on the point of leaving the room when Clench added: "I had better stay here in case the doctor comes, and you can go and soak that stamp off. You know how to do it without my telling you, but be very careful. The clue may prove important."

Grenfell soon removed the stamp, dried it, and returned with it to his friend. Clench laid it on a sheet of white paper and lightly passed a brush full of ink over it, and then lifted it. On the paper beneath, in the form of a stencil were the words, 'Royal,' 'Brockley,' one above the other.

"Now what does that signify?" asked Grenfell.

"Well, you saw the stamp was a perforated one," Clench whispered. "As a business man, you know that large firms always perforate their postage stamps to prevent pilfering. I noticed the hotels as I looked at the envelope through the magnifying-glass. To make certain, I notched it with my knife. It is clear that the stamp came from some firm in Brockley called 'Royal.' Partridge is in close touch with it, or he would not have got the stamp. It may be a business house, or it may be a hospital—probably the latter. Let me assume that Partridge is in the hospital."

"Won't do," Grenfell said crisply. "The handwriting on the envelope is too dashing for that. It's a showy fist, but quite firm. No invalid addressed that letter."

"That's one to you," Clench answered. "Then we'll rule out the hospital. We can also rule out the suggestion of a business firm. Partridge is most assuredly no man of business."

"I've got it," Grenfell said, after a pause, "it's a theatre. 'Royal, Brockley' suggests a place of amusement. Partridge was a fair actor, and a clever conjurer and card manipulator. He could have made a living that way, and it's possible he's doing so now. A wandering life like that would about suit him."

Clench nodded approvingly, and began to consult the Post-office Directory. He found what he wanted presently, and fluttered the leaves, triumphantly. He pointed to a 'leaded' line with his finger.

"You've guessed it," he said. "The Royal at Brockley is a music-hall. Two performances every night, and all that sort of thing. Not a classy place, apparently. If Partridge has come down to conjuring for a living, it's the sort of place that would suit him. At any rate, it's fair to assume that he was engaged a little time at some place of amusement. But there is a good deal to be found out yet. We don't know what kind of show Partridge actually went in for, nor the name he had for the stage. You may depend upon it, he's not performing under his family name. On the whole, I am encouraged to go to town to-morrow—"

"Let me come with you," Grenfell suggested eagerly. "I may be of assistance, and can do no good by remaining here. My disguise is effectual, and there is not the slightest chance of Partridge recognising me. What do you say?"

Clench pondered the point for a few minutes.

"Very well," he said. "It will be a change for you. I don't know Partridge by sight, and he might slip through my fingers, especially as I don't know his professional name. You won't be in much danger. But there's the doctor! Lock up the safe and give me the key."

"Presently," Grenfell said. "Go and see the doctor while I look round a bit. I have an idea that may help us. Partridge has been writing to Draycott, though how he got to know him I cannot tell; and it's likely he has been writing for money. We may find that he has been demanding and getting cash regularly. If money was sent, it probably took the form of a cheque. Do you follow me?"

Clench went his way. With a feeling that he was secure from interruption, Grenfell turned to the safe again. He hoped to discover a bank-book, and perhaps a sheaf of returned bankers' cheques. These are the things that most people preserve without in the least knowing why. The bank-book was not to be seen, but from a long envelope Grenfell produced a batch of long, pink slips, which he proceeded to examine. About half-way through he withdrew one that caused him great satisfaction. He placed the slip in his pocket, restored the cheques carefully, and locked the safe.

Clench bustled into the room presently. "The doctor has gone," he said. "Our interesting friend upstairs is to live to do a great deal more mischief. Two or three days in bed will put him right. He will be out of the way for that time, however, so we can count him as non-existent. I should like to see Draycott's face when they meet. The doctor brought a nurse with him, so that we need not worry. Give me the key of the safe, so that I may replace it. Have you had any luck?"

"We'll talk about that when you come back," said Grenfell. "Replace the key first, in case of accident."

Clench returned at once.

"Now will you kindly cast your eye over this?" said Hugh. "It is a cancelled cheque I found in the safe. It is for twenty pounds, and is drawn upon his bankers by Draycott. I have no doubt there are similar cheques in the safe, but this one is sufficient for my purpose."

Clench took up the cheque and turned it over.

"Drawn in favor of Oscar Lee," he muttered. "Who the deuce is Oscar Lee? You don't suggest that he has anything to do with the case?"

"I do," Grenfell said. "He has a great deal to do with it. Look at the endorsement on the back of the cheque. Does it convey nothing to you? It's Oliver Partridge's handwriting. There is no mistaking it. Though the name 'Oscar Lee' is strange to me, the writing isn't. I can see Partridge's hand at a glance. That is the name under which he is performing. We have to find one Oscar Lee, lately playing at the Royal, Brockley. It should not be difficult."

"Upon my word you are doing pretty well," said Clench admiringly. "Beyond question, you're right. Is it wise to keep that cheque, Hugh?"

"I think so. Draycott is certain not to miss it, and when we find Partridge that cheque may come in uncommonly useful. It's a piece of valuable evidence, anyway. Now, what do you say to going to London to-morrow to look for Partridge? He will never guess who I am. I feel sure that we are on the eve of startling developments, Clench."

"Very little doubt about that," Clench agreed. "In any case, we shall be able to get enough evidence to establish your innocence. Not that that would satisfy me—I will not be satisfied until our host is exposed and this amazing conspiracy brought to light. We will give the Dartdale public something to talk about before long."

"Meanwhile, to bed!" said Hugh. "I am eager for the fray, and have a weapon to cut my way to freedom now."

Things were beginning to move at last. For an hour or more Clench sat on the side of his bed smoking cigarettes and putting the pieces of the puzzle together.

"It's an amazing story," he muttered. "The sort of things we'd scoff at in print. But in real life these things seem natural enough."

Despite the exacting events of the night, Hugh slept well, and awoke next morning with a sense of lightness and exhilaration he had not experienced for an age. Everything promised to be going his way, and there was nobody to stand in the path of progress. Moler was not likely to do any mischief for some time, and Draycott, in his present mental and physical condition, was a force that it was hardly necessary to reckon with. Therefore, it was a small party that breakfasted together in the morning. There was nothing said at the table, nothing beyond ordinary small talk, for it was necessary to think of the servants. Clench was occupied with his letters; he had a good deal of work to do, and hoped he might be excused for an hour or so. He would be busy with his correspondence in the library for quite that time.

"We will go and see if we can find any trace of that Purple Emperor butterfly," Hugh said lightly. "Would you like to give me an hour for that purpose, Miss Kearns?"

Alice agreed, demurely enough; but when they were in the recesses of the park her manner changed. She looked eagerly at Hugh.

"My dearest," she said. "You have discovered something, have you not?"

Hugh kissed her tenderly. There was no chance of being seen here, so that he put off his disguise and the real Hugh gazed into Alice's eyes.

"It is good to see you as you," she murmured. "Hugh, do be careful. Suppose you are seen."

"What a terrible disgrace for Dr. Gordon Blaydes!" Hugh laughed. "But, we are safe here, darling."

Alice dropped her head contentedly on her lover's breast.

"Your presence makes me feel reckless," she said. "But tell me the good news."

"My dearest girl, how on earth do you think there is any good news?"

"I saw it in your eyes, when you came down to breakfast. They are very expressive eyes, Hugh, but I don't suppose anybody noticed besides myself. Mr. Clench, too, seemed so satisfied?"

"We have every reason to be satisfied," Hugh explained. "We had a great night, darling. In the first place, we know that Oliver Partridge is alive."

A happy expression broke from Alice's lips, and she looked at Hugh with the tears in her eyes. If this were proved, then Hugh would be free.

"It sounds incredible. Did you actually find that out in this house?"

"We did, sweetheart," Hugh exclaimed triumphantly. "Of course we have not been over-scrupulous in our methods. We have had to fight those fellows with their own weapons. We took advantage of Draycott's being drugged and Moler crippled, to borrow Draycott's keys."

"How queerly you said that word, Hugh. Don't you think that Dr. Moler met with an accident?"

"No, I don't, darling. I think he was attacked by some enemy. I don't want to put any accusation into words yet, but Clench and I have a shrewd notion at whose hands that accident happened."

"Hugh!" Alice cried. "Do you really mean that Mr. Draycott—"

She stopped as if unable to finish the sentence. Hugh nodded grimly.

"That's the truth," he said. "We have practically proved it. This will give us a tremendous hold on Draycott when the time comes. Well, we got his keys and overhauled his safe. There we found a receipt from Oliver Partridge for money paid him quite recently, so that beyond doubt, the man whom I put out of the way is still alive. We gained the clue from the envelope containing the receipt, and we hope before long to find Partridge. When he is found, and the truth extracted from him, I shall be in a position to prove my innocence."

"Oh, Hugh, that will be delightful. The mere thought of it fills me with joy. But if Mr. Draycott has known all the time that Partridge was alive, it was a dreadful thing to keep the secret to himself and let you suffer so terribly. Why did he do it?"

Hugh's face grew dark, and his lips were firmly compressed.

"That we have yet to get to the bottom of," he said. "It is clear that Draycott has been pressing Partridge to keep silent. Possibly because he has the handling of your money, and a marriage between you and me would have exposed the fraud. There may be other reasons besides that of which we know nothing. But the great fact remains that we know where to find Partridge. We are very nearly at the end of our troubles, darling."

Alice slipped her arms about her lover's neck and drew his face down to hers. For a long time neither of them spoke. It was only when the distant luncheon gong sounded that Alice rose with a start.

"Is it really half-past one?" she asked. "How time flies when one is happy. I must go on ahead, Hugh. I look so pleased that the servants will notice me. You are not to forget what is due to your age and dignity! I hope your eyes won't betray you."

Hugh approached the house a little while after Alice. Clench was walking slowly up and down the terrace.

"Don't go in yet," he said. "I've something to tell you, my boy."

"Nothing amiss, I hope," Hugh responded; "nothing calculated to upset all our plans?"

"Oh, dear, no," Clench said. "On the contrary. The plot is thickening, Grenfell. Our old friend, the Countess D'Arblay, is in the neighborhood. She is staying at the Tor Hotel. Now, is she here by design, or by chance?"

CHAPTER XVI

"OSCAR LEE."

Next morning Hugh and Clench were up betimes and in the garden. Breakfast was usually a late function at Rawmouth, and there was never any appointed time for it. Hugh hoped Draycott would not put in an appearance at the meal.

"You need not worry about that," Clench said grimly. "Unless I am greatly mistaken, Draycott is in no state to see anybody. He'll hang about his room as long as possible. It's any money he wishes he hadn't touched Moler. You may be sure he wants the doctor badly now. It's a funny state of things altogether."

"How do you mean?"

"Well, take our position as a case in point. Isn't it odd that we should be guests here, and guests without a host? In point of fact, we ought to make our excuses, and go. Never was there such a menage since country houses were first instituted. And Miss Kearns is without another woman on the premises except the servants. Absolutely alone, mind you."

"There's another one, anyway," Grenfell muttered.

Clench started, and looked over his shoulder at the tall, graceful figure in black that was coming up the drive. She walked with the air of one thoroughly at home and nothing seemed likely to escape those dark, penetrating eyes.

"It's the Countess," Hugh gasped. "We must not be seen. If she recognises—"

"How can she recognise either of us?" Clench demanded. "I suppose you had forgotten that we are both in disguise. What would she say if she only knew! Don't let us take it too seriously. There is comedy here, if you look at it in the right light."

Clench walked towards the approaching visitor. His disguise laid his fears, if he had any, effectually to rest. He removed his hat politely.

"Can I be of any service, madam?"

"It's very kind of you," the Countess said, with a winning smile. "I came to inquire after a friend, who has met with an accident. You are Mr. Draycott?"

"Mr. Draycott is my host," Clench explained. "I am afraid he is not well. The startling events of last night were too much for him. Mr. Draycott suffers from nerves. If I could take any message to him—"

"I'm sorry," the Countess murmured. "My visit is to Dr. Moler. I am his sister—the Baroness Von Linden. Is he well enough to be seen?"

Clench glanced at his companion. He was thoroughly enjoying the situation. Hugh turned aside so that his face might not be seen, for the very sight of this woman filled him with sadness. She recalled to him a score of follies that he had tried to forget.

He was vexed that Clench should enjoy the humor of the situation.

"Now, what do you think, Dr. Blaydes?"

"I—ex—excuse me; I was hardly following what you were saying. I can scarcely speak as Dr. Moler's medical man. Personally, I should say he ought not to see anybody."

"Not his own sister?" the Countess pleaded. "Don't be hard on me, doctor. Consider my anxiety."

There was no question of her anxiety. The Countess was not acting a part now. Evidently she had dire and pressing need to see Moler at once. Her voice shook with emotion and there was an appealing look in her eyes that Hugh knew only too well. A good many men still lived who bitterly regretted they had ever seen it.

"Well, leave the matter to the patient," Hugh said. "Will you ascertain what he says, Mr. Bassett?"

When Clench departed off on his errand, Hugh forced a platitude to his lips. He wondered what the woman would say if she only knew whom she was talking to. It was strange she should be here, of all places in the world, practically under the same roof as Alice Kearns. And for the sake of this handsome, black-eyed adventuress, he had once faltered in his allegiance to Alice. A flush of shame rose to his face as he thought of it. Well, he had paid a heavy price for his folly. Others, too, had paid a similar price, and where were they now?

Apparently the Countess had forgotten her companion. She stood gazing absently at the ground, her trim little foot tapping the gravel path impatiently. Plainly, she had not come out of mere curiosity. A look of relief lit up her face as Clench returned.

"Your brother will see you, but I am told to say that he hopes you will not stay long. Will you be good enough to come this way?"

Hugh drew a sigh of heartfelt gratitude as the others vanished into the house. The very sight of the woman tried his patience to the uttermost. Still, the situation had its humorous side, and Hugh was smiling when, a minute or two later, Clench came back.

"This is a very remarkable position, Clench. There's something wrong with my lady. What did Moler say?"

"Moler was far from amiable. In fact, on the spur of the moment, he asked me to tell his sister to go to the devil."

"He didn't say he had no sister, I suppose?"

"Oh, no! He is not quite so stupid as that. For an instant he was nonplussed. In was clear my message conveyed no impression to him. But when I mentioned the 'Baroness' by name, he smiled. He knew then who was his visitor. Only he wasn't pleased, and suggested five minutes as the outside limit for the interview. Now, what does she want?"

"Something pressing, you may depend," Hugh replied. "She seemed very much upset. I've seen her in one or two unpleasantly tight places, but never did she betray such anxiety as she displayed just now. Fancy seeing her here; it's almost like the 'curtain' of a story."

"It is a story," Clench said, "and a very, strange one, too. Do you know that I should not have the least objection to hearing the breakfast bell ring? It can't be far short of 10 o'clock. If this goes on much longer I shall raid the peaches. Ah, here she comes."

The slim, graceful figure of the Countess D'Arblay appeared again. She came from the house with her head high in the air, her face white and wet. The anger in her eyes did not leave them as she swept up to the two men.

"I am obliged to you," she said. "I am glad my brother is no worse. I may perhaps be permitted to come and see him again in a day or two. Good-morning."

"She doesn't seem to have scored."

"So much the better for us," Hugh replied. "There goes the bell at last. May the Fates keep Draycott from the table!"

Hugh's fervent wish was gratified. Mr. Draycott deeply regretted that he was unable to join his guests at breakfast. He had had a shockingly bad night, and was not equal to the strain of meeting them. Meanwhile he hoped they would contrive to amuse themselves. He was greatly distressed to hear of the accident which had happened to Dr. Moler.

Hugh, who had come over early for the latest news, exchanged glances with Clench. Alice followed Hugh into the garden presently.

"Won't you confide in me, Hugh?" she asked. "All this mystery disturbs me. Did Moler meet with an accident after all?"

Hugh looked down into the white, anxious face fondly. He saw the grey eyes were steady and courageous.

"It was no accident, dear," he said. "I told you what I suspected yesterday. By a lucky chance I was saved from being arrested on suspicion. Draycott was the culprit right enough."

"But why should he do that?" Alice asked. "I have not forgotten what you said yesterday, but the motive puzzles me. Why did he do it?"

"Well, the man is hardly accountable for his actions. What, between drinks and drugs he is a poor wreck There is no doubt that Moler is blackmailing him. Moler has discovered some shameful secret, and is trading on it. Clench has the key to the mystery, and will expose the conspiracy before long."

"I'm not sure that I don't hold the key also," Alice said. "But my theory is so wild, that I hesitate to debate it even in my own mind. Still, so long as you are here—"

"I'm going to London to-day with Clench," Hugh explained. "It is in connection with the discovery we made last night that Oliver Partridge is alive. We will hunt him up and make him speak. Do you realise what that means?"

Alice drew a long breath. Her face blushed with pleasure, and grateful tears filled her eyes.

"Oh, if you can only find him!" she gasped. "What a wonderful thing it will be. But how did it happen? You had no time for details yesterday."

Hugh told the story in a few words.

"For your sake I cannot be too glad," she murmured. "This will clear your name, Hugh; for you can satisfy the whole world of your innocence. Partridge must be made to explain why he kept out of the way and let people suppose that his watch was stolen. Yet I am puzzled. All through this tangle the string leads back to Draycott. Why is he connected with it? Why should he, a total stranger to you, be so anxious to get you out of the way?"

Hugh shook his head. These questions were not to be answered off-hand.

"It is bound to come out presently," he replied. "We are safe to learn a good deal when we meet Partridge face to face. Of course I will not divulge myself to him; he will be left under the impression that I am in prison. He will not have the remotest idea of the connection between Dr. Blaydes, and Hugh Grenfell. But if you are afraid to stay here alone, I will remain behind."

"I am not afraid. All this mystery frightens me because it affects my imagination, but I am not alarmed. I admit it is necessary you should go to London; I see what you have gained by your escape from prison. Besides, it is as well there should be somebody here on the spot looking after your interests. When you return I also may have something to divulge."

It was getting dusk before Hugh and Clench arrived in London. They snatched a hasty meal at Paddington and made their way by taxi-cab to Brockley. The early performance was over, and the audience was beginning to file in for the second show as they reached the Royal. As Clench had anticipated, it was a small and somewhat shabby hall, patronised, for the most part, by people drawn from the meaner streets in the neighborhood. The name of Oscar Lee did not figure on the programme, but this contingency had been anticipated. A man with a huge curled moustache, and sporting a large sham diamond in his dingy shift-front stood inside the door. Clench accosted him; he had no hesitation in spotting him as the manager. He was quite affable, in spite of his splendor, and genially fell in with the suggestion of alcoholic refreshment.

"You seem to know a good deal of our profession, sir," the manager said.

"Well, yes," Clench smiled. He spoke the truth, for some of his clients were connected with the theatre. "I come from America, you see. I'm on the look-out for talent, Mr. Brabazon—I think you said your name was Brabazon. I never find that I am wasting my time. As a matter of fact, I came here to-night to look for Mr. Oscar Lee. I'm told he was with you for a short season." Mr. Brabazon grunted, as he passed his glass to be filled again.

"No use," he said. "A bally rotter; an absolute wrong 'un. Clever, mind you; quite an artist in his way. He's got a new dodge at table-rapping and conjuring spirits that might have filled the Albert 'All every night, but he's rarely sober. It's only when he's broke that you can rely on him. More than once he nearly gave the show away. Had to get rid of him, my dear sir, simply had to. Insolent beggar, too. Always bragging about his family."

"Many thanks for the hint," Clench said. "I'll not trouble you any more about him. But I've got something for him, and must deliver it personally. If you could tell me where I am likely to find him, you will confer a further obligation on me."

Mr. Brabazon called to a subordinate and asked a few questions. Partridge, it seemed, was not very far off. He had no regular engagement, but was earning a precarious living living from public-house to public-house exhibiting a few tricks for a handful of coppers. He had been seen to enter a house of call close by, not more than an hour before.

"So far, so good," Clench concluded, as the two left the hall together. "We are pretty certain to bag our man before the evening is over. Come along and make inquiries."

It was past eleven before they got on the track of the wandering player. They found him at last at the bar of a flaring gin-palace, which was packed with people, fresh from the music-halls. The atmosphere of the place was hot and sour and stuffy, and the room reeked with the smell of foul tobacco. A space was cleared at one of the marble tables, and a man stood there facing a more or less indifferent audience. At the sight of him Grenfell's face grew hard.

"That's Partridge," he said. "Doesn't look like a 'Varsity man and a blue,' does he? My word! he has changed since I saw him last!"

The man at the table was dressed in what had once been a fashionable grey frock-suit, but it was a dingy green now, and the coat and trousers were horribly frayed. His boots, full of holes, had been patent leather, and the brown rag over them might have passed for spats. He had a dilapidated, grey hat on the side of his head.

He carried his story in his face. There is nothing more pathetic and at the same time more repulsive than the broken-down 'swell,' who owes his fall to drink and dissipation; and a child could have given the history of Oliver Partridge. His face was red and coarse from the ravages of drink. The once easy manner had given place to a vulgar swagger.

"I'm Oscar Lee," he said insolently. "Familiar with the crowned heads of Europe. What am I doing in a place like this? Well, my noble sportsmen, I'm stony broke and want money. Throw me a shilling and I'll show you something the Palace or the Tivoli can't match. Only a bob: one dozen dirty coppers! Come along, lads; don't be mean."

The coppers began to accumulate amidst a fire of chaff and blasphemy. Slowly the pile accumulated until something like half-a-crown had been collected. Partridge called for a drink.

"No, you don't my lad," one of the crowd said truculently. "Not till the show's over. You had me that way last Saturday in the 'Green Man.' Earn your money first."

With a bitter smile and something that suggested shame on his face, Partridge proceeded to do a number of exceedingly clever tricks with cards. There was no mistake about his abilities as a conjurer. He proceeded with some of the elementary feats of thought-reading, and then, without any word of warning, went on to rap messages out of the table. He stood quite clear of the table, asking questions and receiving answers by means of knocks, the sounds of which were clear and distinct.

"Now, that's really clever," Clench whispered. "I've never seen this sort of thing done in the light before. If that chap only kept from the liquor he could earn a pile of money in the West End. I'd like to put one of the questions."

"Wait a minute," Hugh said grimly. "If you don't mind, I'd like to put the question. An idea has just occurred to me. The proper moment will come presently."

A man who looked as if he had spent most of his time abroad was asking questions. He appealed to a dead friend of his for instruction on certain matters, and the knocks in reply came thick and fast. The man's brown face turned slightly pale and his lips quivered. He called for and hastily swallowed a glass of brandy.

"Do you want to hear any more?" Partridge asked, defiantly.

"No, I don't," the stranger said thickly. "I've heard too much already. You're either a wizard or you're in league with the devil. I was going to expose your show, but you have convinced me that I've come up against some irresistible force. You've told me things to-night that were only known to me and the man who is dead. Here, take this you've earned it."

He tossed a sovereign on the table, finished his brandy, and vanished. Partridge picked up the gold coin and moved towards the bar.

"Didn't I tell you so?" he cried. "Didn't I say that I'd show you something that you had never seen before? Anybody else like to know anything of the dead, or the living, or both? Ask me, and the spirit under the table does the rest."

Hugh moved forward. He looked strangely out of place in his disguise.

"Yes, sir," he said quietly. "I'd like a speech with the dead. Will you be so good as to favor me with the departed spirit of Mr. Marcus Gainsforth?"

The smile faded from Partridge's face, and his jaw dropped as he reeled against the table. He stood swaying to and fro as Hugh flickered before him.

"Give me some brandy," he stammered. "I'm ill, I'm dying. Open a window, please, somebody. I want air, I can't breathe here."

CHAPTER XVII

A MORAL FORCE

The strolling player stood till his hat fell over his eyes and dropped to the floor. His jaunty impudence had gone as clean as if it had been wiped out with a sponge. Grenfell might have been some horrible shade from the nether world from the way that Partridge glared at him. The unexpectedness of it all paralysed him completely. The onlookers began to jeer, being ready, with wonted fickleness, to jostle the dejected cheat on the slightest provocation. This mild-eyed, middle-aged stranger had in some way got the better of Partridge, and that was sufficient.

One or two were shrewd enough to see that there was something beneath the surface. They sufficed to sober the rest. They were looking for something in the way of a dramatic development. But Grenfell gave no further sign. He would have been more than human had he not been pleased with the success of his shot, but in spite of the thrill of triumph he kept his head. He had to remember that he was not Hugh Grenfell, but the grave and learned Dr. Blaydes.

He wondered what Partridge would have said had he known the truth. It was as well for the present to keep his identity in the background. Moreover, he had made a most important discovery in the last few minutes. He had never suspected foul play in connection with the disappearance of Marcus Gainsforth; but now he changed his mind. If this had not been so, what was the cause of Partridge's dreadful agitation?

"I asked you a plain question," he said, "and I am waiting for the reply. You say you can call up spirits from the vasty deep, and I am waiting to see them come. Yours is a very clever performance, Mr. Lee, and is worth far more than the few coppers you have received for it. Now induce my late lamented friend, Marcus Gainsforth to come to the other end of the telephone, so to speak, and I'll give you a five-pound note. Ring up, please!"

The wretched Partridge stood in trembling silence. A beady moisture gathered on his face and rolled down his cheeks, but no reply came. Hugh felt sure of his disguise now, and began to see his way clear to the end.

"I understand," he went on. "The atmosphere is uncongenial. You shall have the chance of earning the money elsewhere. Come along with us!"

Partridge accompanied them obediently. He followed like a well-broken dog—not sullenly, but with a fawning desire to please. In the street Hugh paused.

"We want a room where we can be alone for an hour," he said. "If you only knew it, Mr. Lee, this is going to be a fortunate evening for you. If you play the game, a nice sum of money is coming your way without risk or hindrance to present employment, as the advertisements put it. If you try to deceive me, the consequences will be obvious. Now, where can we go?"

To all this Clench listened approvingly. Hugh Grenfell was carrying out the thing admirably. The introduction of Gainsforth's name was a stroke of genius. That one question had delivered Partridge gagged and bound into their hands.

"Come to my lodgings," Partridge said humbly. "They are quite respectable. A—a friend pays the rent of them, so that I may have a roof over my head. The house is not far off."

Hugh indicated that Partridge might lead the way. A little later they were seated in a comfortably-furnished sitting-room, and cigarettes were produced. Clench lay back in his chair watching the others critically. He meant to leave the matter in Grenfell's hands for the present, and prepared to enjoy himself.

"Will you gentlemen please tell me what you want?" Partridge suggested humbly.

"Let me revert to your very clever performance. A finer piece of trickery I never saw, and the way you gauged the intelligence of your audience was masterly. But I fancy the summoning of Mr. Marcus Gainsforth was beyond your power."

"I was not well," Partridge muttered. "The strain was too much for me."

"Let us call it shock instead," Hugh said drily. "You were astounded to hear the name of a man whom you knew mentioned in such company."

"Why should you assume that the name of—er—Gainsforth conveyed anything to me, sir?"

"Now, Mr. Lee, you are beginning to prevaricate. We both knew Gainsforth. I am going to show you presently that we both have an interest in tracing him. Is he alive or dead?"

"I don't know," Partridge said sulkily. "He disappeared."

"Is that really so? What a lot of disappearances there must be in London every year! One might almost write a book on the subject. First, Gainsforth vanishes, then another friend of his, called Oliver Partridge, also disappears. Do you know anything of him?"

Partridge passed his tongue over his dry lips.

"He'll never be seen again," he muttered. "Gone regularly to the bad."

"Most amazing! Gainsforth and Partridge vanish. Hugh Grenfell is put into gaol, on the suspicion of having murdered Partridge for a gold watch. Then Waterhouse also is imprisoned for forgery. Now, these four young men began life together, and I may say made fools of themselves together. Two are in prison and two have vanished. The only one I sympathise with is Grenfell. He was never anything more than a fool, and when he once started work he stuck to it. He was falsely convicted on suborned evidence. He never did Partridge any harm and he never stole the watch. Mr. Lee, you are going to find Partridge for us and help to prove Grenfell's innocence."

The wretched man wriggled about in his chair. How much did this old gentleman really know? He had an uneasy feeling that he was being made game of.

"I will do my best to help you."

"That's right," Grenfell smiled, approvingly. "Produce Partridge, and you shall have as much money in reason as you like. Get Partridge to tell the world how his watch came into the possession of Grenfell, and you—well—you will get off lightly. But if I have to find Partridge myself, I shall have no mercy on him. He will be arrested and charged—with others—for conspiracy, and he will be certain to do five years."

Partridge was not accustomed to subtlety of this kind. What did his tormentors know? Would he be justified in concealing any of the truth? He wished they would be a little more explicit.

"Is Mr. Hugh Grenfell a friend of yours?"

"You may take it for granted that he is," Hugh said drily. "He is a man in whom I take the greatest possible interest. For years I watched his career carefully. He was very badly used, Mr. Lee."

"The law did not think so."

"My dear sir, I am not in the least concerned with what the law thought. I know that Grenfell was convicted on what looked like clear evidence, and had I been on the jury I should probably have concurred in the verdict. Anybody who read the evidence at the trial would have come to the conclusion that Grenfell was a scoundrel and that he was very lucky to get off as easily as he did. All the same I have clear proof that he was not guilty, and he would have been honorably acquitted, had Partridge come forward."

"But—but Partridge was supposed to be dead."

"Precisely: supposed to be dead. He may have kept out of the way from interested motives. He may have been paid to stop his ears and say nothing to anybody. These are all possibilities. Now I want to find Partridge, and you must help me."

Partridge squirmed in his chair. How much longer were these strangers to remain and torture him? If he could only be alone he might evolve a plan of campaign.

"I am not well to-night," he gurgled. "You can see for yourselves that I am not myself. Perhaps you'll say I've had far more to drink than is good for me. Well, I'll not deny it. I was a gentleman once and in a good position, though you may not think it. I had plenty of money, and I daresay I should have had it still but for a woman I met—"

"The old story," Clench smiled drily. "A foreign lady, by any chance?"

Once more Partridge felt most uncomfortable. What did these fellows know? Why were they taking the whole thing so confoundedly easy? They were laughing at him. He would much prefer to see them stern and angry. He felt like a poor miserable mouse in the presence of two cats who happened to be in a sportive mood. He was hot and cold by turns, and his heart was pounding with suffocating force against his ribs.

"That's my business," he said sulkily. "She robbed me of all I had, anyhow."

"Don't be silly," Clench said. "Tell us about it, my dear sir. We are men of sympathetic nature, if you will only give us the credit for it. I have had some experience of the class of woman you speak of, and so has my friend. Who was that foreign lady that called herself Countess—Countess—what did she call herself, Dr. Blaydes?"

"D'Arblay," Hugh answered with a smile. "Ah! I see it is the same lady."

For Partridge gave a sudden start. The mouse was under the velvet paw of the cats again, but behind the velvet he could feel the steel points. He wished they would crush him and put him out of his misery.

"That's right," he quivered. "Hit a man when he is down."

He did not realise how near he was to getting more than he bargained for in that respect. There was a smile on Hugh's face, but his hands were clenched, and he longed to shake by the throat the man who was responsible for all his sufferings.

"We'll find Partridge," he said, "and you will help. I'll not be content till Partridge takes the place of Grenfell, and stands in the dock in his turn."

The cold moisture broke out on Partridge's face again. He would have given five years of his miserable life to learn what this man knew. And who was the other fellow sitting there tranquilly smiling behind his cigarette.

"I assure you, sir," he said presently, "I will do all I can for you."

"I had an idea that I might so far trespass on your amiability," Hugh answered gravely. "I will ask a further favor. What you need is change of air. You are run down, and must have a holiday. I invite you to come and stay with me in the country for a few days. Meet me at Paddington tomorrow at ten minutes to twelve, don't be late, for if you fail to turn up I shall be much annoyed. Subsequently you will also be annoyed—with yourself. My dear friend, give Mr. Lee five pounds to reclaim his wardrobe from the custody of an obliging and even too careful relative. I think that is all, to-night, Mr. Lee. Paddington Station to-morrow, or—well, we'll not discuss the alternative."

Partridge smiled anxiously as he showed his visitors out, and the two friends hastened in a cab to Clench's chambers. The matter of Partridge was not mentioned till supper had been discussed. Clench lighted a cigarette as he turned over his letters. He read one with a smile.

"There's a letter from Waterhouse. He sends me a key to open a box of his in a certain place, and tells me I shall find some startling evidence against Moler. His letter was posted by Mrs. Copping. I must find this box before I return to Dartdale. You'll have to put Partridge off, Hugh."

"Not a bit of it. I've frightened that fellow nearly to death. He hasn't the least idea who I am, and he can't for the life of him make out whether I have solved his identity or not. All he has to go upon is the fact that I am a friend of Grenfell's, working on his behalf. Under that impression he shall remain for the present. I mean to make use of him in another way. He will stay with me at Dartdale, and you shall see some fun presently. Remain till you have ransacked that box, and then come on to Dartdale."

"That's the idea!" Clench exclaimed. "Splendid! You should turn your attention to play-writing, Hugh. I think our friend will turn up tomorrow."

"I fancy he will," Hugh said gravely. "He will be afraid to stay away."

Grenfell was right. A subdued and chastened Lee awaited him on the platform. He was well and neatly dressed, without any of his over-night insolence and swagger. A question as to their destination elicited no reply from Grenfell. It was late in the afternoon when they dismounted at the farmhouse, where Hugh was staying, from a derelict old fly. After dinner, and a generous allowance of wine, Partridge grew more cheerful.

"Quite a bracing air," he said. "I feel all the better for it already. You have been very discreet, Dr. Blaydes, but I presume this is some part of Devonshire. What do you call the place?"

"Well, the village is Dartdale Magna," Hugh said dryly. "You will be interested to hear that that stone building yonder is the prison where Hugh Grenfell is serving his sentence. Do you see that nice old house in the trees?"

"I have noticed it," Partridge admitted. "Friends I suppose?"

"Well, yes, recent friends. The place belongs to Mr. Raymond Draycott. Quite an interesting man. You are sure to take a fancy to him when you meet."

"Great heavens!" Partridge groaned, as he wiped his face. "What the devil will happen next? How much does he know?"

But Hugh did not appear to know anything. He dropped the remark as if it had been purely casual. He did not even so much as glance at Partridge. He was content to feel that his words had gone home.

"You—you like Draycott?" Partridge contrived to stammer.

"He has his good points," Hugh said. "So have most of us, for that matter. I merely remarked that you will appreciate Draycott when you meet, which will be soon. You are my guest, and I will provide you with pocket-money. It will not be much, because I want you to keep sober for the present. There is no public-house within four miles of your rooms, and I will take the liberty of telling your landlady that you are a patient, and that if she sees any signs of liquor about she is to inform me at once. You are getting over a dangerous illness, and stimulants are deadly poison to you. I hope you understand."

At any other time Partridge would have resented the suggestion. But he was utterly and helplessly crushed, and his power of resistance was gone.

"It shall be as you like, my dear sir. Perhaps if there is no temptation in the way I shall be all right, and the air is sure to do me good."

Hugh turned and surveyed the speaker steadily. Partridge had done him a mortal injury, but they had been friends at one time. Perhaps, if Partridge had never come under the influence of the Countess, he might have been a very different man to-day.

"It is entirely in your hands," Hugh said sternly. "If you would be safe, do as I tell you. For as sure as death, if you play me false, you shall stand where Hugh Grenfell stood. I'll do my best to make a man of you yet—to give you another chance. But you must earn your reward, and have to go through danger and trouble yet. Pull yourself together and play the game as I—I have no doubt you used to play it in the old days when you knew Grenfell first. Now follow me."

Partridge groaned to himself. "What does he know? Is he aware that I was in these parts only a little time ago?"

CHAPTER XVIII

TURNING THE SCREW

Draycott came down to lunch the following afternoon, to Alice's secret annoyance. She would willingly have dispensed with his company till Clench's return. It was no time for the exchange of ordinary civilities, and she was glad to find him disinclined for talk. He was gaunt and hollow-eyed, and the trembling nervousness about him was not entirely due to his recent excesses. He sat down with a surely nod and made some show of eating. Alice noticed that he touched nothing but soda water.

"What has become of Bassett?" he asked irritably, "and Dr. Blaydes? Have they deserted me? Everybody seems to be fighting shy of me Where are they?"

"They had to go to London on business," Alice explained. "Dr. Blaydes is back, for I caught sight of him this morning. He gave me a message to say that he would walk in after dinner. I understand he has a friend staying near him."

Draycott grunted ungraciously. It was his mood to believe that everybody was avoiding him. His nerves were terribly worn and shaken, apart from the ravages of alcohol. He had an uneasy feeling that he was being gradually involved in the toils of a net. Moler was out of the way for the present; he was better, but still confined to his bed, and resolutely refused to see Draycott. The latter was doubtful whether to give way to relief or fear. He was anxious to ascertain what the German knew, and at the same time he dreaded an interview.

"Perhaps you would like to see Dr. Blaydes this afternoon?"

Draycott muttered something under his breath. Apparently he did not know what he wanted. Alice had never seen him in such a peevish and contrary mood. There was something about him that frightened her. He looked as if he might burst out at any moment.

"I shouldn't," he said ungraciously. "Why does Moler bring these men here? Who is Bassett? What is he? He never says anything about himself or his people. Depend upon it, the fellow is up to no good. What do you think of him?"

The question was flung at Alice with startling abruptness. Draycott's sombre eyes were full of malice and suspicion. Perhaps he wondered, whether Alice was so simple as she seemed to be.

"Really, I have not given him a thought," she said coldly. "I like what I have seen of Mr. Bassett. He is very interesting and quite a gentleman. So is Dr. Blaydes."

"Then you don't think Moler brought them here as spies?"

There was something almost childlike in the question, as if Draycott's brain had suffered. There was something almost pathetic in the way in which he hung on Alice's reply.

"Certainly not," she said. "They are gentlemen. They care for nothing but science. Whatever Dr. Moler's faults may be he is a brilliant scientist. I expect he is glad of congenial company."

The moody frown on Draycott's face lifted a little, and he played with the food on his plate, his gaze appearing to go over Alice's head.

"I thought they were spies," he said. "You have seen more of them than I have. Perhaps they have money and Moler is blackmailing them. He blackmails everybody, for everybody has a secret, if you can only find it out. Moler is a genius in that way. He gets to the bottom of everything in time, and then he is like a leech for money. He's getting money out of Bassett and Blaydes. He has actually found out something about old Cobham."

"What Cobham do you mean?"

"Why, old Cobham of the Holland Farm," Draycott said. "How stupid you are to-day! Old Cobham the miser, who is always complaining that he can't pay his rent and is known to be worth thousands of pounds. His people before him were just the same. It must be five-and-twenty years since the old chap fell out of his cart coming home from market and was picked up by the gipsies. I recollect my father—"

Draycott's voice trailed away to a whisper. He had forgotten the presence of Alice altogether. Without the slightest doubt, he was wandering in his mind. The drink and the drugs had sapped his intellect. His eyes were blank and his lips worked about constantly. He was talking of things what had happened quite a quarter of a century ago. It was not the first time he had spoken thus, but never before had he been so definite.

It was amazing. Draycott, the comparative stranger, was familiar with incidents of the distant past! They were not incidents that a man might glean from idle gossip. Alice wondered whether she should go a step farther.

It was dangerous, but she decided to risk it.

"I thought that was Squire Langster?"

"Well, you are wrong," Draycott went on. "It was old Cobham. He had ten pounds in gold on him, and a five pound note. The gipsies saw that he was drunk, and took care of his money. It was in changing the note at a public-house in Exeter they got caught. When he got the note back, Cobham broke down in court and cried like a child. Everybody knew it."

Alice listened with vague alarm. There was something uncanny about these reminiscences from the lips of a man who had so often posed as a stranger to the locality. The usually reticent Draycott seemed to know more about Dartdale than he did of the Argentine. The latter country he never mentioned at all. More than once Alice had introduced the subject only to be rebuffed.

"There was another brother who went abroad," she suggested "To Buenos Ayres the capital of the Argentine, Mr. Draycott?"

"Upon my word, I don't know," Draycott said carelessly. "Here, you're trapping me! What do you mean by asking me a question like that? If you try that again—"

Alice glanced up with haughty surprise in her eyes. Startled as she was, she concealed her feelings admirably.

"I am at a loss to understand what you mean!" she said. "I was asking for information from one who knows South America well. Really, your manner is very strange, Mr. Draycott."

In a hazy kind of way Draycott realised he had said or done something foolish, and stammered what was meant for an apology.

"You'll pardon me, my dear, but I am not well," he said, almost humbly. "My memory is not what is used to be. I'm afraid the medicine I take for my neuralgia does my brain no good. And I have to see a man before long on important business. Moler could help me, but, I don't trust Moler. I don't know why Hillditch and Co. should bother me as they do. Anyone would think I was a thief, from the way they address me."

"Who are Hillditch and Co.?"

Draycott suddenly flamed into violent anger. The sombre, hesitating mood vanished, giving place to a frenzy of passion. He smote his fist on the table, setting the glasses jingling, and his eyes gleamed wildly. He raised a shaky hand above his head.

"If you don't know, I'll tell you," he said. "They're a set of sneaking, prying lawyers, a gang of low scamps, whose business it is to suspect everybody they come in contact with. They have tools everywhere prying into other people's business. But I'll let them know what it is to meddle with—with— Now, what the deuce is my name? Oh, Draycott, Raymond Draycott. Funny that I should have forgotten my name for the moment. Do you ever forget your name?"

"I don't remember an instance of the kind," Alice said gently.

"No? Well, perhaps not. It's a curious failing with the cleverest people, professors, and that class. If Hillditch and Co. think—Look here, I haven't a friend in the world. I cannot go to a single individual and confide in him I've got plenty of money, at least I had plenty of money before Moler came, but that does not help me. Why can't people let matters alone? I proved my title to the property."

His wild rage was dropping with every word, as the wind drops when the rain begins to fall. It was a pitiful spectacle to watch him, and Alice could not altogether withhold her sympathy. The man was so utterly and entirely alone.

"I think Mr. Bassett and Dr. Blaydes," she suggested, "might probably—"

Draycott turned upon her with a snarl.

"I'll not have either of them," he snapped. "They are spies. If you have finished your meal, I'll go. I've got plenty to do this afternoon. It will require all my cleverness and attention, but I'll get the better of them yet."

Draycott spoke the bare and bitter truth. Never had he needed a clearer head and a cooler brain. He cursed his weakness which had led him into his present position. He rose from the table and went to the library. It was almost impossible to concentrate his attention on any one point, and he must have recourse to the drug that was the cause of all his mischief. It would be for the last time, he told himself. He swallowed two of the shiny grey tablets, with a weary smile at his own weakness. He ceased to pace restlessly up and down the floor, the clearness came back to his eye and the strength to his limbs. Raymond Draycott was himself again.

He unlocked his safe and took from it a letter received that morning. The full significance of it had not appealed to him before. It was plain enough now.

"Dear Sir,

"The representatives of the late Mr. Marcus Gainsforth have placed the affairs of that gentleman in our hands. A dispute has arisen between our clients and the Grand National Insurance Company in regard to a policy of assurance, and we understand that you can give us certain information, the want of which seriously hampers us in pressing the claim.

"We believe that you are in a position to supply actual proofs concerning the death of Mr. Gainsforth, and certain letters of yours which have come into our possession point to the fact.

"Our Mr. Hillditch will do himself the pleasure of calling upon you this day week at four o'clock, when the favor of an interview will be esteemed. In the interest of all parties, we will press you for a prompt reply.

"Yours faithfully,

"Hillditch and Co."

Draycott shook, despite the drug he had swallowed, and wore the look of a man who is in the grip of deadly fear.

"A threat!" he muttered. "Very crude and evasive, but a threat all the same. If I refuse to see this lawyer I am to take the consequences. I wonder whom I have to thank for this? What letters have these people got hold of?"

Clench, had he been present, might have replied to the question. He might also have had something to say in regard to the mysterious key to a mysterious box received by him from Waterhouse. But, meanwhile, it was all coming back to Draycott. There had been letters; but he had every reason to believe they had been destroyed; indeed, he was under the impression he had destroyed them himself. If they had fallen into the hands of Hillditch and Co., then very awkward questions might be asked. The threat could be detected between the lines of the courteous letter from these solicitors. Draycott's brain was clear enough to see that.

He shivered with apprehension, for he could see no way out of the coming trouble. He would need all his nerve and resource and cunning. Well, he would have to fall back on the morphia. That always made a man of him for the time. He blessed it in a way, but at the same time he cursed Moler under his breath for introducing him to that fascinating anodyne. Moler himself was another trouble he had forgotten for the moment. The German knew too much, and when the time came Moler would play entirely for his own hand. Moler must be removed—

Draycott was still considering the vexed question at dinner-time. Under the influence of the drug he made something of a meal. When he returned to the library, Hugh, in the person of 'Dr. Blaydes,' was announced.

Draycott greeted him with effusion. He was tired of his own company, and eager for companionship. He slipped one of the grey pellets into his mouth, conscious he would need it before the evening was over. Hugh was perfectly at home. Things were going very well and the clearing of his name was only a matter of time. That his disguise was impenetrable he did not doubt. He had undergone torture and humiliation at the hands of this man, and the hour for retaliation had come; but there was no suggestion of this in the bland smile on his face.

"I am exceedingly glad to see you," Draycott began. "Take a seat and a cigarette. It will do me good to have a chat with you."

"I came on purpose," Hugh smiled. "You seem to have had a lot of trouble lately. By the way, how is Moler getting on?"

"Much, better, I am glad to say," Draycott responded. "Not much harm done."

"Well, that's a good thing, anyway. No arrests made in connection with the affair?"

Draycott shook his head. This was not precisely the line he had intended the conversation to take.

"Most mysterious!" Hugh went on. "Strange that so distinguished a man should have an enemy in these parts. Have you formed any theory about the case? Do you suspect anybody?"

Again Draycott shook his head. Hugh had grown suddenly grave and thoughtful.

"Crime always fascinates me," he said. "Did it ever strike you how utterly unnecessary certain crimes are? This looks to me like one of them; a deed committed on the sudden impulse of the moment. It might have been by you or me."

"Aren't you talking nonsense, Doctor?" Draycott asked roughly.

"Not at all, my dear sir, not at all. I tell you I have devoted a considerable amount of time and thought to the fascinating subject. Look at that Baldon case the other day. He is a man in good health, a good sportsman, who had led a clean life. He has a lovely old place, a heap of money, and a beautiful wife to whom he is passionately attached and who is fond of him. They sit down to dinner, talking and laughing gaily, and suddenly he gets up and tries to kill his wife with a knife. But for the intervention of the butler he would have succeeded. He has no excuse to offer—he simply acted on the ungovernable impulse of the moment. Obviously that was the truth. It is possible the same thing happened in the case of Dr. Moler. It is just possible that you did it!"

"That's a lie," Draycott said hoarsely. "Change the conversation, please."

"One moment," Hugh went on. He appeared to be full of enthusiasm for his subject. "I don't say that you did it any more than I accuse myself. I say it might have been done by either of us. You might have gone to bed that night with the full intention of getting a good night's rest. In fact, you did retire quite early. But suppose you rose and dressed again, putting on a tweed suit and shooting boots. Without the slightest idea of what you were doing, you meet Moler. You attack him from behind and leave him for dead. You return home and go to bed, forgetting the tweed suit and the muddy boots. You may laugh at the theory, of course, but this thing has happened before and it will happen again. It is only when servants notice these things and begin to gossip that the truth comes out."

Draycott listened with angry fascination. His impulse was to strike in rudely and demand that Blaydes should talk sense, but some feeling restrained him. How much did Blaydes know? Was not this more than coincidence? Yet it would be a mistake to treat the matter too seriously.

"Why not say that I tried to kill Moler?" he asked. "Call me a murderer!"

"My dear sir, few of us are not murderers at heart occasionally. Of course, you will understand I am fully building up a theory. But theories of this kind have hanged a man before now, and at any rate ensured his proper conduct for the rest of his life. I don't insist that I am correct, but that is my theory so far as Moler is concerned. Perhaps you imagine I can't prove it."

"In the name of common sense, how?"

"By occult means," Hugh said grimly. "By getting behind the veil. I have found the force I need in a most extraordinary man I met in London the night before last. With my knowledge of the subject and his amazing powers, I believe it possible to discover everything. I brought the man from London, and he is with me. With your permission, I propose to bring him here to-morrow. You may say that it is trickery, but I know better. Depend upon it, he will show the whole secret of the attack on Dr. Moler."

Draycott smiled. He was a little easier in his mind. Obviously Blaydes had been talking at random; he was only a harmless crank, after all. Thousands of clever men had been bitten by some craze.

"As you like," he said, with careless good humor. "Like most people, I am fond of clever conjuring tricks. What is the name of your medium?"

Hugh reached for a fresh cigarette. He watched Draycott through half-closed eyes.

"The man's name is Lee," he said. "Oscar Lee. May I bring him along?"

There was no reply for a moment; then Draycott forced himself to speak.

"If you please. I—I shall be glad to see him."

CHAPTER XIX

IN THE GARDEN

Draycott braced himself for an effort. The comforting stimulus of the drug was still soothing and potent, so that the shock was not what it might have been. He was conscious that danger threatened him, but he was not afraid; he could have heard his death sentence with something like equanimity.

The man was an enemy. Blaydes was declaring war upon him. The ultimatum lost no force because it was delivered in a charming voice and with a pleasant smile. Who was this amiable old gentleman? He had come as the friend of Bassett, himself a harmless person upon whose money Moler had designs. Hitherto Draycott had regarded Blaydes with a certain good-natured contempt. His remarks about spirit-rapping had apparently been on a par with his intelligence. But he could not so readily explain away those hints as to the way in which Moler might have been attacked, nor the astonishing allusion to Oscar Lee.

Possibly it was nothing more than a coincidence. Blaydes might not know Lee had another name. Draycott studied the face of his companion keenly. There was nothing in that benign countenance to give him comfort. It would be useless to ignore the thrust. He must carry the war into the enemy's country.

"Mr. Blaydes," he said, "tell me why you are here. What do you want? Do you know that Lee has another name?"

"Perfectly," Hugh said coolly. "His proper name is Oliver Partridge. He is the man whom Hugh Grenfell was supposed to have murdered, or at least put out of the way and robbed. You will recollect that after Partridge had mysteriously vanished, his watch was found in Grenfell's possession. Grenfell is now in gaol for the transaction."

"Very extraordinary," Draycott said, with fine unconcern.

"Is it not? Now, as Partridge is alive, Grenfell must be innocent. He was also innocent of stealing that watch, as Partridge could have proved had he come forward. You would naturally ask why he did not come forward. He would not have suffered by doing so, therefore the obvious inference is that he benefited by keeping out of the way."

"Very interesting," Draycott murmured. "But why should he keep out of the way?"

"Because he was paid to. He was paid to keep out of the way by Martin Faber, who had very urgent reasons for wishing Grenfell to stop in gaol. You see, as the former secretary to a certain insurance company, Grenfell could have asked some awkward questions about the policy that Faber took out in his office. If that had been done, you would not be here at the present moment, Mr. Draycott, for the simple reason that Faber would have had nothing to leave you. Partridge had more than an idea of this, and that is why he was not allowed to show up. He was to remain lost to the world and to draw money from Faber—and others."

"You are not alluding to me, I hope?"

"I am speaking generally," Hugh went on. "But this is true, and when the time comes I shall produce documentary evidence to prove it. Letters—and cheques."

Draycott started at the last word. He restrained an eager question. He was wondering whether Partridge had betrayed him. He would have to find that out.

"Does Lee, or Partridge, know that you are aware of his proper name?"

"He doesn't. He only knows that I have a hold upon him and will stand no nonsense. I am only concerned with one thing, and that is to clear the name of Hugh Grenfell, and I invite you to help me in the work. Turn it over in your mind, try to think how you can be of assistance. It will pay you in the long run."

Hugh changed the subject and refused to say more.

He had attained a certain object, and for the present he was content.. It was all very well for Draycott to take a cheery view of the matter now, but when the effects of the drug had worn out the outlook would not be quite so agreeable. Hugh left Draycott ruminating over a cigarette. It was still early, as he turned toward his lodgings, and the evening was pleasant. As Hugh passed through the shrubbery at the back of the house Alice, followed him.

"I wanted to see you," she whispered, "I am anxious to know how things are progressing, Hugh. We shall not be seen here."

The spot was quiet, and there was no fear of Draycott's leaving the house. Hugh slipped his arm round the girl's waist and kissed her.

"These stolen moments are very sweet, darling," he said. "You need not be afraid; there is nobody about."

Alice returned the caresses tenderly. With Hugh by her side she had no fear of anything. His mere presence seemed to inspire her with another and less troubled view.

"I am not alarmed, Hugh," she said. "Only we have to be so very careful. Consider what a terrible scandal it would be in Dartdale if one of the servants were to catch Miss Kearns in the arms of an elderly gentleman to whom she was supposed to be almost a stranger! My dear boy, you have lived in the country long enough to know that the effect would be electrical."

Hugh smiled at the suggestion. He could imagine how the floodgates of gossip would be raised. Nevertheless, he held the girl close to him and looked down into her eyes.

"Is there anything you have to tell me, dear?"

"Well, there is a good deal, I think," Alice said. "I was anxious to learn what happened this evening, or I should not have waylaid you, Hugh. But perhaps you had better hear my news first. Hugh, do you think that Raymond Draycott murdered Martin Faber?"

Hugh started at the suddenness of the question.

"Is this some new theory of yours?" he asked. "Have you discovered anything?"

"My dear boy, I am as utterly in the dark as I was when you came back. The more I think the mystery over, the more puzzled and confused I get. I start to work out one theory and I find that it leads me to some absurdly exasperating conclusion. Still, that is my fixed idea. I should not mention it; I ought to have whispered it in your ear instead of speaking out loud. But I should not be surprised to find that I have hit upon the truth."

"I don't think so," Hugh said. "I fancy that when we do get to the truth we shall find it far more startling even than you imagine. Mind, I believe that there has been murder, but we have a long way to go before we can prove that. But why do you say that?"

"Because I have been making discoveries, Hugh. At luncheon Mr. Draycott and myself were alone—I have never seen him so queer in his manner before—one moment beside himself with passion, the next almost weeping because he has no friends. He is horribly frightened of a firm called Hillditch and Co. But that is by the way. He was talking of a matter that happened a quarter of a century ago and was familiar with all its details. He spoke as if he had been present. And he actually didn't know that Buenos Ayres was the capital of Argentine. He said I had laid a trap for him; and indeed I had. He nearly struck me. It was very significant, that remark of his about a trap. Why should he suspect me of laying a trap for him? Hugh, I don't believe he ever saw the Argentine."

Hugh listened gravely; there was a good deal in what Alice said.

"But that does not prove murder."

"Oh, I admit that," Alice replied. "He might have induced Faber to make a will under false pretences. He might have lured him on to the line and stunned him. He might have placed the body where the train would cut it to pieces. He might have come secretly to England to do all that. Then after the deed was done he had only to go to Paris and wait for them to find him out, so that he could come and take possession of the property. I daresay it sounds very improbable, Hugh, but—"

Hugh stooped and kissed the quivering, red lips tenderly. He would not waste these precious moments talking of Raymond Draycott.

"Let us make the most of our time, darling," he whispered. "Never mind Draycott. How good it is to be with you again, to know that my name will be cleared, and to be conscious that everything is coming right! It can only be a matter of a few days at the outside. The rascals will never know how they were brought to book. 'Blaydes' will disappear, and Hugh Grenfell will emerge from prison a free and innocent man."

Alice smiled at her lover's face. She was growing accustomed to his disguise.

"It is funny to be made love to by an elderly gentleman," she said, "but very pleasant. Still, I shall be glad to see my own Hugh again, stripped of his disguise. I am sure that you have some good news for me, dear."

"Couldn't be better," Hugh said cheerfully. "That trip to London was the most successful day's work I ever did in my life."

"Hugh!" Alice cried. "Do you mean to say that you have found Partridge?"

"You've guessed it. We found Oliver Partridge, beyond the shadow of a doubt, and, what is more, he knows all about Marcus Gainsforth. I haven't tackled him about that yet, because the time is not ripe. But we shall oblige him to speak in a day or two."

"But are you sure he will not disappear again?"

"Absolutely; you can make your mind easy on that score. Partridge, at the present moment, is under the same roof as myself. He isn't aware that I know his real name; in fact he is puzzled as to who I am and what I am driving at. On the other hand, I've told Draycott I am a friend of Grenfell's and have found

Partridge. I also dropped a few other hints that will give him a sleepless night. My game is to scare him, to make him fear some terrible danger hangs over him. When his nerves are all shattered—"

"I think I understand. You want to frighten him into some confession."

"That's the idea, Alice. It doesn't really matter, as we shall expose him in any case. Partridge will try to see Draycott and come to some understanding."

"But what connection is there between these two, dear?"

"That I am not in a position to prove. But there is some connection, because Draycott has been supplying Partridge with money all this time. I can prove that, because I have one of the cheques in my possession. These two rascals will try to meet, and I shall be present when they do. It was for this purpose that I compelled Partridge to come with me. If—ah! what did I tell you?"

Hugh dropped his voice to a whisper. He drew Alice aside into the shadow, as the sound of a footstep was heard in the shrubbery. A moment later Partridge came furtively along. He was evidently trying to find his way to the house. Hugh smiled grimly as he passed.

"This is what I expected," he said. "You must go indoors at once, Alice, and leave me to follow that man. There are strong reasons why these two must not meet until I am ready for them. Probably Draycott has gone to bed by this time."

Alice slipped into the house through the drawing-room window, which she had purposely left open. Partridge stood in the shadow of the porch talking to the butler. In the stillness of the night Hugh heard every word that passed.

"I'm very sorry, sir," the butler explained. "My master has gone up to his room, and I dare not disturb him at this hour. It would be more than my place is worth."

Partridge argued in vain. He had to fall back upon the conventional method.

"Tell him Mr. Lee called," he said. "I will come again to-morrow afternoon about four. I shall come by way of the wood, and perhaps, Mr. Draycott would meet me there. I am an invalid, and find the hill to the house a little trying."

The butler repeated the message respectfully and closed the door. As Partridge made him way back through the shrubbery, Hugh joined him.

"I thought I asked you to remain indoors," he said. "I warned you of the danger of the fog and mist. I presume the opportunity of seeing Mr. Draycott again was too great a temptation."

"Mr. Draycott is nothing to me."

"Whom are you talking about?" Hugh smiled. "You will say next you have never heard the name of Draycott. Never seen it on a cheque, perhaps? Well, if you like to go your own way, you must. But you will be bitterly sorry for it afterwards. I've been talking to Draycott about you."

Partridge's jaw dropped. The evening had grown unpleasantly warm.

"Who are you?" he asked hoarsely. "What do you want? Why have you dragged me down here? I won't put up with it, and so I tell you. I'll go back to London to-morrow."

"As you please," Hugh said. "It's a free country and people can do as they like. At least, they can do as they like if the police do not interfere. Perhaps it may be better to tell me quietly how Marcus Gainsforth came by his death than to have the story dragged out of you in a police-court. Then there is the story of the conspiracy between you and Martin Faber, whereby Hugh Grenfell was clapped into prison. That would be an ugly thing to come out in examination before a magistrate."

Partridge found it difficult to breathe in comfort. He was terribly afraid of this benign old gentleman who seemed to know so much.

"I'll—I'll do what I can," he stammered. "I don't want to cause trouble. But I swear I know nothing of the matters you speak of."

Hugh smiled as he led the way into the sitting-room.

"Yes, you do," he said, "and, what is more, you could tell me the whole story of the death of Martin Faber."

Partridge shook his head obstinately. He did not disguise from himself that he was in a desperate place, but he would not put his head in the noose for all that. He had had time to study his position and think matters over. His head was clearer than it had been for weeks, and the power of thought and concentration was coming back to him.

He assumed an air of virtuous indignation. Why should he be treated in this unfriendly fashion?

"I've had nearly enough of it," he exclaimed. "You order me about as if I were a dog. Who are you, anyhow?"

Hugh waved him towards a chair.

"Sit down," he said. "You ask who I am. Well, you will know before long. It will be the surprise of your life when you find out."

"Then I'll take my surprise now."

"Oh, no, you won't, my friend," Hugh said grimly. "You'll wait till you get it. I have not suffered in silence all this time to have my plans ruined at the last moment for the sake of a rascal like you. Had I behaved like an ordinary man, you would be cooling your heels in gaol at this moment. If I raise my little finger, I can get you ten years in prison. Oh! you may smile, but suppose I call Hugh Grenfell as a witness against you."

Partridge changed color, and his truculence departed as suddenly as it had come.

"I can't think who the deuce you are."

"Well, that's satisfactory," Hugh went on. "Now let us go farther afield, if you don't mind. You know the story of the death of Martin Faber. If you cared to, you could tell the world how he died. I know what you are smiling at. I am speaking in a figurative sense, now. You think that, if you play your cards right you will pacify me and keep in the good books of Draycott at the same time. But don't forget the Scriptural warning that no man can serve two masters. If you offend me, who will befriend you after Draycott is hanged?"

Partridge sat in his chair white and silent. His bluster and aggressiveness had vanished. His gaze followed Hugh mechanically as the latter rose and put a tantalus and soda-water on the table. He pulled out one of the stoppers, and the odor of whisky permeated the room.

"I don't wish to be accused of lack of hospitality," Hugh said cheerfully. "There are cigars in the box, and I can recommend these cigarettes. Help yourself to whisky."

Partridge's hand shot out eagerly, his fingers clutching the neck of a decanter. It seemed years since he had touched anything, the smell of the whisky caused his mouth to water, and there was a queer kind of catch in his throat. He saw Hugh regarding him with a smile on his face. He pushed the decanter back, and jammed in the stopper.

"I'll not touch a drop," he said hurriedly. "You're a devil to tempt me. You know my one great weakness, and you are going to play on it. That's why you brought me here. But I'll not fall into the trap, and so I tell you. Now go on."

He folded his arms resolutely and glared at Hugh defiantly. Really, there was more manhood in the creature than Hugh had expected. He rose and put the spirits away.

"I want none," he said, "and I'll not tempt you further. You have possibilities that I had not reckoned upon. So much the better for you, my friend. In time I may be able to trust you. Now let us have a quiet smoke and a friendly discussion. Of whom shall we talk? Shall it be of Raymond Draycott or Martin Faber? It's your lead."

CHAPTER XX

WHOSE HAND

Clench returned from London satisfied with his progress, and he had an interesting story to tell Grenfell.

"I found those letters of Gainsforth's," he said. "You remember Waterhouse sent me the key to a certain box. I managed to trace the box and get hold of the batch of letters. Most of them were from Faber."

"They throw no light on Faber's death, I suppose?"

"Of course, not precisely on that, but certainly, on the causes that led up to it. Faber passed for a simple country gentleman, and that kind of thing; but, in fact, seems to have been a sorry scamp. Apart from his drinking habits he had other vices. He was up to his eyes in debt, and there were one or two transactions that smacked rather strongly of fraud. There was fraud, as we shall find when we get to the bottom of things. Situated as he was, it is a mystery how he procured the money to pay his insurance premium, and why he insured his life for such an enormous sum, when he was pressed even for a few pounds."

"Haven't we both a pretty good idea?"

"I know we are both working from the same basis," Clench went on. "But the trouble is to prove our suspicions, Two men know all about it, and so did Gainsforth. Moler knows and Partridge knows, or Draycott would never have supplied him with money. We must make one of these men speak. The question is, how."

"I fancy I have solved that problem," Hugh said. "We'll make both Draycott and Partridge speak. Partridge was almost frightened out of his wits when he realised I had him close to Draycott's house, and Draycott himself was only a little less agitated when I said 'Oscar Lee' was here. I dropped mysterious hints to Draycott about my friend Hugh Grenfell, and the bait was swallowed. Draycott is thoroughly disturbed, and obviously anxious to know whether Partridge has betrayed him. He will make it his business to see Partridge. On the other hand, Partridge is anxious to see Draycott; indeed, he took advantage of my absence to try it on last night. Those two must meet, but we must contrive to be present, or, rather, in a position to hear what is going on. There is no time to lose, for we cannot keep Collier in gaol much longer. I should not like Copping to suffer after he has done so much for me."

"How do you propose to manage it?"

"My dear fellow, I don't propose to do anything. This affair will manage itself. Draycott will contrive to communicate with Partridge or vice versa."

Hugh's forecast was correct, for on the following morning a small boy connected with the farm set out for Rawmouth with a note in his hand. It was easy to gain possession of the letter and open it. Sure enough, it was a line from Partridge to Draycott, asking for an interview in secret without delay.

"What do you take me for?" the letter ran. "Anybody would think that I didn't know you. I'm coming to your house this afternoon at five o'clock, and don't you forget it. I'm coming to the front door, and I'm going to ask for you. That library of yours looks like a snug place, and it is very open and sunny. I think I'll see you in the library."

Draycott appeared to agree, for the reply was verbal. A little after four Partridge set out for a walk to see something of the country.

"All this is rather fortunate for us," Hugh remarked to Clench. "One of us will be able to be present at the interview, and hear every word that is said. On the whole, I had better undertake this work, since I know the house so well. I'll get Alice to help me."

"What do you intend to do?" Clench asked.

"Well, I'll hide in one of the big cupboards in the library. Alice will lock me in and put the key in her pocket. They are big oak cupboards, almost empty. It's worth the risk."

Clench was of the same opinion. It was an opportunity of solving the whole problem at one blow.

There was no difficulty in making ready. Alice listened eagerly to what Hugh had to say.

"I can manage that easily," was her comment. "Mr. Draycott never uses the cupboards, and I don't suppose he knows whether they are kept locked or not. He is in his bedroom now, and has given orders that he is not to be disturbed till five o'clock. After that, if anybody calls, he will be pleased to see him."

"That brings Partridge on the scene," Hugh said to her.

"I expect so—I don't know what instructions the butler has had. You can sit here and talk to me till we see Partridge coming up the drive. It must be something very important, or he would not run those risks. Now tell me, has Mr. Clench found anything fresh?"

Hugh was explaining in some detail the state of affairs, when Alice, standing by the window, faced round upon him excitedly. She pointed down the drive.

"There's your man. I'll go and make sure there is nobody in the hall before I show you into the library."

Five minutes later Hugh was in the dark, with the key turned upon him. The great cupboard was old and worn and the panels had shrunk from the beading. He found he could command a glimpse of what was going on in the room. Partridge was moving uneasily about. He took up a Japanese paper knife in the form of a dagger and hid it under a pile of papers.

The action was eloquent of his feelings and of his fear of Draycott. Hugh saw Partridge start and change color as Draycott lounged into the room. The man was afraid of his host, and it was more than probable he had good cause to be.

Draycott pointed to a chair with a contemptuous wave of his hand.

"Sit down and cut it short. What do you want? What are you doing here? It was part of our contract that you were never to try to see me. I was to send you money from time to time, and you were to stay in London. What does this mean?"

"I didn't come of my own free will," Partridge protested. "Nor am I here altogether on my own behalf, as you will see before I have finished."

"Why do you come at all?" Draycott insisted.

"Because I was compelled to, confound it," Partridge burst out irritably "That interfering old fool Blaydes made me. He's found out that I know a great deal about Gainsforth. God only knows how much he really has discovered. He forced me to come down to this district, though I had not the least idea he was luring me so close to your house. He looks like an amiable old fool, but it's my belief he is nothing of the kind. He wants to know about Gainsforth, and the true story of the plot to ruin Grenfell. And he'll find it out: he'll find out everything if you and I don't pull together. That's why I wanted to see you to-day."

"Oh, that's why you wanted to see me to-day, is it?" said Draycott, repeating Partridge's words as if he were learning a lesson. "Really, now and what have I to do? You've only to put it into words, and I'll do anything you require. I always do, you know."

Draycott showed his teeth in a savage grin. He was in a reckless and dangerous mood. Partridge regarded his companion uneasily.

"Now, don't be sarcastic," he said. "What's the good of sneering at me? I can't help it. You must see for yourself that I've every reason to keep clear of Blaydes. I wish he was at the bottom of the sea. But if you take him for nothing but a doddering old fool of a scientist, then you are mistaken. He and his friend Bassett fairly ran me to earth and gave me a a fearful time. They regularly frightened the life out of me! Mark my words, they know a lot more than they pretend. Oh! they looked like a pair of benevolent old donkeys as they sat at the other side of the table, but the questions they asked and the way they put them would do credit to an Old Bailey lawyer. Now, who are they?"

Draycott broke out into one of his violent moods.

"The Devil knows and the Devil cares," he cried. "It's Moler. Moler is at the bottom of the whole thing. These chaps are his spies. He brought them into the house. They dropped in here by accident, but it wasn't any accident, and have been spying on me over since. They look like benevolent old men, but they are nothing of the kind. They're detectives in disguise."

"Oh! come off it," Partridge said irritably. "What's the good of talking that nonsense? As if Moler would be such a fool! It's his game to keep the house quiet, to have you to himself, so that he can get your money."

"Yes, and he has done well," Draycott said bitterly. "When I came here I owned the property and had nearly a hundred thousand pounds in money. It's only a comparative short time ago, and what have I left? I could not put my hand on twenty thousand. Moler has had the rest."

"His greed was always boundless," Partridge said.

Draycott flashed round upon him angrily.

"Yes, and what about yourself?" he demanded. "Do you ever leave me alone? Don't you apply for your cheque regularly every month? I wish I had got rid of you both when I had the chance. I could have done it easily two years ago. If you two had been out of the way there would never have been any of this fuss and bother, and I could have laughed at Grenfell till he came out of gaol. As it is, I've never had a moment's peace from either of you."

"What's the good of going over all that ground again?" Partridge asked. "Moler is not your enemy, and has no more to do with your difficulties than I have. What we three must do is to stick together in the face of the coming danger. Our interests are yours—"

"Yes, and my money seems to belong to the three of us," Draycott sneered.

"Why not?" Partridge said coolly. He was beginning to feel at home. "The money is as much mine as yours. You wouldn't have got it without me, and you wouldn't have kept it without Moler."

"I took a risk to get it—a fearful risk."

"You did, and you'll have to take another fearful risk to keep it, my friend. The main question now is, what we shall do with Bassett and Blaydes?"

Draycott protested no further. He may have expected the talk to take this turn, but Hugh fancied that Partridge's information had a disturbing influence on him. With moody and anxious face, he paced up and down the room, almost oblivious of Partridge's presence.

"What do you know of Blaydes?"

"About as much as you do," Partridge replied. "If you ask me, he is one of those confounded private detectives, and Bassett is another."

"Bassett came as the friend of Dr. Moler."

"What if he did? Moler's a precious scamp, and clever at that, but he doesn't know everything. These two men hunted me out and tried to frighten the life out of me. They are on the right track, and the sooner you grasp that the better. I'm taking a risk in coming here to-day, but I've to study myself as well as you. If they find out about Gainsforth—"

"But they can't," Draycott exclaimed. "Nobody could. The scheme was too intricate for any detective. There's not a soul in this place, where Faber lived all his life, that dreams of the truth."

"Moler knows about it, anyhow."

"Moler knows when he is well off. He'd never kill the goose that lays the golden eggs, Partridge. My advice to you is not to go too far nor ask for too much money."

"I wouldn't touch a penny of it if I could help it," Partridge said. "If I could only keep off the cursed drink I'd never take a sou from you. But it's idle talking like this. What are you going to do? I may not get a chance to come here again—"

"Well, why not meet me in the wood behind the house?" Draycott asked.

Partridge shuddered. Something was appealing to his imagination.

"Not me," he said viciously. "I don't want to be served as you served Marcus Gainsforth."

CHAPTER XXI

"OUR MR. HILLDITCH."

This news was worth running some risk for. Grenfell hugged himself as he stood listening in the cupboard. If Partridge meant anything, he was accusing Draycott of the murder of Gainsforth. This was an illuminating flash, but for a moment the light was too dazzling for Grenfell's mental vision. Why should Draycott have murdered Gainsforth, and what could he gain by the crime? How could he have done it when, by all accounts, he was in South America?

Hugh waited breathlessly for an indignant denial. He expected a violent outburst from Draycott. But nothing of the kind followed.

"Be quiet, you fool," Draycott muttered. "You mustn't say these things. Walls have ears."

"We need not worry about that," Partridge replied. "The walls of this house are thick and nobody suspects anything."

"You have forgotten Dr. Blaydes, and probably Bassett."

"Blaydes ought to be a few miles away. Better look under the table and see whether he is there. But what's the good of talking like this? I know you, my friend, and I'm not taking any risk. When I meet you I shall meet you openly. I'm not going to have my head bashed in when I'm off my guard. I came to-day to be of service to you—"

"Not forgetting yourself."

"Why not? In the ordinary course of events I should not mind hearing that you were dangling at the end of a rope, as perhaps you will before the finish. There are times when I am bound to have money, or I'd never touch a penny of yours. Still, I am in it now, and there is no getting away from that fact. We're both in danger, and that is a common bond. Blaydes is hot on my track, as well as yours, and we must find out how much he knows and act accordingly. I'm taking a risk in coming here to see you—"

"Then why not meet me where we shall be safe?" Draycott urged.

"In that wood? Not me!" Partridge laughed insolently. "I haven't the pluck, my boy. I have no desire to share Gainsforth's fate, or to try the effects of the game you played the other night with Moler. I didn't see what happened to him, but I can guess. The question is, what are you going to do?"

Draycott pondered it moodily. His mind was clear in the presence of this new danger, and he was striving hard to see a way out. He fully recognised the peril. He knew Blaydes was not the innocent old gentleman he professed to be. He would have to give the whole situation his serious consideration, and this meant more morphia. Indeed, he was not capable of any physical or mental effort without it.

"Go away and leave me," he said. "Leave me for a day or two. Keep your eyes open, and don't ask too many questions. You shall hear from me as soon as possible."

Partridge departed more or less satisfied. He was relieved to find that Dr. Blaydes had gone fishing. It was clear the good old man had not followed him. About the same time the supposed antiquary was talking to Alice in the garden at Rawmouth.

"I have picked up much useful information," Hugh said casually. He shrank from telling Alice what he had discovered. The mere fact that she was under the same roof with Draycott filled him with apprehension. "One or two things were said that help me materially. In the course of a day or two you may look for developments. By the time I change places with Collier again, the evidence will be complete. I can promise you that you will see very little of Draycott, and Moler is safely out of the way. This will be a relief to you."

"It is, indeed," Alice said, with a sigh. "You can't imagine how their presence stifles me. I was losing my nerve. If you had not come back I fancy I should have been ready to do anything they asked me."

Hugh took Alice in his arms and kissed her. His heart was beating high with happiness, and he thrilled with the consciousness of coming triumph. The world looked very bright and fair.

"It will not be for long, darling," he said, as he held Alice's face between his hands. "Your troubles and mine are nearly over. A few days more and I shall be free. I will resume my old occupation and prepare a home for you. My old chief, our managing director, always declared I was innocent. He came to me after the trial and said so. I will be reinstated."

"Does it matter?" Alice asked gently. "Don't forget that I have come into my money since the trouble begun. There will be plenty for us both, Hugh. After what has happened, I want you all to myself for quite a long time. You must not go back to the City again; we will take a lovely old house in the country, and you can farm or do something of that kind. I am so glad for your sake that this money has come to me."

Hugh smiled into the pretty, sympathetic face. It was more than possible, he thought, that the money was already gone. On the other hand, he might be in time to save it.

"It is a tempting picture," he laughed. "Nothing would please me better than to stay by your side and care for you. But there is stern work to be done first, dearest. I must leave you for the present. Draycott won't trouble you, that's one comfort. He has plenty to occupy his mind for the next few days."

Hugh's prophecy was correct. Draycott kept close to his room on the plea of illness, pondering his difficulties, and driving off madness by doses of morphia. He inquired for Moler from time to time, and professed satisfaction that he was progressing favorably. The latter already felt well enough to dispense with his nurse.

Draycott's lips compressed ominously as he heard this. A plan had taken shape in his mind. It was a wild and desperate scheme, but he was a desperate man. He did not realise his dangers any the less because the foe had so artfully concealed them. He recognised the strength and skill of his enemies, but would carve a way out even at the cost of human life. If he failed, then a double dose of morphia would end it all.

He sat polishing up his scheme, his brain fresh and vigorous after a touch of the hypodermic syringe. The butler came into the room with a card on a tray.

"Tell Mr. Hillditch I will see him in the library."

He took a turn up and down the room, holding the card of Mr. Harold Hillditch in his hand. He had forgotten this danger.

"Another of them!" he muttered. "How many more? I wonder what this damned lawyer knows! Is he in league with Blaydes and Bassett? Strange I should have overlooked him! Now, to see whether he can get the better of me or not."

Mr. Hillditch resembled an athlete—which indeed he was—rather than a solicitor in good practice. He was like a sporting barrister out for a holiday. There was something about his square, clean-shaven jaw that Draycott did not like. Here was a man to be afraid of; he watched as a cat watches a mouse.

"I am not likely to detain you long, Mr. Draycott," the stranger said. "As a matter of fact the papers relating to the estate of the late Mr. Gainsforth—"

"Why do you call him the late Mr. Gainsforth?" Draycott asked. "Is he dead?"

For an instant a shrewd smile flickered over the face of Mr. Hillditch. It was a sort of tribute to the powers of his antagonist and Draycott recognised it as such.

"We have every reason to believe so," the lawyer said. "But I will touch on that point presently. Our late client was a poor man in the sense that he wasted his money. What little he had left goes to a niece that needs it all. We found amongst his papers some securities, worthless at the time, that now are of great value. But before doing anything on behalf of the niece, we must prove death. We must satisfy the court that Mr. Gainsforth is no longer alive. This is not a very easy matter because the court requires more than mere supposition."

"But how does this concern me?"

"If you will have patience, I will explain," Hillditch answered. "Gainsforth was on very intimate terms with Mr. Faber. We have documentary evidence to prove this. A mass of letters has come into our hands from a certain source—to be quite frank with you, they were delivered to us by a convict called Waterhouse."

"The devil!" Draycott ejaculated. "I—I mean please go on, Mr. Hillditch."

Hillditch ignored the agitation of his companion. "Amongst the letters were many from Mr. Faber. I am bound to say that they show Mr. Faber in an exceedingly bad light. He seems to have been a scamp of the very worst type. They also show that he was at his wits' end for money. In the face of all this, it is extraordinary he should have insured his life for a hundred thousand pounds. We shall probably find before we have finished where he obtained the money for the premium. Mr. Faber, I imagine, was the last man in the world to put himself to inconvenience to benefit others. He cared little for his wife and, in any case, she was a dying woman when the insurance was affected. Before the second premium became due Mr. Faber was killed in a railway accident; or rather on the railway line near here. At the same time our late client vanished."

"I was in the Argentine then."

"That appears to be unfortunate for my case," Hillditch replied. "Still, there may be a satisfactory explanation. Here is one of the letters written to Mr. Gainsforth by Mr. Faber. Please take great care of it as it is an original. You will see that the signature is that of 'Martin Faber' and the name is in inverted commas. Now, can you explain why the name should be marked like a quotation?"

Draycott took the letter in his hand and read it. Hillditch paused for a reply. At the expiration of five minutes he was still patiently waiting.

CHAPTER XXII

THE FLESH-COLORED GLOVE

Draycott found his voice at length. He took up the Japanese paper-knife and toyed with it nervously. Something in the way he gripped the handle impressed his companion, whose keen glance never wavered. Hillditch had a fair idea of what was passing in Draycott's mind—rage despair, madness, and the wild lust of slaughter reigned there.

"Why do you come and worry me in this fashion," Draycott demanded fiercely.

"I thought I was acting in your interest," Hillditch replied. "Can't you see that?"

"No, I can't. What has all this to do with me? I was abroad at the time."

"We will take that for granted for the moment. But you must admit that this letter would be a serious matter for Faber if he were still alive. It connects him with the disappearance of Gainsforth. It suggests fraud. It gives Gainsforth a hold over Faber who wrote it to blind him and obtain his confidence. Possibly Faber expected to recover the letter. If we could find Gainsforth—"

"If you could," Draycott interrupted. There was sneering triumph in his tone. He regretted the words almost before they were uttered. "But you can't."

Hillditch's lips were compressed again, and his eyes glistened like steel.

"My dear sir, you are mistaken," he said impressively. "We can lay hands upon Marcus Gainsforth at any moment. We know where his body lies."

Draycott started. It was as if a strong hand suddenly gripped him by the throat.

"We can prove a very pretty conspiracy," Hillditch went on. "We can prove fraud, and worse. On behalf of the Grand National Insurance Company I tell you this. When our proof was completed, Faber's estate would cease to exist. The money you came into would have to be refunded. I am not using this as a threat—merely as an argument to induce you to give us all the information you can. I have written out a series of questions for you to answer. I want you to go over them at your leisure, and reply to the best of your ability. You might post the answers in the course of a week."

Draycott took the long sheet of brief paper with a shaky hand. He began to understand that this was another foe to contend with. He forced a smile to his lips and affected a geniality of manner.

"Of course, I will help you all I can," he said. "Now may I offer you anything? A cigar and a whisky-and-soda?"

Hillditch declined politely. He had to see another client in the neighborhood, and never drank between meals. It was true he had another client, but Draycott would have been still further agitated had he known that this client was Russell Clench, whom Hillditch called upon without delay.

"I can give you only a few minutes," Hillditch said. "If I hasten I can catch a local train, and reach Exeter this evening, where I have business to transact. It will be safe for you to walk with me as far as the station."

"That's what I was going to propose," Clench said. "How did he take it?"

"Draycott? He took it rather badly. My dear sir, that man is a homicidal lunatic, and the victim of drink and drugs which render him all the more dangerous. He seriously debated in his mind whether or not he should stick me with a dagger he uses as a paper-knife. His one idea is to get out of this mess by slaughtering his enemies wholesale. But I gave him a rare fright over that letter."

"I expected something of that sort," Clench replied. "I did the right thing in placing these facts and papers in the hands of your firm. As I am here in person looking after Grenfell's interests, I could do nothing else. The information you fished out of Waterhouse's box will hang Draycott."

"Give him rope enough and he will hang himself," Hillditch remarked sententiously.

"Precisely. You gave him that list of questions, I suppose? Good! And he promised to answer them in due course? Instead of doing so, he will destroy all the evidence he can. If we have him closely watched he will tumble into our hands. For the sake of Miss Kearns, I want as little scandal as possible. We may get all we need without exhuming the body of the man who is supposed to have been buried as Martin Faber."

Hillditch nodded; it was a complicated business, but he was seeing his way clearly now.

All this time Draycott was pacing anxiously up and down the library. He read the questions on the sheet of paper a score of times. They were pertinent questions, couched in a curt, business-like way, and sent a cold chill down his spine. They were the very questions a judge would ask of a prisoner who was giving evidence in his own defence.

"That rascal suspects something," Draycott muttered. "It looks as if he were on the right track. Yet for the life of me I can't see how I can be connected with it. No one knows the facts but Moler and Partridge, and even Partridge does not know everything. Moler is the only one to be really feared. Still, he's not fool enough to kill the goose that lays the golden eggs, though heaven knows the goose has laid eggs enough lately. That scoundrel will have every feather I've got. If I could only get him out of the way! If the blackguard would only die!"

Draycott's voice trailed away to a whisper. The hate in his eyes boded ill for Moler, who lay upstairs more or less helpless, who was, however, so far better that he had discharged his nurse. For reasons of his own, Draycott had kept out of Moler's way; but it was necessary to see him now. Unwillingly he ascended to Moler's bedroom. The latter was seated in a big armchair in the window, going over some papers. He thrust these hastily aside as he saw Draycott.

"What do you want?" he asked, in anything but a friendly tone.

"I've come to have a chat with you," Draycott replied. His assumption of ease and assurance was overdone, as Moler did not fail to note. "I've had a lawyer from town, asking all kinds of questions about Gainsforth. I hardly know what to do."

"Murder him," Moler said harshly. "Lure him into a quiet place and cut his throat. Creep after him in the dark and attack him from behind. That's the game. Act on the presumption that dead men tell no tales. Only make sure that they are dead."

Draycott flushed uncomfortably. There was no mistaking the significance of Moler's suggestion. But he could not afford to quarrel with the astute German.

"I can't murder the lot," he said. "I may not see this lawyer again, and Blaydes is not here. He passes as an amiable old cleric, as you are aware, but he is a detective. He knows pretty well everything, and so does your precious friend Bassett, or he would not have brought Blaydes here."

"Your nerves are out of order," Moler said contemptuously.

"Oh, are they! Listen to the gist of a conversation I had with Blaydes, and what that Hillditch had to say."

With that, Draycott briefly recounted the sum and substance of the talks he had had with the two men.

"Now, what do you think of that, my friend? I'm surrounded by people who are plotting my downfall. They don't know everything, because the whole secret is confined to you and me. What shall I do?"

"Really, I don't know," Moler said indifferently. "I don't see why I should concern myself about it. As soon as I am fit, I shall take a sea voyage. I may be away three or four months. I hope to start at the beginning of the week, and I shall need money, say, ten thousand pounds."

"Ten thousand devils!" Draycott burst out furiously. "You'll not get that out of me. Have you ever troubled to count up what you have had of me already?"

"I'm a poor arithmetician," Moler yawned. "You may console yourself with the reflection that the money never really was yours. I'm going to have it, mind you. It will come back to you in time."

Moler closed his eyes, apparently in slumber, and Draycott slipped sulkily from the room. He knew what Moler meant as plainly as if the intention had been put into so many words. Moler intended to abandon him to his fate. He was going to extract one big loan, and then Rawmouth would see the wily German no more. And he had chosen the time for his last exaction just when Draycott sorely needed a clear head and clever brain to aid him.

Moler should never have that money, Draycott told himself so over and over again as he sat reviewing matters in the library. He declined to go in to dinner, and would not have the lights turned on. He was still sitting in the darkness when Alice went to bed. She could hear him coughing as she turned the key in the door. She was looking forward eagerly to the day when this mystery and trouble should come to an end. The weight of it was beginning to press on her nerves. She sat undressed for an hour or more. Presently she turned sleepily towards her dressing-table, when she paused and listened.

She thought she heard a choking cry at the end of the corridor. The cry rose again, this time clearly and distinctly. Without a thought, Alice opened her door and ran along the corridor in the dark. She knew now whence the noise came. Undoubtedly a struggle was going on in Moler's room.

"Who is there?" she cried. "Who is there, and what are you doing?"

The noise and heavy breathing stopped instantly. In the utter darkness a shadowy figure dashed past her and a door at a distance closed quietly. With trembling hand Alice fumbled for the switches; and flooded the corridor with light. Moler's bedroom door stood open, and the German saw her.

"I beg your pardon," he said, with a gasp. "I am sorry to have alarmed you, I have had a horrible nightmare, and I always call out when that kind of thing overcomes me."

Alice uttered some apology and closed the door. She did not believe Moler for an instant. She heard him quietly turn the key in the lock. She had noticed his white face and the way he had gasped for breath. Still, if the German refused to speak, it was no business of hers.

As she turned to extinguish the light, an object on the floor attracted her attention. It looked like a hand severed at her wrist from somebody's arm. It was a flesh-colored glove, apparently made of fish-skin, for it was greasy to the touch and oily inside.

"I had better show this to Hugh."

CHAPTER XXIII

VOLUME FIFTEEN

Alice had very little doubt as to what had happened. Draycott had attempted Moler's life. The mere thought of it set her heart beating painfully fast. She was looking forward anxiously to the time when she should leave this hateful house. It was bad enough to have Moler watching and prying, but the knowledge that Draycott was a cold-blooded assassin came in the nature of a shock. Draycott had deteriorated so rapidly that it might be her turn next.

With a half-smile at her weakness, she shot the bolts of her door. She was too excited to think of sleep. Many singular things about this business puzzled her. Moler must have known whence this attack on his life proceeded; it was impossible to believe that he was ignorant of his assailant. Alice had no doubt, and yet Moler had lied to her when he pretended he was merely suffering from nightmare. All the same, he had been careful to lock the door of his room.

Hugh and Mr. Clench must be told everything in the morning. She examined the curious greasy glove in her hand, and its clamminess caused her to shudder. She had never seen anything like it before, and wondered what it was. It was reasonable to infer that the glove had been dropped by the would-be murderer as he fled from Moler's room. Therefore, the article belonged to Draycott. But what could he use such a glove for? Alice had read that gloves were used by thieves to prevent traces of finger-marks, but she was under the impression that ordinary gloves would serve this purpose.

Alice hid the glove carefully and put out her light. No doubt Hugh or Mr. Clench would be able to explain the strange business. She fell asleep, pondering the matter, and when she opened her eyes again it was past eight. When she came down to breakfast, to her astonishment, Draycott was already in the room. He stood in front of the window, apparently admiring the landscape gleaming in the sunshine. He was more carefully dressed than had been his custom of late. He was humming a frivolous air, and his whole manner was one of gaiety and good humor. Not for many months had Alice seen him like this; assuredly not since Moler had become an inmate of the house. He turned to Alice with a smile on his face. The only thing unnatural about him were his eyes. There was a strange glazed look in them, a peculiar deadness, as if they were made of glass. Alice looked at him, marvelling—she was not familiar with the effects of morphia.

She forced herself to smile, but was thankful Draycott did not offer to shake hands. She could not have done so with a man who was at heart a murderer.

With a barely suppressed start she saw the reason presently. Draycott's right hand was clumsily bandaged, and she observed the strips of plaster across the back.

"You have hurt yourself," she said gently.

"A trifle," Draycott said lightly. "I scratched myself during an experiment. Lovely morning, isn't it? What are you going to do to-day?"

Alice responded in the same mood. It would never do to arouse his suspicion. For some reason he was going out of his way to make himself agreeable to her, and it was policy to deal with him in a similar spirit.

"Not much," she said. "I have plenty to do in the house. A walk after lunch, perhaps."

"You ought to invite a friend to stay with you," Draycott went on. "An old schoolfellow, perhaps. I'm afraid I have not realised how dull you must be. Moler and myself are selfishly interested in our experiments. The only callers are people like Dr. Blaydes, who are learned, but dull. Don't you find him so?"

"I have not formed any opinion about him," Alice said indifferently. "He is an old man."

"And a little inquisitive, eh?" Draycott laughed. "Haven't you found him so?"

Apparently Alice had not. She spoke as if the subject bored her, as if she and Blaydes were only the most distant acquaintances. All the same, she knew what Draycott was driving at. He seemed satisfied with her reply, for he changed the conversation.

"I'll take you to Paris. But I must finish certain experiments first. They are rather delicate, and a little dangerous. I require to use a certain kind of glove in handling ingredients. I have mislaid one of the gloves, hence the scratch on my hand. I suppose you don't happen to have seen it lying about?"

Alice shook her head. The deceit was necessary, and she stood to it bravely. Draycott was evidently worried about the missing glove, otherwise, he would not have assumed this amiable manner at breakfast; but it was obviously needless to ask further questions of Alice.

"I daresay I shall come across it," Draycott said carelessly. "By the way, what was the matter with Dr. Moler last night? Didn't I hear him making a noise? I went as far as the corridor, but I saw you had forestalled me."

Alice bent her head over her cup lest Draycott might see her face. She had had very little doubt about the author of last night's disturbance, but now that Draycott had confirmed her suspicions out of his own mouth, the shock left her pale and trembling. She would have liked to rush from the table, for reflection that she was seated opposite a murderer gave her a sickening sensation of fainting. But Draycott must see nothing of this. Not for a moment must he guess that Alice had any suspicion of the truth.

"It was alarming," she said. "At first I thought something dreadful had happened. It required all my courage to ascertain the cause. But it was nothing worse than a violent nightmare. Dr. Moler was very sorry he had disturbed me."

Draycott looked relieved. The meal came to an end at last, and with a deep feeling of thankfulness Alice was free. No sooner had she discharged her few household duties than she went at once to Grenfell's lodgings. She had the mysterious glove in her pocket and the sooner she could get rid of it the better. She met Hugh by a stream, fishing-rod in hand. He looked all over the elderly gentleman enjoying a quiet holiday.

"Hugh, I am so glad to meet you," Alice said. "There are many things to tell. The most dreadful business happened last night."

"No more murder or attempt at murder?"

Alice proceeded to explain, Hugh listening gravely, almost anxiously.

"You ought not to stay in that house any longer," he said.

"Oh! I am not afraid, dear. There is not much fear of that man attacking me. And consider how useful I am. If I had not been at Rawmouth you would never have heard of this. But I have not quite finished. Let me tell you the story of the glove."

"What glove?" Hugh asked. "Where does the glove come in?"

"I am just going to tell you. Then I will ask you to account for Mr. Draycott's unexpected appearance at breakfast to-day, and the curious questions he asked. Perhaps you will also be able to explain what is the matter with his hand. What do you think of that, Hugh? Here is the glove. It is a hideous thing, and I am glad to be rid of it."

Hugh turned the glove over and over in his hand. It was plain he could make nothing of it.

"Let us consult Clench," he said. "He may be able to throw some light on this mystery. Anyhow, the glove is of importance, and is in some way connected with the bandages on Draycott's hand. Clench is at the cottage waiting for a telegram from London."

Clench listened to the story gravely. There was a queer smile on his face and a look of assurance in his eyes.

"I fancy you can enlighten us, Mr. Clench," she said.

"Well, perhaps I can," he answered modestly. "There are so many complicated features in this case that one is apt to overlook some of the threads. I have had this in view for some time, and it was very careless of me to forget it. The loss of that glove is a serious matter to Draycott. But it has no connection with anything in the way of dangerous poisons."

"I thought it might be used to avoid leaving finger-marks," Alice said. "Then it struck me that an ordinary glove would serve the purpose."

"Very good, Miss Kearns. You have it off exactly. Did you notice Draycott's hand at breakfast. Was it bandaged?"

"Yes, it was," Alice explained. "There were straps of sticking-plaster all over it."

"Especially on the back of the hand?"

"You are quite right. If you had been present yourself you could not have described it better."

Clench asked a few more questions, and then put the glove aside carefully.

"Is this really of use?" Hugh asked.

"My dear boy," Clench explained. "It is of vital importance. Miss Kearns has simplified our task wonderfully. I confess I have been puzzled to demonstrate the motive for all this tangle of crime and conspiracy. I could not quite see my way to establish certain connections between Draycott and somebody else. I have been working for that end, more especially to bring Moler into the net. Moler must be made to speak, and the weapon to open his mouth is now in my hands. Only give me a little time."

"You are sure of all this?" Alice asked.

"My dear young lady," Clench went on exultingly, "I am by nature a cautious man. My legal training renders me so. Now I wonder whether there is a file of the 'British Medical Chronicle' in the hospital at Dartdale."

"Why do you want it?" Hugh inquired.

"I am deeply interested in certain branches of surgery," Clench smiled. "Also I wish to study the various papers contributed to the 'Chronicle' by Dr. Moler. I'll go to the gaol hospital and try to make friends with Dr. Flack. If he has what I want, then I shall be able to show my hand. You may be surprised to hear that the 'Chronicle' contains the clue to the whole mystery. Produced in court it will go far to give Moler and Draycott a long acquaintance with the interior of an English prison."

CHAPTER XXIV

A LADY IN THE CASE

Dr. Flack was pleased to meet Mr. Bassett. He had heard of his visitor, and strangers interested in criminology were extremely welcome. The doctor had an hour to spare, and was entirely at Clench's disposal.

"Sit down, please," he said. "May I offer you a cigar?"

"I think I had better explain first, I am going to make a confession, doctor. I place myself entirely in your hands. As a matter of fact, I have no claim to the name of Bassett. That is assumed for private reasons. Here is my card and the name of my firm. Perhaps you have heard of it?"

Flack was properly impressed. He began to scent a mystery.

"I presume you are engaged in some delicate business?"

"I am endeavoring," answered Clench, "to get to the bottom of one of the most ingenious frauds ever perpetrated. I might be less keen were it not that this conspiracy has led to the imprisonment of an innocent man. There is a convict here who should never have been sentenced at all. Strangely enough, the man Waterhouse lately released is in a position to clear up the matter."

"Dear me," Flack exclaimed. "Quite a sensational story! You want to see Waterhouse?"

"That is so. Dr. Moler was attending him till he met with an accident. I suppose Waterhouse is in the care of a local man now. I understand that he is much better."

"I hear so," Flack said, "thanks mainly to Moler's remarkable skill."

"Well, we are on the eve of important developments, and it is a great relief to find that you are ready to assist. At the proper time I will take you further into my confidence. Now, doctor, do you file the 'British Medical Chronicle?"

"Naturally," Flack answered. "The authorities pay for them and they are bound at intervals. If you are looking up any statistics, I shall be delighted to help you."

Half an hour later Clench had all he needed. He found exactly what he had expected, made copious notes and when he returned to the doctor's sitting-room he believed he had gone far to solve the mystery.

"You appear to be satisfied," Flack suggested.

"My dear sir, I am more than satisfied," Clench said. "Everything is fairly plain. If I had gone to Scotland Yard and expounded my theory they would have laughed at me. Now I am able to prove to them that I am right and, strangely enough, Moler is going to help me. One of his articles in the 'Medical Chronicle' and his evidence will complete my case. It's a pity so brilliant a man should be such a villain."

"Really!" Flack said, with an elevation of his eyebrows. "Has Moler that reputation?"

"Not yet, but he will have," Clench said drily. "Oh, the affair will make a tremendous sensation when it comes to be told. I am greatly obliged to you Flack, and I thank you for all your trouble and attention. May I see you again in a day or two?"

"Use me when and how you like," Flack responded. "I am entirely at your service."

Clench hesitated, as if about to say more. But he thought it might be well, considering his official position, that the doctor should not know too much.

A little later Clench went on his way rejoicing, happy in the knowledge that he was going to strike a real blow for Grenfell at last. At the outside it would only be a matter of a day or two. He had merely to make out his plan of attack, and the thing was done. He would take a few hours' holiday meanwhile. The world was full of glorious sunshine, and a breeze fresh from the distant sea gave a sense of buoyancy and strength. A walk across the moor, followed by an afternoon on the trout stream, was the programme that suggested itself.

Clench struck out boldly across the heather. At the end of an hour he paused to light his pipe. As he rose from the shelter of a gorse-bush he saw a big touring car coming towards him along the white strip of road. The car pulled up presently and the solitary occupant got out. She was a tall woman, magnificently dressed, a beautiful woman, too, dashing and audacious, with that vague hint of 'Miladi' which stamps her class. She was either that, or a foreign princess travelling under a nom de guerre. Clench whistled softly, as he saw her, and a queer smile flashed over his face.

"I'll remain here," the lady said to the driver. "Go back along the road till you find it, you fool. It must have been dropped in the last six miles or so."

The chauffeur touched his hat humbly; he was accustomed to this imperious mood. The car hummed away until it was out of sight. Clench stepped forward and raised his cap, removing a part of his disguise at the same time. There was a mocking light in his eyes.

"This is a piece of good fortune I did not expect," he said. "I am delighted to see you. Your old admirer Clench, very much at your service. It would facilitate matters if you told me your present name."

"Countess D'Arblay, of course," the woman said, with a flashing smile.

"Of course," Clench responded gravely, "Countess D'Arblay to me beyond question, for to me anything like prevarication is useless. What does your chauffeur call you?"

The woman laughed. The irony of the question appealed to her.

"Your Highness something or other," she said. "After all, what does it matter? What's in a name? as Shakespeare so pointedly asked. I am a Russian princess touring in England. I am looking for a place in Devonshire where I may spend a quiet month or two. I wish a big house in a park and that kind of thing."

"Taken by means of false pretences and all that kind of thing, I suppose."

"My dear man," the Countess said coolly, "you don't know what you are talking about. At the present moment I have more money than I know what to do with. With all my faults, you must admit that I always paid when I had the money."

"The vilest of us has his redeeming trait," Clench allowed. "Go on."

"I mean to spend it; I always do. And I must have rest; I'm beginning to develop nerves. The ozone in this air will set me up again."

"And this is the only reason why you are here?"

"Honest Injun! You won't give me away, Clench? I never did you any harm."

"I always took precious good care of that," Clench said coolly. "But you are lying to me. You want me to believe that your appearance here is an accident—that you are ignorant that Moler and Draycott are not many miles away. And you lied to me the day in the train when you were coming down."

The Countess smiled—she was getting no news from Clench. Then she laughed steadily. Clench knew he had touched a chord that responded to his touch. He had made a mistake in mentioning these people, perhaps, and it was therefore necessary to move quickly. He tightened his lips, and the glint in his eyes was hard and flinty. He took the woman's hands in his and held them firmly.

"Attend," he said, "and listen to me. Hugh Grenfell is in gaol. You know why and what he was charged with. You must know he is innocent, and that till lately Waterhouse was in the same prison. Partridge has gone to the dogs and Gainsforth has disappeared. The chances are these men might have made good and useful citizens had they not come under your baneful influence."

"Not Partridge," the woman said coolly. "Oliver Partridge was always a bad lot."

"I don't agree with you," Clench said. "There was not very much the matter with Oliver Partridge before he met you. Had he come in contact with the right woman he would now be a respectable member of society. But I am not here to discuss his character."

"I suppose not," the Countess said demurely. "By the way, why are you here? Is this a chance meeting, or have you engineered it for some purpose of your own?"

"Call it luck, if you like," Clench went on. "To some extent this is a chance meeting, but I was going to look you up. I have known for a few days that you were in the neighborhood, guessed you were on some mischief when I met you a little time ago. It wasn't for me to say whether you were here on pleasure or not. Is it pleasure or business?"

"I have already told you," the Countess said. "I am looking for a house."

"Yes, but that does not preclude business altogether, my dear Countess. All the same, you mustn't stay here. Before long Moler and Draycott will be—"

"But, my dear man, they are nothing to me," the Countess protested. "I'd rather not see Moler."

"Really!" Clench smiled. "Not see your own brother! The brother whom you visited under Draycott's roof. How callous! And the poor man may be dying for all you know. It won't do, Christine, it won't do at all. What mischief you are up to is no concern of mine, but it is my business to see that you can do no more of it in Devonshire. Try Cornwall, if you like; and there are some lovely spots in Somerset. But you must not remain here."

The Countess's dark eyes flashes dangerously.

"Why not, pray?" she asked. "Who will prevent me?"

"I will. There are urgent reasons why I want you out of the way. Now, I know a good deal about you. I was one of your set in the old days, but I flatter myself I was one of the few who kept his head and managed to steer clear of your fascinations. My wings were never singed. I found you a most interesting woman, Christine, but nothing more. I made it my hobby to collect fragments of your interesting history. I could write your memoirs for Scotland Yard without many mistakes. I can assure you that Scotland Yard would be pleased to read them. Unless you promise to clear out of Devonshire this week they shall have the opportunity."

The woman's face was hard and defiant, but her lips were white. She had admired this man always, and, in her reckless way, she feared him. He had always understood her; from the very first she had never got anything out of him. Moreover, if he chose, he could be a dangerous enemy. What was he doing here, and why was he in disguise? Why was he frequently visiting Draycott's house? She recollected that he must have paved the way for her to see Moler. She bit her lips with anger and vexation when she thought of this.

"I'm up to no harm," she pleaded. "Honestly, I came to find a house where I could pass the summer in peace and quiet. I've plenty of money, and no temptations to make more. I'm sick of the old life, with its dangers and troubles. I'm not too old to marry and settle down, Clench. Give me a chance, and I promise you—"

But Clench shook his head firmly.

"Your promises are worthless," he said, "and I don't want you here. You are in the way, my dear lady. Why should you spoil the life of some honest man, as you spoilt the life of Hugo Grenfell and Marcus Gainsforth and Oliver Partridge and—"

"As I said before, Partridge was a bad lot from the start."

"Well, I'll throw you in Partridge, if you like. But what I say about the others is correct. What I have to do now is to make Draycott and Moler speak. Moler regards me as a middle-aged dreamer with money to spare. He looks at me with a predatory eye; he has designs on my purse. To him I am merely Mr. Bassett. He has not the remotest idea that I am here to save Grenfell. It is possible you may be of assistance."

"I will do all I can for you," the Countess said cordially.

"I am aware of the fact," retorted Clench. "Now listen to me. You know what I am and what I can do. If you play me false, I'll crumple you up like a piece of paper. If you betray me by so much as a thought, I'll land you in prison, where you ought to have been long ago. If I raise the hue, plenty of your victims will take up the cry, and I'll do it without the slightest compunction if you don't go as straight as a die."

The words issued from Clench's lips in a hissing whisper. He was holding the woman's hands in a grip like a vice. He saw the defiant smile fade from her face, that her lips had become pale, and that they were trembling. Her bold, black eyes fell at last.

"You were always a hard man," she said bitterly. "I could never do anything with you, Russell. I suppose that is why I liked you better than all the rest put together. What do you want me to do?"

"That's right," Clench said, as he released the long, slim hands. "That is how I expected you to speak, my lady. I want you to place yourself entirely at my disposal. My present address is on this card. Let me have yours as soon as possible. Then, if it is not too far, I'll come over and lunch with you. Possibly I may bring Moler. There's your man coming back—perhaps it would be as well not to be seen talking any longer. But you'll leave here for good at the end of the week."

Clench touched his cap carelessly and strode off towards Rawmouth. This chance meeting had entirely altered his plans. He strode into Moler's bedroom an hour later, ostensibly to see how the invalid was progressing.

"I am glad to hear you are better," he said. "I am curious to have your advice on a matter that is interesting me, I should like a chat with you on the subject."

"Anything I can do, I shall be delighted to do."

"Thanks," Clench replied. "The matter is skin-grafting. I find you are the authority on the question. May I sit down and discuss the subject?"

CHAPTER XXV

A LESSON IN SURGERY

"I should have thought that that kind of thing was quite out of your line," Moler said. He appeared to be completely at his ease. The look of suspicion had gone from his eyes. "But I will give you all the information in my power, Mr. Bassett."

"I should prefer you to call me by another name," said Clench, "Bassett is merely my nom de guerre. I am really Mr. Russell Clench—a lawyer with a considerable criminal practice; the name may be familiar to you."

Moler smiled. He was not in the least disturbed. It was plain he had a clear idea of what was going to happen.

"The name and reputation of your firm are well known to me," he said, "I presume you are here on important business, Mr. Clench."

"I will be quite candid. It is my business to clear the reputation of Mr. Hugh Grenfell, and restore his good name. I am able to prove that he was the victim of a vile conspiracy. He was got out of the way to prevent awkward questions about Mr. Martin Faber's insurance money. The man who calls himself Oscar Lee—otherwise Oliver Partridge—will be a useful witness, and Waterhouse will be another. Waterhouse was good enough to inform me where I could find certain papers belonging to the late Marcus Gainsforth."

"What has all this to do with me?" Moler asked quietly.

"Oh! I shall come to that presently. I want to clear the way first. But surely most of these facts are already familiar to you?"

"I will admit it, but only for the sake of argument."

"That is exceedingly kind of you," Clench smiled. "I have seen Waterhouse. We have had a long talk about this matter. The conspiracy will be revealed in due time. Are you prepared to deny that Marcus Gainsforth was murdered?"

"I had nothing to do with that."

"Granted; the thing was done before you came on the scene. Gainsforth was murdered, and Grenfell was in gaol before you met Draycott in Paris. I will ask you presently to tell me what happened during the time you two were in Paris together. You may refuse if you please, but your refusal will only delay matters for a day or two. In any case, I can prove what took place."

"You are beginning to threaten me," Moler blustered.

"Well, what of it? In fact, I am only showing you how strong my hand is. You well be well advised to regard me more in the light of a friend than an enemy. But, being master of the situation, I prefer to conduct the case in my own way. You parted from Draycott in Paris, and he was under the impression he had seen the last of you. Whether you followed him here or met him by accident is a matter of no importance. You did find him again, and you have been living here ever since. Blackmail is not a nice word, but, in the circumstances, I can think of no other."

The color crept into Moler's cheeks.

"Do you mean to be offensive?"

"I mean to speak the truth," Clench said bluntly. "After what happened in Paris, you had a hold on Draycott, and have used it to the best advantage. Trading on that secret, you have extorted thousands of pounds from him. The extortion became so heavy at last that Draycott made up his mind to get rid of you. He tried to murder you, and you are still suffering from the effects of that attempt. One attempt having failed, he made a second one in your bedroom late at night. A man must have a very strong motive when he risks his neck in that fashion. You may deny this if you like, Dr. Moler."

"Who is denying it?" Moler asked sulkily.

"Ah, that is precisely the kind of reply I expected," Clench went on. "Really, I am obliged to you for saving me so much trouble. But does not your tacit admission justify me in using such a word as 'blackmail'? You may say that Draycott is a drunkard and the slave of the drug habit as well. But even this will not account for two serious attempts on your life. I am willing to concede that Draycott is a dangerous, homicidal lunatic, but the impulse to kill for killing's sake was not present when Marcus Gainsforth was done to death by the man who calls himself Raymond Draycott."

Moler was stirred at last. His color came and went, and he seemed to have some difficulty in breathing. The half amused vigilance had left his eyes, and his manner changed to one of almost sickening fear and anxiety.

"You are a clever man, Mr. Clench," he said, slowly and painfully, "a very clever man. You mean to say you can prove this against Draycott?"

"In the course of a few days, certainly, but I hope you will save me the trouble. If I obtain an order from the Home Secretary for the opening of a certain grave, I can prove that Gainsforth was murdered. After that hint I am sure you will not put any obstacles in my way."

Moler smiled with the air of one who is anxious to please.

"What first put you on the right track?" he asked. "It was very clever of Draycott."

"Clever! There has been nothing so daring and so ingenious in the whole history of crime! There was only one flaw in the scheme—Draycott was bound to have a confederate. He had to come to you, for the simple reason that nobody else could serve his purpose. Mind you, there was no really plausible excuse for adopting your treatment. Only a criminal would have done so. You guessed something of the motive from the first. That is why you kept an eye on your patient and afterwards tracked him here and blackmailed him. Why a man with your wonderful gifts should act like this passes my understanding. With your brains I should have made a fortune long ago—your knowledge is a fortune in itself."

"I know," Moler said softly. "The misfortune is that I cannot stick to one thing for any length of time. My brain is full of ideas, and I have to test them as they come along. Give me twenty thousand pounds, and I could set the world by the ears. That is what I came here for. But I found Draycott a harder nut to crack than I expected."

"You pieced the story together after you got here?"

"Partly so, and partly from what Draycott told me in his drunken fits. Drink was the one great danger he had to fear."

"So I should imagine. Those drunken bouts must have caused you a deal of anxiety. I may tell you that it was these periodical attacks that set a certain young lady thinking. She was inclined to laugh at her wild ideas till she consulted me."

"To say nothing of Dr. Blaydes," Moler remarked drily. "Who is he, Mr. Clench?"

"Ah! that is the leading incident in the sensational drama," Clench smiled. "Directly I went into matters I saw at once that Miss Kearns was right. Her instinct had carried her to the root of the mystery, and on the night of the attack upon you in your bedroom she found some useful evidence. You will recollect how she came to your help. No doubt she saved your life. She also found this."

Clench produced a flat cardboard box containing the mysterious glove Alice had picked up in the corridor. He handed it to Moler.

"This article would puzzle most people," Clench went on. "But I fancy I can understand it. Permit me to compliment you on the cleverness of the workmanship. It looks exactly like the genuine thing. Did you make it yourself?"

"Not wholly," Moler explained. "I designed the component parts and mixed them. You can see that the lines of a human hand are there, as well as the hair on the back. I cannot understand how Draycott came to lose it, unless it was torn off in the struggle. The glove was made by a man in Paris."

"Really! Now I understand how the Rue de Rivoli murderer escaped ten years ago. If they could have established certain marks on his hand he would have died. I presume it was your ingenious discovery that saved the ruffian's neck?"

"That is so," Moler admitted, with a degree of pride in his tone. "I received a large sum of money for that operation. But is a mere nothing by comparison."

"I know that," Clench said drily. "Your wonderful powers go a long way farther. What a pity you were not born with a fortune! In that case you might have done humanity invaluable service."

"I have done so already," Moler said defiantly. "I could show you things that would entitle me to a statue in every capital in Europe if I liked. But what does it matter? You are bent on placing me where I can do no good or harm for many years to come."

"I have done nothing of the sort," Clench said. "Tell me everything, and you will be free to go where you please. Tell me the story of the inception of your wonderful article in the 'Medical Chronicle.' Prove that you can do only half what you claim, and your debt is paid."

Moler looked up with an eager light in his eyes.

"You give me your word of honor for that?"

"I have already done so," Clench replied. "You place yourself in my hands. I am very loth to deprive mankind of a mind like yours."

"Then I'll do everything you ask."

"Good;" said Clench. "Can you walk a little, do you think? If so, we will go and have the matter out with Draycott now!"

Draycott sat in the library with a litter of paper before him. For an hour or more he had been pondering a certain step, and was calculating his forces. There was more than a possibility that it would be expedient for him to leave England for an indefinite period, and he had to put his house in order first. He would take a long rest in some quiet place where his foes would not find him. He would rigidly abstain from drugs in future. Meanwhile, of course, they were necessary. He had just injected a heavy dose of morphia, and his brain was acting under that splendid but treacherous spur.

His imagination was carrying him far, when the door of the library opened and Clench and Grenfell entered. There was something stern and business-like about them both—something that aroused all Draycott's fighting instincts at once. He was ready for the fray, too—his foes could not have arrived at a more opportune time.

"What can I do for you, Mr. Bassett?" he asked harshly.

"Call me by my proper name," was the crisp reply. "I am a solicitor acting on behalf of Mr. Hugh Grenfell, and my name is Russell Clench. It will be as well that you also should be called by your proper name, Mr. Martin Faber!"

Draycott jumped to his feet, then as abruptly sat down. He was breathing hard.

"This joke is quite beyond me," he said. "My name, as you are perfectly aware, is—"

"Martin Faber," Clench said firmly. "You are Mr. Martin Faber, of Rawmouth Park. You are the man who insured his life for a hundred thousand pounds and shortly afterwards died, as the result of an accident, on the line not far off. The victim was mutilated beyond recognition, but as his clothes and linen belonged to Faber, he was supposed to be Faber, and buried in that name. This may sound very much like a comic opera, but there is a precedent for the tragic occurrence in a similar case that happened some time ago in France. The man found on the line was Marcus Gainsforth. You lured him there and murdered him, battered his head till it was impossible to identify him, and subsequently laid him on the line in front of the express, which cut him to pieces. Obviously you had, somehow, induced Gainsforth to dress himself in a suit of your clothes and linen before the murder. It was planned with extraordinary care, and proved entirely successful. You had next to vanish. This was easy. You went to Paris and lay there perdu until you could return as Raymond Draycott, Faber's old friend from the Argentine, to whom he had left everything. It was smart of you to make a will to this effect some seven years old, but unfortunately the document was written on paper that had not been fabricated till long after the date it bore. When you were installed here, passing as Raymond Draycott, all appeared to be well. You had the money from the insurance company, and nobody seemed likely to suspect the facts. But Mr. Grenfell discovered a dangerous flaw or two, and it was imperative to put him out of the way. That was done by the aid of Oliver Partridge, who is now in this locality, under the name of Oscar Lee. In this drama everybody has posed as somebody else, and, not to be out of the fashion, I followed your example. But the game is up, Mr. Faber."

"Draycott," the other said stubbornly. "Draycott. Do I look like Faber?"

"You don't," Clench admitted. "But that difficulty is not insurmountable. You are not the first man whom Dr. Moler has altered out of all knowledge."

Draycott, or rather Faber, gripped the edge of his chair and glared at Clench impatiently.

"Do you think any court of law will listen to this infernal trash?" he demanded.

"We will try if you like," Clench replied. "Moler will probably be prepared to go into the witness-box now that he sees no chance of exhorting any more money from you. Naturally, he is exceedingly anxious to save his own skin, and I have given him the opportunity of doing it. He will prove his wonderful skill in skin-grafting and other amazing surgical exploits. He will show us how he changed your face beyond recognition, how he made you two inches shorter than, well, than you were before. He could not change your eyes, and that is why you wear glasses. By a slight operation on your throat he modified your voice. The transformation is a marvellous one and would probably have proved sufficient if Moler could also have changed your habits. But unfortunately for you, the real Faber and the suppositious Faber, alias Draycott, were much alike in one respect. They gave way to drinking bouts at regular intervals. These intervals came at the same time in both cases. Then you forgot things. At times you displayed a singular knowledge of local events, and people dating back years. Again, Martin Faber had a singular malformation of one hand; hence arose the need for that wonderful flesh glove which you lost on the night you attempted to murder Moler as he lay asleep. I see your hand is covered with bandages now, but there is really nothing the matter with it. The bandages are merely disguises till you can recover your glove. Need I carry this any farther, Mr. Faber? Do you still pretend you are Raymond Draycott?"

Faber sat, apparently unheeding. At last the purport of the questions appeared to dawn upon him, as though they had travelled a long way before they reached him.

"What is the good?" he asked sullenly. "Every word you say is true. You have not overlooked a single fact of any consequence. I was on the verge of ruin and in danger of arrest. I was a decent man till the demon of drink sapped my moral strength. I speculated and I lost. I was going to take Miss Kearn's money when I saw the French case you speak of in the paper. That gave me my basic idea. I had also read Moler's articles in the 'Medical Chronicle.' I thought my plan out till I saw the way quite clear. I managed to pay the first insurance premium and to hold out for a year so as to avoid suspicion. I chose Gainsforth for a victim because he had some physical resemblance to me. He had no money, and readily fell into the trap. I hurried off to Paris in disguise and saw Moler. He had a thousand pounds for his job. By the time I was presentable again, 'Raymond Draycott' turned up from the Argentine. You can see how nicely everything seemed to fit together. Then danger threatened from Grenfell. He had suspicions, and I was afraid of him. I thought I was done with Moler, but there I was mistaken. He found me out and bled me freely. That is why I tried to kill him on two occasions; I wish I had, I'm sorry I failed. He would have drained me of every penny in time. Tell Grenfell that Alice's fortune is safe. Now what are you going to do?"

"That will be a matter for the police," Clench remarked.

A bitter smile crossed Faber's face. He had been fumbling with a little bottle in the desk drawer, and more than once had slipped a grey tablet between his lips under cover of his handkerchief.

"I think not," he said, "at least, not as far as I am concerned. I took a strong dose of morphia before you came in, and have supplemented it several times during our interview—I wish you good-bye, gentlemen. Allow me to—compliment you upon the skill—the skill—what was I saying? Oh, yes, the skill—"

He fell back, his eyes closed, he spoke no more. He was dead, as Moler a little later assured Clench, without emotion. Though Alice was shocked, her relief was great. The doctor had come and gone, and Moler had vanished also.

"We must have you into Dartdale when the next fog comes," Clench said to Grenfell. "At the outside it will only be a matter of a day or two, and we must not get Copping or Collier into trouble. I'll see Copping tonight and tell him what we will do. It will be a weight off his mind. There is another matter I must see to at once."

"Not more trouble, I hope?" Hugh asked.

"Well, it ought to be a pleasure," Clench said, with a smile. "Our friend the Countess D'Arblay is in the neighborhood. I had special need for her services, and was willing, in certain circumstances, to permit her to settle here for a time. I did not foresee that our task would be simplified. Naturally, I anticipated that Faber would give us trouble. Now I will tell the Countess to leave the country instantly. That is why I must see her to-day."

The story of the Rawmouth Park Romance, as the papers called it, caused a tremendous sensation when the details became public. But before this Hugh, under cover of a friendly fog, had returned to Dartdale, and Copping's mind was at ease. He and his wife had gone to another district before Hugh recovered his freedom, which was only a matter of a comparatively short period. A disposition was shown to make a hero of him, and it was with enormous difficulty that he shook off the newspaper men who besieged him. He could not be so mean as to appropriate kudos that was Collier's by right.

"They offered me five hundred pounds for my experiences," he told Alice. "I believe I have a splendid opening as a journalist. Shall I take it up?" half in jest, half in earnest.

"Why should you?" Alice asked. "So long as I have you again as you used to be and without that disguise, I am content with things as they are. It was a clever disguise, but it made a difference. Mr. Clench tells me that all my money is intact. This place is to be sold for the benefit of Mr. Faber's creditors, so I can't stay here much longer. Dr. Moler is believed to be in South America, and Partridge has gone no one knows where. Mr. Waterhouse is off to Canada. As for you, Hugh, you will have to marry me now whether you want to or not."

Grenfell gazed into the pretty smiling face.

"I have loved you long and truly, Alice, and we shall climb life's hill together. I am sure you will be only too glad to get away from this dreadful place. But, you see, I have no money, and must regain my position. Everything will be on your side, and—"

Alice put her hand gently on Hugh's lips.

"I'll not hear another word," she said. "Write these articles; the five hundred pounds will pay for our honeymoon. We can discuss the future afterwards."

"Then, you will take me as I am, dearest?"

Alice laid her hand on his shoulder, and her eyes were filled with a happy light.

"Dear," she whispered, "I have been waiting for you."

FRED M WHITE – A CONCISE BIBLIOGRAPHY

NOVELS (A-Z)

Ambition's Slave (1916)
The Argus Eye (1919)
Blackmail (1902)
The Blue Daffodil (1934)
The Brand Of Silence (1911)
A Broken Memory (1929)
The Bubble Reputation (1908)
By Order Of The League (1886)
The Cardinal Moth aka The Accused Orchid (1903)
The Case For the Crown (1918)
Claxton's Mill (1912)
A Clue In Wax (1930)
The Corner House (1905)
The Councillors of Falconhoe (1922)
Craven Fortune (1904)
A Crime On Canvas (1909)
The Crimson Blind (US title: The Mystery Of The Crimson Blind) (1905)
A Daughter Of Israel (1892)
The Day: Or The Passing Of A Throne (1914)
A Deal In Letters (1923)
The Devil's Advocate (1924)
Dropped From The Fast Express, or A Daughter's Sacrifice (1911)
The Edge Of The Sword (1907)
The Ends Of Justice (1906)
A Fatal Dose (aka Behind the Mask) (1907)
The Fight For The Child (1925)
The Five Knots (1907)
"Found Dead" (1930)
The Four Fingers (US title: The Mystery Of The Four Fingers) (1907)
A Front Of Brass (1910)
The Garden O' Dreams (1909)
A Golden Argosy (1886)
The Golden Bat (1924)

The Golden Rose (1909)
The Green Bungalow (1923)
The Grey Woman (aka Sinister House) (1928)
The Happy Exile (1920)
A Harbour Of Refuge (1918)
Hard Pressed (1910)
The Honour Of His House (1920)
The House Of Mammon (1913)
A House Of Sorrows (1911)
The House Of The Schemers (1906)
The House On The River (1925)
In Trust (1892)
Jim Crowshaw's Mary (1911)
The King Diamond (1927)
Lady Clara (1913)
Lady Edna's Awakening (1920)
The Lady In Blue (1915)
The Law Of The Land (1906)
The Leopard's Spots (1920)
The Lonely Bride (aka The White Bride) (1907)
The Lord Of The Manor (1907)
Love, The Foe (1910)
A Maker of Millions (1909)
The Man Called Gilray (1911)
The Man Who Found Christmas (a novelette) (1915)
The Man Who Knew (1932)
The Man Who Was Two (1921)
The Man With The Vandyk Beard (1925)
The Midnight Guest: A Detective Story (1907)
A Mummer's Throne (1910)
My Lady Bountiful (1905)
The Mystery Of Crocksands (1923)
The Mystery Of The Ravenspurs (aka The Black Valley) (1911)
The Mystery Of Room 75 (1922)
Naboth's Vineyard (1889)
The Nether Millstone (1906)
Netta, The Story Of Sin (1909)
New Century Calendar Clue (1948)
Number Thirteen (1914)
The Old Secretaire: A Christmas Story (novelette) (1887)
On The Night Express (1930)
The Open Door (1907)
Paul Quentin (1908)
Paul, The Sage (1910)
The Phantom Car (1929)
Powers Of Darkness (1912)
The Price Of Silence (1925)
The Psalm Stone (1905)

Queen Of Hearts (1930)
A Queen Of The Stage (1908)
The Riddle Of The Rail (1926)
The Robe Of Lucifer (1896)
A Royal Wrong (1913)
The Salt Of The Earth (1918)
The Scales Of Justice (1908)
Secret Of The River (1934)
The Secret Of The Sands (1911)
A Secret Service (1913)
The Seed Of Empire (1916)
The Sentence Of The Court (1913)
A Shadowed Love (1905)
The Shadow Of The Dead Hand (1926)
The Silver Stream (novelette)
The Slave Of Silence (1906)
A Society Jezebel (1917)
The Sundial (1908)
Tregarthen's Wife: A Cornish Story (1901)
The Turn Of The Tide (1923)
The Weight Of The Crown (1904)
The White Battalions (1900)
The White Bride (aka The Lonely Bride) (1910)
The White Glove (1910)
The Wings Of Victory (1919)
The Yellow Face (1906)

SHORT FICTION SERIES

THE MASTER CRIMINAL (1897-1898)

A series of 12 short stories featuring Felix Gryde, who describes himself as "a really clever soldier of
fortune."

The Head Of The Caesars
At Windsor
The Silverpool Cup
The "Morrison Raid" Indemnity
Cleopatra's Robe
The Rosy Cross
The Death Of The President
The Cradlestone Oil Mills
Redburn Castle
"Crysoline Limited"
The Loss Of The "Eastern Empress"
General Marcos

THE LAST OF THE BORGIAS (1898)

A series of stories featuring Professor Victor Colonna, a vigilante physician who murders undesirable people with undetectable poisons.

The Scrip of Death
The Crimson Streak
The Holy Rose
The Saving Of Serena
The Varteg Necklace
The Three Carnations

DRENTON DENN - SPECIAL COMMISSIONER

Drenton Denn is a tough newspaper reporter on the payroll of The New York Post. His hallmarks are a straw hat, a Norfolk jacket, a perennial cigar, and a terrier by the name of "Prince."

The Yellow Moth
The Red Speck
Dust
The Fire Bugs
The Great White Moth

THE ROMANCE OF THE SECRET SERVICE FUND (1900)

This series features Newton Moore, the top agent at The Secret Service Fund.

By Woman's Wit
The Mazaroff Rifle
In The Express
The Almedi Concession
The Other Side Of The Chess Board
Three Of Them

THE DOOM OF LONDON

This sci-fi series of six stories describes a variety of catastrophes which ravage London.

The Four White Days
The Four Days' Night
The Dust Of Death
A Bubble Burst
The Invisible Force
The River Of Death

THE SAGE OF TYBURN (1905-1906)

Each of these stories was preceded by the header The Sage Of Tyburn.

No. 1 - The Chronicle Of The Yellow Girl
No. 2 - The Chronicle Of The Blue-Eyed Syndicate
No. 3 - The Chronicle Of The Inconsequent Princess
No. 4 - The Chronicle Of The Elderly Adonis
No. 5 - The Chronicle Of The Libelled Velasquez

THE DRAGON-FLY (1909)

Six stories about an impecunious but brilliant amateur criminologist, entomologist and ornithologist by the name of Horace Daimler. Each of the stories was preceded by the header The Dragon-Fly.

No. 1 - How Horace Daimler Got His Name
No. 2 - The Three Red Rats
No. 3 - [title unknown]
No. 4 - [title unknown]
No. 5 - A [illegible] Crime
No. 6 - The Mirror Over The Fireplace

REAL DRAMA (1909)

A series of stories published under the subtitle "Being Some Leaves From The Notebook Of A Late Theatrical Agent."

His Second Self
An Extra Turn
"Not In The Bill"
The Plagiarist
The Man In Possession
A Pair Of Handcuffs

THE TELEPHONE STAR (1912)

A series of stories about Keith Marrit, a star journalist working for a fictitious newspaper called The Telephone.

No. 1 - The Case Of El Hamid, The Seer
No. 2 - The Case Of The Genuine Counterfeit
No. 3 - The Case Of The Yellow Car
No. 4 - The Case Of Lord Wintercotte

No. 5 - The Case Of The Rusty Nail
No. 6 - The Case Of The One-Eyed Chauffeur

GIPSY TALES (1903-1916)

A series of stories describing the adventures of a wily British navvy with Romany roots, who is known only as "Gipsy." In his fantasies Gipsy portrays himself as a playwright, and tries to stage-manage the dramatis personae and the situations that feature in the stories.

A Matter Of Kindness
A Liberal Education
A Stranger In Bohemia
Drops Of Water
The Unpremeditated Curtain
Mere Details
Out Of Season

THE DIARY OF A LONELY SOUL (1915)

The Diary Of A Lonely Soul - Story 1 [title unknown]
The Diary Of A Lonely Soul - Story 2 [title unknown]
The Diary Of A Lonely Soul - Story 3 [title unknown]
The Diary Of A Lonely Soul - Story 4 [title unknown]
The Diary Of A Lonely Soul - Story 5 [title unknown]

AN A-Z OF OTHER SHORT FICTION

According To The Statute
The Ace Of Hearts
Adventure (aka A Trick of Fate)
After Reynolds
Alias "James Jones"
An Ally
And This Is Fame
Anonymous
The Apple-Green Plate
Applied Mechanics
The Arms Of Chance
Art Critics
At Short Notice
Aunt Mary
Autumn Manoeuvres

The Azoff Diamonds
A Bad Cold
The Balance Of Nature
The Barrister At Bay
Below Zero
The Better Way
Big Fish
The Big Thing
Billy's Xmas
A Bit Of Egypt
The Black Admiral
The Black Cat
The Black Narcissus
The Black Prince
Blind
Blind Chance
The Blindworm
A Block Of Marble
A Bootless Errand
Brayton's Secret
The Broken Lute
A Broken Sceptre
The Broken Trail
The Buff Gauntlet
Burglar Bill's Pupil
By Grace Of His Majesty
By Wireless
A Call On The Phone
A Captious Critic
The Case For The Prisoner
The Charlatan
A Christmas Bride
A Christmas Deputy
Christmas Cards
The Christmas Carol
A Christmas in Peril
A Christmas Star
The Clock Struck Twelve
The Colonel's Christmas Pudding
Compounding A Felony
The Convict
Coralie And The Pearls
A Corner In Elephants
The Courage Of Despair
Crossed Swords
The Dancing Shadow
The Daughters Of The Moon
A Daughter Of Nature

The Dawnstar
A Deal In Diamonds
Denny
A Derelict In Clover
The Desert Ship
A Dog's Life
The Doll's House
The Dormer Window
A Dose Of Quinine
The Doubting D, or, A Cranky Cryptogram
A Draught Of Life
Early Closing Day
An Eastern Princess
The Eavesdropper
The Ebbing Tide
The Egg Of The Little Auk
The Emsdam Dispatches
The Empty House
An Error Of Judgment
The Evidence For The Prisoner
Excess Profits
An Eye For An Eye
The Eye Of The Camera
The First Stone
The Foil
Forget-Me-Not
For Love's Sake
For Once In A Way
For Value Received
A Foster-Father
Found!
The Fourth Man
Free Labour
A Friendly Call
From Information Received
Full Fathoms Deep
Gabrielle
A Gamble In Love
A Game Of Draughts
A Garden Of Pearls
Gentlemen Of The Jury
The Gates Of Ramshi
The Grey Bat
The Grey Raider
The Guiding Star
The Half-Crown Princess
The Hand Invisible
Hardy's Big Coup

The Heart Of The Anarchist
Heavy Metal
The Heels Of The Dawn
Her Christmas Dawn
His Christmas Gift
His Majesty's Mails
A Hole In The Net
The Hospitallers
Ice In June: A Playwright's Story
Icky Of Oluk Lake
Imperial Preference
In Black And White
In Rosemary Lane
In The Dark
In The Fog
In The Pit
Introducing Mr. Pentsymon
The Joinville Tunnel
Judgment Reserved
Karma
Kindergarten
The Kingmaker's Token
Lady Mary's Bulldog
The Language Of Flowers
The Last Drive
The Law Of The Jungle: A Tale Of Mean Streets
The Leather-Pushin' Private
The Left Hand
The Lesson The Ants Taught
The Livery Of Death
The Lonely Furrow
The Long Arm Of Bronze
Love In Aether
The Luck Of The Game
Made In England
The Man Himself
The Man Who Got Through
The Man Who Rang The Bell
The Man With The Eyeglass
A Masked Battery
The Master's Voice
A Matter Of Habit
'Merica
A Message from the Flood
The Midnight Call
The Missing Blade
The Missing Note
The Mistletoe Bough

Moray The Traitor
More Than Coronets
The Morning Glory
Music Hath Charms
A Musical Treat
The Mystery Of Room Five
Natural Selection
Nerves
The Night Express: The Story Of A Bank Robbery
The Northern Light
Not On The Records
An Object Lesson
The Odds On Zero
One Day With A Working Ant
One Foggy Night
One Of The Old Guard
On Peace Night
The Onus Of The Charge
The Orpheusia
Ostentation
The Other Man's Story
The Pardon
A Parrot Cry
The Path Of Progress
The Pawn And The Rook
Pearls Of Price
Photo By Lesterre
Pictures In The Snow (a Christmas story)
A Place In The Sun
The Platinum Chain
A Popular Novelist
Poste Restante
A Prize Crop
Proof Positive
The Purple Terror
A Queen In Hiding
A Question Of Money
Rachel's Seventh Year
Rawhide Science
The Real Dramatic Touch
A Record Round
Red Petals
Rob Peter—Pay Paul
A Rope Of Snow
Rose Of The Desert
A Royal Bag
The Royal Train
The Salmon Poachers

Santa Anna
A Satisfactory Reference
Saviour From The North
The Second Chapter
Second In The Field
The Shebeeners
A Single Hair
Sir Jeremiah's Big Shoot
Sister Louise
The Sixteenth Chapter
A Sleeping Partner
Sleeping Partner
A Sound In The Night
"Special" To The Telephone
A Stolen Interview
The Straight Game
The Stranger Within The Gate
Sub Rosa
The Substitute
The Superman
The Supreme Test
The Sword Of Justice
A Table Tragedy
The Thirty-Seventh Month
This Little World
A Thrilling Exit
The Throat Of The Wolf
The Ticket
To Be Let Furnished
Treasures Three
The Two Bon-Bons
Two Of Them
The Unbelieving Eye
Unbidden Guests
The Unexpected
An Unrecorded Crime
The Vital Spark
The Vital Spot
War Ribbons
The Waterwitch
The Western Way
When The Moon Set
The White Geranium
The White Spot
White Wings (1922)
The Wings Of Chance (1922)
The Witness (1920)
The World Next Door (1916)

www.ingramcontent.com/pod-product-compliance
Lightning Source LLC
Chambersburg PA
CBHW071351170626
46811CB00003B/1086